# Christmas Under a Cold Moon

*A Moonrise Inn Novel*

*Book 2*

## JENNIFER SAFREY

Sibylline Press

Copyright © 2025 by Jennifer Safrey
All Rights Reserved.

Published in the United States by Sibylline Press,
an imprint of All Things Book LLC, California.

Sibylline Press is dedicated to publishing the
brilliant work of women authors ages 50 and older.
www.sibyllinepress.com

Sibylline Digital First Edition
eBook ISBN: 9798897409655
Print ISBN: 9798897409662
Library of Congress Control Number: 2025939362

Cover Design: Alicia Feltman
Book Production: Aaron Laughlin

This is a work of fiction. Names, characters, places, brands, media, and incidents are either the product of the author's imagination or are used fictitiously. Any resemblance to similarly named places or to persons living or deceased is unintentional.

**HUMAN AUTHORED: Any use of this publication to train artificial intelligence (AI) technologies to generate text is expressly prohibited.**

Sibylline
Press

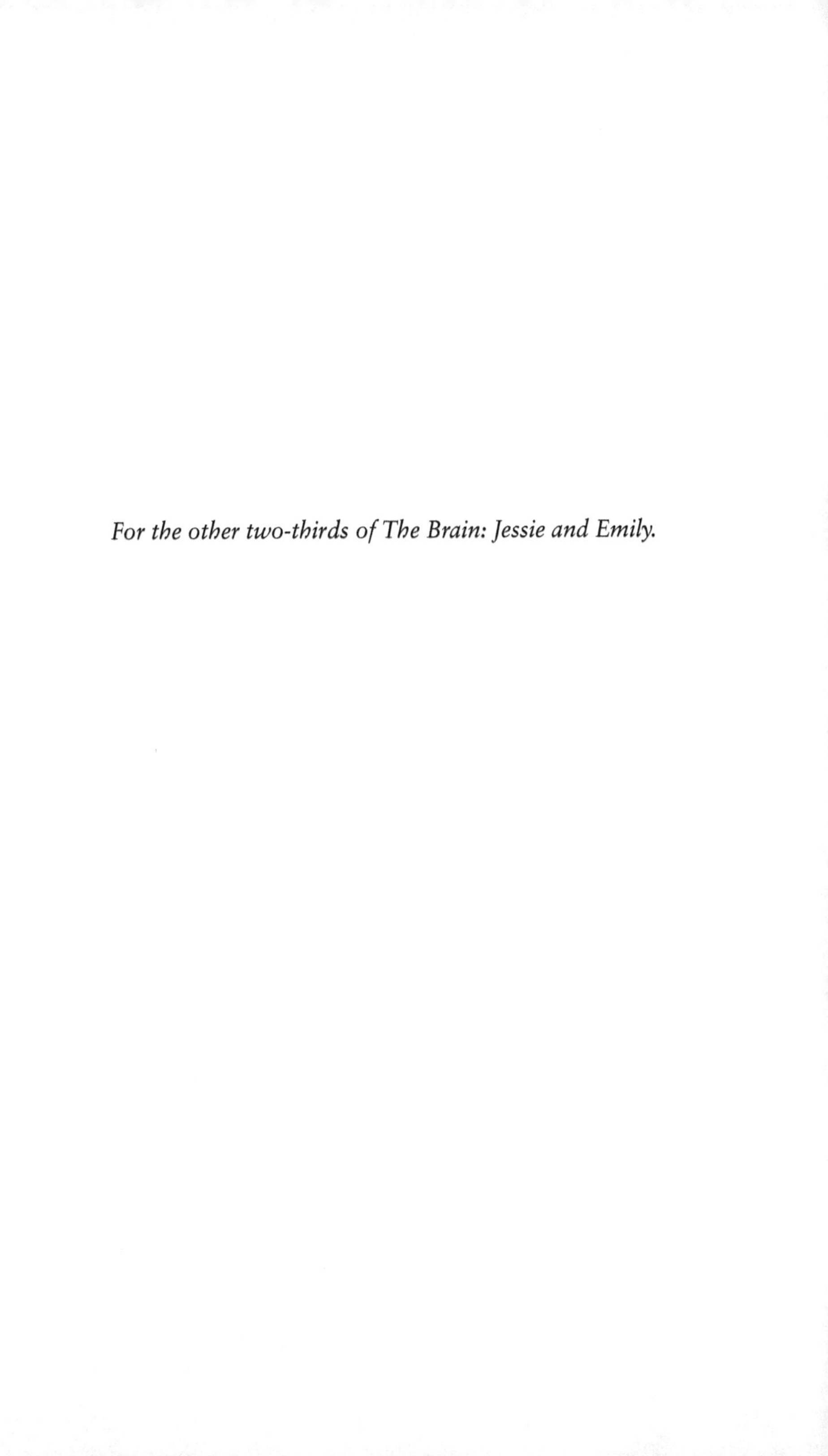

*For the other two-thirds of The Brain: Jessie and Emily.*

# CHAPTER ONE

Carter glanced in the rearview mirror, and Rudolph the Red-Nosed Reindeer stared back at him.

Well, not really. It was a cherry-colored VW Bug sporting brown felt antlers on each side mirror, a little black dot in each headlight, and a big red pom-pom nose on the grill.

He returned his gaze to the highway before him, but after a few seconds, he couldn't help but peer in the mirror again. Even in the dark, he was almost positive he could see jingle bells on each antler.

Jingle bells? So wherever this driver went, they were accompanied by an insistent sleigh-bell soundtrack?

Who on this entire *Earth* would do that to themselves deliberately? Who would decorate a vehicle to transform it into a relentless monster of holiday cheer? On purpose?

And there was no way those headlight eyeballs were legal.

Carter shook his head, checked his blind spot, and changed to the middle lane. His green alpaca-wool scarf suddenly felt suffocating in the warmth blasting from the vents, so he worked his fingers underneath it to his collarbone, then pried it loose from his neck. He dropped it onto the passenger seat, on top of his leather weekender bag and charcoal-gray knit hat.

He silently commended himself for the decision to leave Jersey City in the evening, so he'd mostly missed rush hour in New York. Now, on I-95 in Connecticut, it was free and clear and hopefully would be for the rest of the trip to Seasalter, Rhode Island.

Before checking into the inn, he'd stop somewhere for dinner and a couple of beers. He'd be spending the next two days as a working tourist, posting content for Man Cave Adventures, so he might as well start things off with some comfort food. Selene, the owner of the Moonrise Inn, had said she would leave the key for him because he was arriving late.

Rudolph the Red-Nosed Bug changed lanes and came up on his left.

Carter couldn't help it; he had to see what kind of lunatic would drive such a cutesy abomination.

He looked to his left.

The driver was bouncing in her seat, her enthusiastic and likely loud singing muted by both cars' sealed windows. Her hands drummed the steering wheel, and her long blond hair rippled over her shoulder and elbow.

Carter faced the road again with a snarl. He couldn't even check out a pretty blond woman these days without thinking of Mallory Robson—his rival. Well, he couldn't be absolutely sure she was his rival, but if he were one of the travel influencers in the running for a TV host job, Mallory Robson had to be also.

If anyone had told Carter a year ago that he would be auditioning to host *Wander With Love*, he would have laughed in their face. To be fair, if they had told him a year earlier that he would become a travel influencer at all, he would have told them to bite their tongue.

But his Man Cave Adventures account had resonated with thousands—hundreds of thousands—of followers on social media, more than he'd ever thought when he'd started it on a whim. Just before Thanksgiving, large travel-gear company Wanderlove had approached him, told him about the show they were developing for the Travelworld Channel, and asked him to audition to become the host of the first season. They were auditioning several social media travel stars by sending them to plum holiday locations to create video content.

The compensation for a TV show? Well, they weren't specific with details this early in the process, but the pay, along with the yearlong sponsorship, would likely be substantial enough that it would go a long way toward his dream: buying a house and starting a home-based business. Putting down permanent roots for the first time in his life and staying put.

There had been rumors about the show and who would be chosen, and there were other travel content creators who craved the wide exposure. The most popular one, with more than a million fans, was Mallory Robson, of Sunshine in a Suitcase.

Carter's lip curled. Seriously—Sunshine in a Suitcase. As if traveling were actually fun.

He'd scrolled many times through her feed. *Not* because she was beautiful. Because he wanted to see her popular content. He was in the business, after all. And her account was ... bright. Cheerful. Joyful. Every picture was smiling and sunny, even somehow the photos of her huddling under an umbrella and the photos of her peering through a thick fog.

It was probably that sunshiny hair, brightening her whole head like a stained-glass window of saints and angels with circles of light around their faces.

Carter rolled his eyes.

If anyone would be driving a jangly reindeer on a highway in December, it would be Mallory Robson.

Wait. Could it actually—

He turned his head again, just as the driver turned her head.

They locked eyes, and a smile lit up Mallory's whole face. She waved.

He quickly turned back to the road.

Mallory Robson. What kind of luck was this?

*His* kind of luck. Christmas luck.

Travel influencers likely were scattered all around New England this month—Christmas in New England was picturesque, after all. They'd be here to take their festive photos and write their inspiring captions and post their moneymaking affiliate links. But still, what was the chance Sunshine in a Damn Suitcase was on the same stretch of road he was?

On second thought, this was I-95, the Northeast corridor. Chances weren't *that* slim.

The Bug beeped three times, the sort of beep that wasn't designed to warn another driver or move them along, but the sort of beep that was friendly and asking for attention.

He ignored it and gave his car a bit more gas. Not so much as to be rude; just enough to pretend he didn't recognize Mallory, and he didn't realize Mallory was trying to get his attention.

She could take her suitcases of sunshine to wherever she was going and forget she ever saw him. He had a task he needed to keep his mind on.

He stole a last glance in the rearview mirror, where Rudolph was getting smaller and smaller.

He let out a breath and added just a bit more pressure to the gas—

And hit a small bump in the road, and there was suddenly a pop, and the car seemed to grow heavy on the passenger side.

He tried again, and the car struggled, bouncing. A rhythmic flapping and slapping was audible even through Carter's closed windows.

Oh, no. A flat. He needed to get off the road before he damaged the rim and exacerbated the problem.

Luckily, he was just about at the next exit. He put on his hazards, edged over one lane, and slid down the exit ramp mostly on momentum. Taking a chance with the tire in order to get out of harm's way, he turned and stopped at the side of the road before parking.

Leaving the car running, he stepped out to assess the tire. Or, what used to be a tire. He must have hit something sharp to destroy it so quickly.

He got back into the car, grabbed his scarf, wound it around his neck again, put on his hat and pulled it down to cover his ears, and yanked his wallet from the center console to search for his driver's assistance card. He knew how to change a flat, but in the dark and the cold, he thought it better to call for backup. Pressing his lips together, he shook his head. Who knew how long he'd have to wait here?

A car slowly made its way down the ramp behind him, then went around his car to park in front of him.

A red Bug with antlers.

Carter cursed under his breath as the Bug's driver's side door opened, and Mallory slid out. She buttoned the top of her hot-pink wool coat, pulled the sleeves over the cuffs of her mittens, and walked toward his window.

Why was she smiling? And why wasn't she wearing a hat in this weather? Her blond hair blew wild around her head, giving her the appearance of an Avenger, but the wind had to be biting into her ears.

When she got to his car, he lowered the window about a quarter of the way—whether to keep out the freezing air or to keep out Mallory Robson, he wasn't sure. He tried not to flinch, waiting for her to say his name, or at least ask if he was Carter Scott.

"What seems to be the trouble, little lady?" she mock-drawled instead.

This woman could find creative content in everything. He didn't need her finding it in him, sitting in his stuck car. It was less than a good look for someone who was supposed to be an expert in travel.

He huffed. "No trouble."

"No?" She looked into his car, then around them. "You're saying you meant to slow to a dangerous crawl on I-95, then creep off the exit to this particular spot? This is your final destination?"

"Yes," he said, because there was no way he was going to give Mallory Robson a chance to feel superior. It was bad enough they likely both knew she was, professionally. "It is. I'm fine."

She nodded slowly, looking into the dark distance. "Nice holiday choice. That empty parking lot with the broken chain-link fence will be the perfect holly-jolly backdrop for Christmas pictures on your socials."

Carter set his jaw.

She pointed, and he followed her finger to find an abandoned car with two flat tires and blue graffiti on the side panel. "Check it out. That must belong to the last guy who refused to ask for help," she said.

"I seriously doubt that someone who drives a reindeer around without irony is someone who can help me with a flat tire."

"A flat tire?"

Did he imagine it, or did she appear delighted by that?

She walked around to the passenger side and stood back, crossing her arms, studying the tire with more interest than was warranted. Then she came back to his window. "That's not a flat tire. That's a *splat* tire. I mean, you really shredded that thing."

Mallory raised a delicate eyebrow, waiting for his response.

He knew, from perusing her accounts online, that her eyes were a strange but hypnotizing violet, but right now, they seemed as dark as the night around them, fringed with long lashes. But they sparkled, along with her very white teeth between two lips slick with cotton-candy-colored gloss.

"Yes, thank you," Carter said. "but I'm about to make a call—"

She abruptly turned and walked away, peeling off her mittens and shoving them under one arm. She went to her car and popped the trunk and began to rummage around.

A gust of wind hit his temple, and he raised the window. He dragged his eyes away from her reindeer car and flipped through the cards in his wallet. No roadside assistance card. Where was it? In his glove box? Had he left it at home when he cleaned out his wallet last week?

He shook his head as if clearing out cobwebs.

Mallory was walking back to his car, carrying a number of items. He lowered his window again.

"Man, it's cold," she said, as if she didn't mind it at all. "Isn't it cold?"

Carter didn't see the need to answer what had to be a rhetorical question.

"I've got a jack and a lug wrench."

"I think I already have all that."

"Well, I have them in my hands, so all we need is a spare. Which I hope you have."

He hopped out of the car, went to his own trunk, moved some bags and boxes around, and extracted the spare from the compartment underneath.

"Nice," Mallory said. But instead of waiting for him, she knelt beside the splat tire and loosened the first lug nut.

"I can—"

"You can give me some light," she said, indicating his phone.

He turned on the phone's flashlight, knowing he should stop her and do this himself, but something about her capable, pink-tipped nails mesmerized him as she loosened the rest of the lug nuts.

"Do you know where to put the jack?" she asked. "Every car is different."

"Yeah," he said, and she put out her hand. He realized one dopey moment later that she was offering to hold the flashlight, so he gave her his phone and jacked up the car. She removed the lug nuts, and he removed the tire, replacing it with the new one. She put the lug nuts back on, he lowered the car, and she tightened the lug nuts.

They did all this while wordlessly passing the light back and forth. When his phone was back in his hand, she grinned. "Teamwork makes the dream work, eh?"

"You didn't need to help."

"Of course you didn't specifically need *my* help." She bent and picked up the jack and the wrench. "But you needed someone's help. You could have called for help, but you might have had to wait in the cold for a while. And this isn't the safest spot if someone decides to speed off the highway. Now you can get yourself on your way."

She strutted to her Bug in that hot-pink coat like some kind of Roadside-Assistance Barbie, without saying goodbye. But she didn't drive away. She went back to her trunk for a bit, then slammed it shut and opened her car door, pushed the seat back, and half climbed into the back seat.

Carter definitely looked at her ass. Not his fault it was all of her he could see while she did who knew what. Finally, she stepped out and skipped—seriously, skipped, in black ankle boots with heels—over to him with her hands behind her back.

"Pick a hand," she said.

"Why?"

"Why? Who asks why to 'pick a hand'? Didn't you ever play this game when you were a kid?"

"No."

She sighed dramatically, with a lot of noise, and looked at the sky as if summoning divine intervention. "Pick a *hand*, and you might get a surprise."

"You mean a surprise other than my flat tire?"

"Was that the surprise? Or was Rudolph the surprise, coming along and saving the day like he saved Santa on Christmas Eve?"

He didn't have time for this. He tapped her right arm.

She drew the hand from behind her and presented him with a tire gauge, with a shiny red bow stuck on it. "Merry Christmas! Two weeks early, but the North Pole has informed me you're on the Nice list."

"*I'm* on the Nice list? If that's true, Santa's HR is not hiring competent staff."

She shrugged one shoulder. "I only know what I'm told. Please, take it. I have an extra, and you should check the pressure of the spare before you go."

He took the gauge.

"You're welcome," Mallory said, though he hadn't thanked her. Yet. Because he had every intention of doing so. He wasn't *that* much of a jerk.

She studied his face, and he shifted his weight from one foot to the other, shivering. Maybe she didn't know who he was. She might have smiled and waved at him on the road because she thought he was attractive—it occasionally happened that a woman thought so—and she might have mentioned taking pictures for social media earlier because everyone was on social media. She wouldn't have helped him if she knew he was on his way to audition for a TV show she probably wanted to be on. She might have unscrewed all the little lugs on all four of his tires and thrown them into the dark night, allowing his car to smush onto four puddles of airless rubber, and screeched her reindeer Bug into the night to take his place for the audition.

He had an urge to touch one of her smooth, cold-pink cheeks, and as he clenched his hand, he suddenly knew without a doubt that Mallory Robson wouldn't have done any of that. She still would have helped him.

Would he have helped her if it were her flat tire? Of course, but that was because a decent man ought to assist a woman in peril.

"What are you thinking so hard about?" she asked.

"Thank you. For stopping, and the help, and the gift."

"It's no problem at all," she said. "Carter Scott."

He frowned.

She laughed and waved her arms in the air. "Behold! I'm an all-knowing sorceress!"

"No, you aren't."

"I am. Ask me what the weather is going to be tomorrow."

"So the all-knowing sorceress can check her Weather Channel app?" He sighed. "I know who you are also, Mallory Robson."

She tucked in her chin and raised her brows. "I didn't think you—"

"Checked out the content of someone else in my industry? Of course I do. Particularly when she's so …" He knew the right word. The honest word. He just had to force himself to say it. "Impressive."

"Huh. I didn't think the creator of Man Cave Adventures would be particularly interested in my aesthetic or my message."

"I'm not." He realized too late that his response was ruder than it should have been, considering what she did for him, but she didn't seem to care. Her expression remained open and warm. "What I mean is, you're right—our messages are diametrically opposed."

"I travel to inspire my followers with the beauty and positive things in the world, and you—"

"Travel to show my followers where they can find the comforts of home when they need to be away from home."

"How to cope with travel, then, instead of how to embrace it."

"Not everyone wants to embrace it. Sometimes people are obligated to travel, for business or for family, and they need help enduring it."

"Of course. Your number of followers proves it."

"It's nowhere near yours."

"Well, you must embrace travel in some way, or you wouldn't do it."

"It's too cold to be psychoanalyzed at the moment."

"Fair enough." She shrugged. "Where are you off to?"

"Where are *you* off to?"

"Somewhere Christmassy. Like you, I'm sure."

"Well. Yeah."

Neither said anything for a moment. Then a strong wind picked up, pinching the tip of Carter's nose and quite possibly freezing his snot. Mallory wrapped her arms around herself.

"Why aren't you wearing a hat?" he demanded. "It's like a hundred below."

"It's like fourteen above," she corrected. "And I never wear a hat."

"Why the hell not?"

She shrugged again and tossed her golden hair over one shoulder.

Of course. Her hair. It was the crowning glory of every photo on her accounts. On the beach, on a ski slope, in a cave—wherever she was, it shone around her face in long layers, in braids, in a high ponytail.

"You're by yourself in your car," he said. "If you can call that thing a car. You can't wear a hat in your own car? Are you honestly that vain?"

"No. I'm that aware that selfie opportunities are everywhere." She pulled her phone out of her pocket and rushed to his side to wind her arm around his waist. "Smile, Carter Scott."

"No," he growled as she extended her other arm in front of them and snapped about ten photos, angling her head slightly differently in each one. He scowled at himself in the screen.

Why didn't he move away?

It wasn't because she was so warm and smelled like coconuts and sand.

Her sunshine hair blew into his mouth, and he sputtered and swiped at his lips with one hand.

She stepped back and scrolled through the pictures, examining. "You know, you'd be a whole lot prettier if you smiled."

He pressed his lips together.

"I'm kidding," she said. "We both look hot."

Her confidence and her compliment were so breezy and simple, he was taken aback. "You're not posting those, are you?"

"No way," she said with a smirk. "Can you imagine what our followers would say if we were together? My dreamy explorer types and your—whatever they are? Grouchy travelers?" She slid the phone back into her pocket and tugged her mitten back on. "No, these pictures are for my private collection. So I can forever remember the night I stopped to help a dude in distress."

"I was not a dude in distress. I was a slightly inconvenienced man."

She laughed. Of *course*, her laugh sounded like a golden wind chime, a morning bird song, a ripple of water on a silvery pond.

Her hair, her laugh, her smile, her generosity, her *everything* made Carter want to put his hands over his head and flee for a cabin in the woods, where he'd make meals for one and huddle alone in front of a fireplace and never have to speak a civil word to anyone ever again.

Why was he like this? Why did she make him feel like this? Like an uncouth, unrefined, antisocial ogre?

"Go on," Mallory said. "Get this sleigh on its way."

She accompanied him to his driver's side door, and he slid onto his seat, which had cooled considerably since he'd left his window open. He nodded once at her. "Thanks again."

She folded her arms on the bottom of the window frame and leaned in a couple of inches. The breeze blew in her coconut smell again, as if they were on a Caribbean island and not in the almost-winter, unseasonably cold dark of Random, Connecticut. "You're very welcome."

She pulled out, tapped the car once, and sashayed back to her VW Bug. He raised the window while he watched her shut her trunk, get in the car, fire it up, and click on her blinker. She drove off, sticking a mittened hand out of the car to wave a final farewell.

He sat, silent, for a few minutes. Partly to let her get a healthy head start on I-95 North again, and partly to clear his head of all the unexpected brightness and laughter.

She was … kind.

He wouldn't have expected it.

Why not? Because she was pretty?

No. Just because … people were people.

And she was so publicly his opposite.

But she was very, very kind.

She'd helped him purely out of the sweetness of her heart and had asked nothing in return. Not even a playful, "You owe me."

He'd sort of wished she'd asked for something in return, so he could have repaid the debt then and there, and he wouldn't feel guilty knowing something she didn't know.

That he had a golden Wanderlove opportunity.

And he'd taken it. He was willing to take all the help he could get with this goal, even if he didn't tell Wanderlove that his eventual goal was to stop traveling for good.

Her smile lit up his brain again.

"Guilt," he muttered to himself, "is a wasted emotion. There's a TV job on the line."

He hopped out and checked the tire pressure—fine—then headed back to the highway.

Mallory's laugh lingered in his ears.

He realized it probably would remain, long after Wanderlove chose their host.

★ ★ ★

"Call Paige," Mallory commanded her phone, and after a moment, her assistant's voice came loud and clear through the car's speakers.

"Hey, you! Are you making good time?"

Paige's voice never failed to make Mallory grin. If she hadn't been already. "I am, but I had to make an unscheduled pit stop."

"Oh? Some pretty holiday lights off the highway?"

"Not this time. You'll never guess who I ran into."

"Dasher? Vixen? Hermie the dentist elf?"

"Carter freaking Scott."

"Seriously? Man Cave Carter Scott?"

"The very one. On I-95."

"You saw him driving?"

"I saw him driving, I saw his car break down, I saw him look mortified when I stopped to help him."

"Oh, my God. That's hilarious. Did he know who you are?"

"He definitely did, from the first second. He pretended he didn't, but I finally got him to admit it."

"Is he as, uh, frowny as he always is online?"

Mallory laughed. "I can confirm his sullenness is not merely a carefully crafted persona. He's humorless. I mean," she added quickly, "he's handsome. Really hot. But man, is he humorless."

Carter's short brown hair had been mostly hidden under his knit cap, and his body was hidden under his navy peacoat, but his grouchily set jaw was sharp under light stubble, his thighs were strong under well-fitting dark-blue jeans, and his wary eyes were the turquoise blue of the Aegean Sea. And Mallory could too easily imagine his long, graceful fingers dancing over piano ivories, or a laptop keyboard, or over her skin ...

And after about three minutes, she was tempted to grab him, pull him close, and kiss the scowl off his face.

"You must have completely overwhelmed him," Paige said, not realizing Mallory was thinking of all the ways Carter Scott had overwhelmed her.

"Maybe. To be honest, I felt sorry for him," Mallory said. "I mean, who's that bereft of holiday cheer this close to Christmas?"

Other than possibly her. But that was something she didn't share. Paige was her part-time college-intern assistant, not her friend. Not staying in one place long meant friendships were tough to maintain.

"I'm sure there are lots of people, for lots of reasons," Paige said.

"Well, this guy is their king."

"He is," Paige pointed out. "King of the man-cave dwellers. Where's he off to, anyway?"

"No clue. I couldn't get it out of him." Mallory beeped at a car about to cut her off, and it swerved back into its lane. As she passed on its left, she waved and smiled at the driver to show no harm done.

"You didn't tell him you're going to Seasalter, did you?"

"I did not. Though frankly, even if I did, I wouldn't have to worry he'd follow me. He seemed eager to put as much distance between us as possible."

"You think he's auditioning for Wanderlove?"

Mallory was taken aback. "Why would he be?"

"Man Cave Adventures is growing in terms of followers and engagement."

"Maybe," Mallory said slowly, not wanting to think about competition. "But even if he did audition, I'm sure I'd win. Thanks to your brilliance, we're doing even better."

"Thanks. Even though the Moonrise Inn was booked when I tried to reserve it. Luckily, there was a cancellation, so Wanderlove could get you in."

For her audition for *Wander With Love*, the travel-gear company had sent Mallory to Seasalter, Rhode Island, which had a reputation as the perfect little town for Christmas. There were original and fun holiday community activities and gorgeous homes, but it wasn't Newport or Boston, so it didn't get quite the crowds the bigger areas did. Even still, enough people knew about its winter holiday appeal that all the hotels and inns were booked solid all month, and though Paige had scoped out Seasalter in October, she couldn't find a room. So when Wanderlove booked Mallory in the exact place Paige had loved online, they were delighted.

"The Moonrise Inn," Mallory said now. "It sounds dreamy."

"According to the pictures on its website, it is. And, get this: The full moon is at the end of the week. Lots of opportunity to be creative with moon imagery in your posts, in addition to all the holiday fun. Wanderlove will definitely pick you. When they do, don't let Hollywood go to your head."

"I wouldn't consider it Hollywood."

"It's as close as we get."

"I don't pay you nearly enough."

Paige just chuckled, which Mallory appreciated. Her assistant worked at Sunshine in a Suitcase solely for college credit, but if she won the TV hosting gig and yearlong sponsorship that came with it, Mallory could afford to pay and keep industrious Paige part time and hopefully send her on her own assignments a couple of times a year.

And if Mallory were chosen to host their new show on the Travelworld Channel, Wanderlove would ensure that she could keep up her own dream job. Seeing the world. Bringing little pieces of the planet to followers who couldn't, and offering advice and tips to followers who could.

As far as she was concerned, this was what life was about: expanding one's horizons out, and out, and out.

She'd travel forever, if she could.

But being a travel influencer wasn't cheap, and though she had sponsorships, expanding her reach and growing her company cost money. With Wanderlove's exposure, backing, and sponsorship, she could keep traveling, keep expanding, for the foreseeable future, anyway.

A little tickle at the back of her mind pushed her eyebrows together.

What was that? Was that guilt?

No. Guilt wasn't necessary. She worked hard, and she deserved to get a great business opportunity. She deserved to follow her happiness.

Carter looked and sounded so … grumpy. Grumpier than a flat tire warranted, in her opinion.

Maybe—he wasn't happy.

That little tickle again.

"I'm *happy*," she muttered through her teeth.

"What's that?" Paige asked.

Mallory brushed a lock of hair out of her face. "Nothing, sorry. Did you let the inn know I'm getting in around seven?"

"I did. Selene is the owner. She sounds like the nicest person."

"Of course she is. Someone who owns a Moonrise Inn couldn't possibly be anything but."

"Enjoy your evening. Let me know if you need anything."

"I promise I'm going to try to need you as little as possible until after the new year. So you can have fun on the holiday." She added a little coolness to her voice, to stay professional. She liked Paige, a lot. But she couldn't let the lines blur between being a boss and being a friend. Paige had tried occasionally to draw Mallory into discussions that were ... friendly, and she didn't want to hurt her intern's feelings.

Paige paused, as if considering saying something else, but only went with, "I appreciate that."

Mallory couldn't help softening. "I meant what I said, Paige. You're brilliant, and you've helped me tremendously. I'm going to do what I can to keep you on."

Paige's smile was audible. "In the meantime, I'll keep helping you until I go back in mid-January. I like working with you. And ... I like you."

"Tha—thank you."

"You're very welcome."

Mallory disconnected, and her Christmas music CD came back on. All Mariah wanted for Christmas was Mallory.

All Mallory wanted for Christmas was a TV deal.

# CHAPTER TWO

The entire inn seemed to be asleep when Carter pulled to a stop in the lot. All the windows were dark, except for a soft golden glow coming from the windows of the front room and the glittering of an elaborately decorated wreath on the front door. Selene had said she was leaving the front door open for him but requested he lock it behind him when he arrived.

After shutting off the car, he leaned forward and rested his head on the steering wheel for a moment. Long drive, then a dinner at a local pub, where he'd met two men at the bar. Kyle and Darryl owned Taco Tuesday, a downtown eatery, and they were the perfect new friends; they all talked sports, drank beer, and told dumb and funny stories until they all remembered they had work in the morning.

The air inside the car was cooling rapidly, so Carter went around to the passenger side and hoisted his duffel bag onto his shoulder before closing the car door as slowly as he could and have it still catch. Then he grabbed his suitcase from the trunk. He flinched at the one-horn beep of the alarm and walked mindfully up the front porch stairs. The Moonrise Inn seemed to be a beautiful, well-restored old farmhouse, but in the dark, he couldn't even confirm the paint color. Above him, the moon was a few slivers away from full, bathing the porch's rocking chairs in celestial white light. Now that he was closer to the wreath, he could see that its twinkle lights illuminated the little iridescent charms that covered it: crescent moons, stars, comets.

Carter nodded, impressed with the inn's keeping to theme.

He pushed the door open softly, but it didn't even creak. As he closed and locked the door, the scent of the sitting room wound around him: cinnamon, chocolate, and a hint of something else, something ethereal.

Carter had lived and traveled to many cities, stayed in many hotels and hostels, and he'd never felt so welcome, so immediately at ease in a new place before. It was …

Magical, his mind said, but why would it say that? When had he ever said something was magical?

That was something Mallory Robson would say.

No, not *magical*. Nice. Not unpleasant.

He picked up the envelope that Selene left on the bookcase for him. Inside was a key and a little index card, on which she'd written:

*Welcome, Carter. I'm looking forward to meeting you tomorrow. Breakfast is seven to ten a.m. You're in the Orion's Belt Suite, second floor. I hope you both have a wonderful evening.*

*Selene*

Carter folded the note and stuck it in his pocket. It wasn't an uncommon mistake for hotels to assume he was traveling with a partner. Front desks and concierges often asked him if he and his companion would need anything special. He'd let Selene know tomorrow that she was mistaken, that he'd never travel anywhere with a girlfriend ever again, not as long as he had any control over his own life.

Well, probably best to keep that last part to himself.

He glanced around. Selene had left a small corner lamp on, as well as a moon-shaped nightlight on the wall and some flameless candles on the windowsill. The long, gauzy white curtains on the window suddenly fluttered in greeting—though in December, all the windows were sealed shut. Maybe there was a heat vent underneath them.

Something came over Carter, just for a moment. A feeling as if … as if he could rest.

Peace.

He closed his eyes, and his shoulders dropped for the first time in—a very long time.

Then he cracked his eyes open again. This place—

He shook his head. It was pretty, that was all. He glanced around, but the room was a little too dark to get a good picture, and he didn't want to wake anyone in an adjoining room by snapping lights on.

Sitting on the soft, velvety sofa, he scrolled through the pictures on his phone and chose a selfie he'd taken that evening at the bar with Kyle and Darryl. He typed a quick caption, tagging them and giving a shout-out and a link to both Taco Tuesday and the restaurant they were at. *You feel at home wherever you are traveling with good guys, good food, and good beer. Man-caving tonight at the Moonrise Inn before exploring Seasalter's Christmas festivities tomorrow.* He added a slew of hashtags, rolling his eyes as he did every time, but they attracted followers. He remembered to tag Wanderlove, then posted, slid the phone back into his pocket, and walked up the stairs, which had a carpet runner to silence his progress to the second floor.

The inn would be full, as was every place in town, Wanderlove had told him, so he opened the door stealthily so as not to wake anyone and was once again impressed with the door's lack of creak. He shut it silently.

Apparently, Selene had left the fireplace on for him, and though it warmed the room considerably, it didn't give off much light to see with. Carter reached out to find a switch on the wall but merely hovered his hand in the air as fatigue hit him again. The long drive, the two beers, the music at the restaurant all caught up to him. He couldn't even fathom flicking on the light, squinting, unpacking toiletries, settling in. He could take care of everything in the morning.

Traveling was the worst, but traveling alone was the lesser evil, because he could do whatever he wanted. And what he wanted was to stumble over to the bed and fall into it.

He put his bags on the floor by the door and kicked off his shoes, then pulled off all his clothes, leaving them in a pile on the floor. He paused for a moment, letting the heat from the fireplace lick his bare skin. The bed's headboard was barely visible in the dark room, so he made his way toward it slowly and carefully, since he had no idea of the layout of the room. He somehow made it without banging an elbow or stubbing a toe. He chose the side of the bed away from the window, peeled back the blanket, and slid in.

He felt his consciousness sliding away even before his head touched the pillow.

His last thought before sleep took him was that usually hotel sheets were cool.

These were warm. So warm.

★ ★ ★

Mallory rolled over and smiled even before opening her eyes. Whenever possible, she didn't bother with alarms, preferring to wake naturally with the sun. The New England sun was unforgiving in December, but this morning, it felt glorious. The Moonrise Inn was a gorgeous gem, owner Selene was as sweet as could be, and Mallory had spent some time last night moving in: folding sweaters in drawers, lining up her shoes on the floor in the closet, arranging her makeup and toiletries carefully in the bathroom, putting her suitcase neatly away in a corner.

A new place. Again.

She stretched, then opened one eye, allowing the light to filter in gradually before opening the other. No early birdsong this time of year, or leaves rustling, which was a bit sad, but she brightened at the thought of Seasalter bustling with Christmas. She couldn't wait to see it, to immerse herself in it. To photograph it.

She reached up and patted the top of her head. She'd trained herself to sleep on her back all night so she wouldn't wake up to a total hair tragedy, and it seemed she'd managed well. This bed was a comfortable cloud while somehow still offering a lot of support for her back. Hotel beds ran the gamut between unsleepable and pretty decent, but this one was top of the line. The pillows were of varied puffiness, and the many-thread-count sheets were soft. She'd had a blessedly deep and dreamless night in this nurturing cocoon of a room.

She'd set the electric fireplace on a timer, and it went off a few hours ago. How was she still so warm? Maybe she'd go back to sleep for a little longer ...

Mallory turned her head, so her cheek sank into her long hair, and her heart stopped.

There was someone else in the bed.

She frantically shuffled through her memory cards. It was unusual but not one-hundred-percent unheard of for her to meet a man while traveling and have one night of fun. But no, she ... she'd come straight to the hotel. She hadn't gone anywhere, she hadn't drunk anything, she—

Oh, God.

Her mouth went dry.

Who—

Then he rolled over, and his eyes shot open.

She screamed.

Carter Scott opened his mouth wide and screamed right back.

★ ★ ★

Before she opened the inn in September, Selene wasn't a morning person. Not at all.

Dan was.

Selene didn't even know exactly what time he woke up every day, only that it was long before she could sit up in bed and form a coherent thought. When she finally did, she'd shuffle into their kitchen. He'd slide a hot mug of coffee into her hand and drop an affectionate, lingering kiss on her forehead—in that order.

Now that Dan was gone, she was awake every morning probably around the time he had been. But twenty-five years made a habitual creature, and each time she awoke, she sniffed the air for her favorite dark roast, and each time the scent wasn't there, she remembered he was gone.

And she had a few moments of grieving all over again.

Life moved on, of course, in the house he'd convinced her they should purchase and turn into an inn. It was the strongest dream that dreamer Dan had ever expressed, so she acquiesced, despite knowing nothing about the business of running an inn. "We'll figure it out," he assured her the night after they'd closed on the house. "Together."

He didn't know that their together would only be for a few months longer.

He didn't know he'd die suddenly and leave her to run his lovingly decorated Moonrise Inn on her own.

Selene already had set all the tables in the dining room with festive, sparkly tablecloths and gleaming place settings. She poured the beans into the coffee press, then put the scoop on the counter and wiped her hands on her full-length apron festooned with stars. She made her own coffee in the mornings now, and enough coffee for the guests who'd stayed the previous night. Along with enough breakfast for all. Her days were filled with fulfilling requests and meeting expectations.

It was hard.

But … she didn't hate it.

She was the one to carry Dan's dream forward.

"Selene," he'd said, long ago, "my moon goddess. I believe in us. I believe in you, even when you don't."

She didn't, at first.

But as guests came and went and left glowing reviews and promised to return, she started to believe.

Just a little.

She glanced at the clock over the sink, then pulled the vat of waffle batter out of the refrigerator, as well as a bowl of fresh blueberries. She deposited everything in front of her, then went back to the refrigerator. Full house this morning. She reached for a carton and worried she might not have enough—

"Eggs!" she heard behind her as the swinging door opened.

Owen stepped into her kitchen, carrying several paper bags.

"Are you kidding?" she asked, leaning her rear against the counter and beaming at him. "You are a Higglytown Hero. How did you know I forgot to pick up more eggs yesterday?"

"I didn't." Owen set the bags on the counter beside her. His sleeve brushed her own, and through the cotton of her sensible pink cotton turtleneck, she could feel the cold air clinging to his ski jacket. "I was up early, craving chocolate croissants. So I hit up Sandy Bakery, and I grabbed a few for your guests also. Then I went next door and got strawberries and eggs, since you mentioned Moonrise is full to bursting this week, and I'm certain you can't have too many berries and eggs."

"You're right about that, and I appreciate it."

He pulled off his hat and sniffled, his straight nose red from the frigid outdoors. He grinned, and she couldn't help grinning back at her friend.

Her good friend.

Emphasis on good. Or friend. Or both.

"I'll reimburse you," she said, changing the subject in her mind the way she always did when she found herself musing about Owen Cardiff's place in her life.

"Whatever."

"It's not whatever. It's my business, and I'm going to pay you for groceries."

"If you really want to."

"I do."

"I'll take a cup of coffee as a tip, if you insist."

"You know I do." Leaving his coat on, he scooped the coffee grinds from the canister on the counter, put them in a filter, and poured water into the coffeemaker chamber.

She'd met Owen on Labor Day weekend, when he'd come in and informed her that he'd grown up in this house, that his father had promised Owen would inherit it, only to leave it instead to his new wife. The woman wasn't fond of Owen, and instead of selling it to him when he offered, she secretly sold it out from under him to Selene and Dan.

Neither Selene nor Dan had had any idea of the dispute or of Owen's existence, but Selene refused to sell to Owen when he asked. She'd only just opened the inn that weekend, determined to honor Dan's dream.

But Owen offered a deal that would protect her: If the Moonrise Inn wasn't in the black in a year, Selene could sell the house to him, recoup her losses, and move on with her life.

Selene agreed to the deal.

As much as this inn was his dream, Dan wouldn't want her to be saddled with debt. He'd understand, as long as she gave it her best shot.

And she did. Every single day. Her guests' reviews showed it, as did the increasing number of reservations.

But what happened next was something she'd never expected: She and Owen became friends.

He'd come over that same week with a telescope, offering to show her the full harvest moon. Knowing Dan would never refuse such an offer, Selene accepted and had a lovely night. Soon, Owen was stopping by once or twice a week, mostly in the evening when she had time to herself, and they talked and sipped wine and sometimes listened to music. As the nights got longer and colder, they moved their talks indoors, first into the inn sitting room, then eventually—as guests began to fill the house—upstairs in her private living room.

They never touched. But it didn't escape Selene that the locations of their get-togethers were becoming cozier, more intimate, and later; Owen often didn't leave until well after midnight, when they finally checked the time and realized they'd been having too much fun to notice the hours passing.

And in the last month, Owen had taken to texting her or even stopping by most mornings—early, since he knew she had to be up. It was as if he wanted to be the first one to talk to her; to be the first one she communicated with each day. Sometimes it was an offer of assistance, like today, and sometimes it was just hello.

"Hey," he said, taking two mismatched, oversized mugs from the cabinet, mugs that were for her and not for discerning diners. "How do those doors sound?"

Selene realized she'd been staring into space instead of doing the zillion-and-two things she needed to do before the first guests wandered into the dining room, expecting sustenance. She spun on her heel and began to heat the griddle. "They sound like nothing. Silent. Thanks for doing that."

"Those hinges need treating every now and then. It's no trouble."

"You could show me how to do it, so you don't have to—"

He slid a steaming cup of caffeine toward her, raising his brows, waiting for the rest of her sentence.

*So you don't have to do it. But I don't mind if you do. I like the help. No, I like the company. I like—*

*Dan, is this—*

*Can you just let me know if this is—*

*Okay?*

She waited. She knew it was crazy, but sometimes he answered. Sometimes he spoke into her mind in that gentle way he always had.

She waited.

Then …

A scream.

A scream?

Selene and Owen stared at each other, eyes wide.

Two people. Screaming. Upstairs. Second floor?

She bolted from the kitchen, Owen right behind her as they raced to the stairs.

★ ★ ★

"What are you *doing* in my *bed*?" Mallory shrieked. She backed up so quickly, she rolled onto the floor. She grabbed the bedspread as she fell, pulling it with her, then scrambled to her feet while covering herself. There was no real need, since she was wearing her flannel pajama set and thick socks. But she needed another layer of distance between herself and Carter Scott.

"*What?*" he yelled, tumbling off the bed on his side and backing into the wall, an arm outstretched as if she was a bloodthirsty gator just emerged from a pond. He was—not in flannel pajamas, or any pajamas. He tried dragging the bedspread, but she was clutching it, so he fell to his knees to let the bed hide him from the waist down. He yanked a pillow off the bed and dropped it in his lap. "Why the hell are *you* in *my* bed?"

"What *is* this?" she demanded. "You decided to *follow* me after I helped you with your car ... all the way to my *room?*"

"This is *my* room! I swear!"

"It's *my* room, you ... you ..."

"Wait," Carter interrupted quickly, his hand still up as though she was interested in going anywhere *near* him. "Before you select the best pejorative—and I'm sure you have some good ones ready—please, please listen to me. I'm guessing we both have reservations at Moonrise?"

He waited until she nodded.

"Okay," he went on. "Which is a coincidence. Or, not completely, since we're both interested in cute New England Christmas town content, and we both happened to end up in Seasalter. But reserving the same room—this is clearly a mistake by ... by someone. Maybe me, maybe you—"

"It wasn't *me!*"

"Or maybe someone else, okay? But I would never, ever hurt you, Mallory. I would never hurt any woman." He didn't move, his arm still outstretched. His eyes searched hers, and the earnestness reflected there unnerved her. "I didn't even know you—anyone—was in the bed. I never turned on a light. I just flopped down and fell asleep in the dark. I woke up in the same position I fell asleep in. I probably never even touched you, and if I did, I was totally unconscious. And luckily ..."

He paused, as if rethinking what was about to come out of his mouth.

"Luckily what?"

"Luckily, you're dressed like you were sleeping in a refriger-ated boxcar."

"I get *cold* at night!" Mallory took in a sharp breath—to say what else, she wasn't sure yet—but there was an urgent rap on the door.

"It's Selene. Is everything all right?"

"Um," Mallory said.

"Can I come in?"

Mallory glanced at Carter. He tilted his head and pleaded with his eyes until she let go of the blanket and shoved it across the bed. He snatched it up, wrapping it around his body, and stood. "Yes," he answered.

The inn owner entered, wearing a pink shirt and an apron. Her blond hair was twisted fashionably in a claw clip, and a pair of reading glasses sat askew on her crown. She stopped in the center of the room, looking from Mallory to Carter as if trying to figure out how to break up two alley cats about to tear into one another. Finally, she repeated, "Is everything all right?"

Mallory noticed a handsome middle-aged man in a jacket hovering outside the door, watching them all anxiously. Maybe Selene's husband? She met Carter's gaze before she forced a smile onto her face. "Good morning. I'm so sorry we woke you—"

"And possibly everyone else in this inn," Carter added.

Mallory glared at him.

"You didn't wake me," Selene assured them. "But something must be very wrong."

Mallory glued her smile back on for Selene. "There seems to have been some sort of mix-up. This gentleman and I seem to have been given keys to the same room, and he came in after I went to sleep"—she glanced at Carter for backup and he nodded—"and he never turned the light on before falling asleep himself. So we, um, we woke up in the same bed."

Selene gasped and covered her mouth with one hand. "Oh, my God," she said through her fingers. "I'm so sorry. I—Wanderlove made your reservation, so I thought you were together."

The man at the door backed away quietly and left.

Mallory frowned. "Wait. Wanderlove did make my reservation here." She turned to Carter. "They—they made your reservation too?"

Carter nodded slowly. "They—" he started, then sighed. "They contacted me last month and asked me to come here and audition for, um ..." He glanced at Mallory. She suspected he was reluctant to tell her about his great opportunity, likely to spare her hurt feelings. But he didn't need to worry about that because—

"The TV show?" she asked, then twisted her lips to one side.

"Oh, no. Let me guess," Carter said. "You're auditioning also?"

"Yes."

They both sighed, realizing what had gone wrong. "It seems Wanderlove's right hand doesn't know what their left hand is doing," Carter said.

"I assumed you were together," Selene said. "The company rep called and said they needed a room for two people and gave me your names and the date. I confirmed just one room with them in an email, and they didn't contact me to correct me, so perhaps there was a misunderstanding?"

"One room?" Mallory asked. "Does someone over there think we're a couple? Why would they think that?"

Carter shrugged. "We'll call them this morning, clear it up."

Selene put a hand on her forehead, distressed. "I'm so, so sorry—"

"It wasn't your fault," Mallory said. "And if Carter and I had both checked in earlier in the day, we would have discovered this before … before …"

"Before it was awkward," Carter finished. Mallory nodded.

"I'm so, so sorry," Selene repeated, putting her hand on her forehead and looking at the ceiling. "I promise you both, this is not how I run things here."

"I believe it," Carter said. "This inn is beautiful and very obviously run with care."

Mallory cut her eyes to him again, surprised to hear such kindness from Sir Grouchiness.

"It seems as though you know each other already," Selene said.

"Sort of," Mallory said, the smile never leaving her face.

"Sort of," Carter parroted, and Mallory saw his fingers whiten as he tightened the bedspread around his lower half.

"Well," Selene said, "breakfast begins in a half hour. Mallory, do you want to go up to my apartment and freshen up there?"

"No," Mallory said. "I think I'll be fine here."

"If you're sure," Selene said.

"I am." She was. If Carter had nefarious intentions toward her, he'd have attempted to follow through with them before she'd realized he was there. And his surprise and horror at the situation, as well as his assurances he was harmless, were genuine.

"All right." Selene nodded. "This is a suite, so there is an extra room with a door for privacy. We'll figure this out after breakfast. All my other rooms are fully booked for the week, but I'll see what I can do about finding one of you another room in town."

"Thanks, Selene," Carter said. Mallory echoed it.

Selene turned, and the three of them realized they weren't alone.

Two women huddled in the open doorway, peeking in with expressions that could have been gleeful or horrified or baffled; it was hard to tell. Mallory placed both of them somewhere between their late sixties to mid-seventies.

"Is everything okay in here?" one woman asked with a frown, clutching the lapel of her purple satin pajama top closed.

Her friend, also in pajamas but having opted for festive red flannel covered with grinning elves, flicked the first woman's arm. "Brenda, what kind of question is that? These two kids were screaming their heads off. Everything is obviously *not* okay."

"It is, actually. We're so sorry we woke you," Mallory hastened to say, smiling at them and Selene.

"Woke us? Honey, it's well past five a.m., when I usually wake up." She put a hand on the doorframe and leaned in, searching the floors. "I'm Jackie, by the way." She lowered her voice to a theatrical whisper. "Did you see a mouse?"

"No!" Selene said, with a note of panic under the assurance.

"No, we didn't," Carter confirmed. "This is the nicest inn I've ever stayed at, to be honest."

"This place is super dreamy," Mallory said. He didn't roll his eyes at her word choice. Not completely. But Mallory sensed his really wanting to.

Selene moved to the door and managed to herd the women away from the door in a way that was somehow far more polite than pushy. "Good morning, ladies! I have coffee, tea, hot chocolate …"

The door closed.

"Are you okay?"

Mallory was surprised at the … something in his voice. Compassion? Gentleness? She considered his question carefully before answering. "Yes, I think so. Just startled to find you in my bed ... or, our bed ... *the* bed. Confused at how this all happened. Relieved that Selene is going to help us. And ... those ladies."

Carter twisted his lips into a rueful expression. "Those ladies." He drew his brows together. "Do you want me to leave so you can—"

"No, no." She glanced at the bathroom door. "I can wash up and change in there, then you can have a turn."

"I don't want you to feel unsafe."

"I don't." He still looked skeptical. "Really."

He nodded slowly.

She sat on the bed, though tentatively, as if it were a spring trap now and not the best bed she'd ever slept in. "Can you believe Wanderlove made such a big mistake? Why would they send us to the same place to make content for them? Maybe some kind of paperwork mix-up?"

He sighed.

"I'm only trying to understand how—" Mallory said.

Carter crouched low. "Hold on," he said. "I'm—"

She heard the rustling of clothing, and she turned to the window. She realized the room had a bit of a sea view. Last night she couldn't see it in the darkness, but the beach was about two blocks away, and between houses she could see a sliver of gray waves, the morning sun glowing golden above.

The bed dipped under her, and she faced Carter, now perched on the farthest corner from her. He was still barefoot, but now he had on jeans and a T-shirt. His shoulders seemed nicely but not overly sculpted. Not that she was looking.

Yes, she was looking. She dragged her eyes up to his, embarrassed, but he was staring into space, biting his lip.

"What?"

"Something's fishy," he said.

"The ocean's not far."

He tilted his head at her to acknowledge her dumb quip. "I don't think this is a mistake. Wanderlove was professional about everything else, then suddenly they send us to the same town, the same hotel?"

"What are you saying?"

"I'm saying we're missing some information."

"Yeah."

They sat in silence for a moment. Then another.

"It can't be that bad, whatever it is," Mallory finally said.

"Probably not bad, but I don't particularly like being finger-puppeted."

"As long as I get to audition, I can play along with whatever they're doing. I'm going to get that show."

Carter kicked his feet up on the bed, leaned back on his elbows, and raised an eyebrow at her. "How self-serving and mercenary of you. I thought you were all rainbow sprinkles and kittens."

"And just what is wrong with rainbow sprinkles and kittens?"

He didn't respond; instead, he scanned the room. "Where's your suitcase of sunshine? Where's ... any of your stuff? Maybe if I'd tripped over a pair of clunky heels on the way in last night, I'd have woken you up and we could have avoided all this today."

Mallory laughed. "Are you seriously making the argument that I should have been a slob when I got in?"

"Maybe not a slob as much as a normal person in a hotel room."

She rolled her eyes. "I unpacked, of course."

"Unpacked where?"

She went to the dresser and opened a drawer, gesturing like a grinning game-show hostess at the folded shirts and sweaters, then opened another drawer to display jeans and leggings. She opened a small top drawer but hurriedly shut it when she realized her bras were on top.

He sat forward, taking it all in. "It looks like you moved in."

"I didn't move in. I made myself comfortable."

"I live out of my suitcase when I travel."

"What? Who does that?"

"I do. I like to keep everything in my bag so when it's time to leave, I can leave. Fast. Who does it like *you* do?"

"Everyone. That's why hotel rooms and inns have dressers. So guests can unpack and feel at home."

"I don't feel at home in a rented room."

"Maybe if you unpacked and relaxed a bit—"

"No."

"Have it your way. And why'd you get in so late, anyway? I bet you stopped for a beer and some sportsball at a pub."

"So what if I did?"

"No, it's good. Manly-man activities are on brand for you."

Out of the dresser, she selected a long red sweater, a pair of black leggings, and a red-and-green plaid scarf. She pulled out underwear also and slid it between the folds of the sweater. But when she turned around, Carter wasn't watching her. He'd flopped back on the pillow and his eyes were closed. His hands were behind his head, and the gesture lifted the hem of his T-shirt, exposing a slice of his abs. Not that Mallory noticed or anything. "Don't feel at home in a rented room, eh?" she asked.

"If you recall," he said without opening those eyes as blue and as deep as a pool at a luxurious Caribbean resort, "I was rudely awakened by shrieking."

"Hey, pal, you shrieked as loudly as I did."

"Maybe," he conceded. "But now I'm exhausted."

She hugged the pile of clothes to her chest. "Well, you can't sleep there."

"Where do you suggest I sleep?"

"Wait," Mallory said, falling into the ivory-upholstered armchair. "What if Selene can't find another room in town?"

Carter sat up again and punched the pillow under his back to poof it. "It's a suite. I'll take the sofa in there."

"I—I—" Mallory wasn't sure what the right answer was. She understood this morning wasn't either of their faults. And she believed Carter had been as horrified and embarrassed as she was. But to agree to be roommates in this beautiful suite—

"I want to be a gentleman here," Carter said. "I do. I want to tell you I'll leave, and you can have the room. But if Selene can't find another room in town, which I'm quietly doubting because of the myriad holiday festivities in this little greeting-card town, the only option is to sleep in my car for a few nights. While I might offer that if it were summer—"

"No, that would be unreasonable."

"We'll be two friends sharing a suite. I promise I'll respect your privacy and any of your wishes."

*Will you? What if I wish you would kiss me?*

What? No! Why did that pop into her head?

This guy.

"Let's see what Selene can do," Mallory said, "and if she comes up empty, okay, we can share the suite. We're both reasonable adults. Well, we're both adults. Well ..."

"Very funny."

She smirked. Something about Carter Scott was so ripe for teasing. It was probably that humorless face. He'd just said "very funny" in a way that suggested he didn't find it funny at all. Which was absolutely funny to her. She couldn't help it.

He lifted his chin as if basking in the sun. "Bathroom's all yours. Unless you need to get more sleep also."

She wondered if he meant she could slide into bed with him and somehow fall asleep with his body right next to hers.

Nope.

She stood, about to carry her clothes to the bathroom, but she stopped. "Are we friends?"

"What?"

"You called us friends."

"We aren't enemies."

"No." Though she felt a small, sudden pang about it. It was easier to go after the TV show opportunity if she didn't personally know anyone else in the running.

*You don't want friends.*

*Shut up,* she told that little critical voice inside her. *He doesn't mean real friends. He means two people who aren't enemies.*

She took a deep breath, let it out, and smiled as she always did. "I suppose so." She made her way to the bathroom.

After she closed the door, he called, "Just because we're friends, doesn't mean you can use all the hot water!"

"It's every man for himself, Carter Scott!" she called back.

She wondered if she heard him chuckle. Then she decided she must have been mistaken, because she doubted Carter often found anything to smile about.

# CHAPTER THREE

The shower spray went on for a time, then off. Bottles rattled, compacts popped open and closed.

Carter turned up the volume on a morning talk show, trying not to hear Mallory, trying not to listen to how she perfected her face, her hair, each morning. Not that she hadn't been perfect when she rolled out of bed. Granted, she was screaming, and so was he, and it wasn't really the best time to assess someone's appearance. But he assumed she must have washed all trace of makeup off her face before bed last night, yet she still glowed as if she'd spent the night with visions of damn sugarplums dancing in her head.

Her rumpled, gorgeous blond head.

Carter growled, shifted on the bed, and pulled the blanket a little more over his hips.

There was so much to be annoyed at here that he didn't know where to start: Wanderlove, for screwing things up, deliberately or not; Mallory, for taking it all in stride after the initial shock; the lady guests, for managing to make an awkward situation even more so; this infernal talk show on TV at the moment, on which a brunette woman was triumphantly folding and unfolding the perfect "packable wardrobe"; or the coffee scent coming from downstairs, beckoning to pull him out of the bad mood he had every right to be in at the moment.

Every right.

He'd really wanted to be done traveling for the year, but then Wanderlove made this un-turn-downable offer for Seasalter. A town he'd never heard of before he was contractually obligated to head here.

The bathroom door opened. He deliberately didn't look at Mallory as she emerged, but when she paused for a few seconds, he glanced at her to see her watching the screen.

"Look at that! The perfect packable wardrobe. Not a wrinkle in sight."

Carter didn't allow himself to roll his eyes because if he did, he'd have rolled them so hard, they would have bounced out the back of his skull.

"Why are you like this?" Mallory asked, but her tone was curious, not combative.

"Like what?"

"Like the way you are."

"Why are *you* like this?"

"Like what?" she asked.

"Like the way you are."

They locked gazes. Her expression was one of a gentle field guide, observing a prickly wild animal but fully accepting of its nature.

He wondered when was the last time someone—well, a woman—regarded him with that kind of easy acceptance. His mother, probably. Even his sister gave him a hard time on occasion. "On occasion" meaning, of course, every possible occasion.

"Are you done in there?"

"Yes." She bustled across his view of the TV and put her pajamas in the dresser. "I'll wait for you for breakfast, if you want."

He pushed himself up from the bed and strode over to his suitcase, which remained on its side where he'd left it next to the door last night. "I don't eat breakfast."

"It's the most important meal of the day."

"Says who?" He knelt on the rug and unzipped his bag.

"Says everyone."

"Says you, who is a morning person."

"You might be too, if you anticipated a delicious breakfast."

He glanced at Mallory before opening his bag, but it seemed she planned on standing there and observing. He noticed she'd freshly styled her hair, and the golden curls framed her face and cascaded over her shoulders. He couldn't really put a finger on exactly what makeup she'd applied, but her skin was a little more dewy, like she'd awakened in a spring meadow of heather and daisies instead of falling out of bed, screaming at the sight of him. Her lashes were long and feathery, curtains on violet eyes that were somehow a little deeper and darker. Her red sweater came down to mid-thigh, and her black leggings ended in combat-style boots with thick socks.

*You look nice.*

He turned his back on her abruptly and opened the suitcase, and a jumble of clothes popped out as if on a timed spring. He began to paw through the pile for his favorite dark-green Henley shirt. After a few moments, he frowned and riffled through the garments with a little more frustration.

"What are you looking at?" he finally asked her over his shoulder, feeling her gaze boring into his back.

"I'm impressed with your advanced organizational system," Mallory said. "I'm trying to learn it, but it might be too sophisticated for me."

He glanced for a moment, because a moment was all it took to notice the mirth dancing in her eyes. He pressed his lips together and might have said something he'd regret, but his fingers brushed the waffle-knit cotton, and he pulled out the shirt. Then he dove back in to find his underwear. If Mallory wanted to get an eyeful of that, she was welcome to it.

But, apparently bored with his failure to find her charming and engaging, she moved toward the door. "I'll see you out there. Since you'll obviously be wanting coffee."

He grunted and ignored her soft chuckle as she let herself out, closing the door softly behind her.

Clean clothes in hand—maybe a bit rumpled, but who cared?—he stomped to the bathroom. The last thing he heard before he closed the door was the talk-show host bubbling, "Next up, a celebrity chef gives us unique ideas for pancakes. After all, breakfast is the most important meal of the day!"

★ ★ ★

The hot, hot water had washed away a bit of Carter's frustration and other uncomfortable emotions, and it was time for him to get to work. To call Wanderlove, find out what was going on, and start taking notes, videos, and photos for his own content.

He pulled his empty backpack from his suitcase and tossed in a notebook and pen—he was old school when it came to capturing ideas—his phone charger, and his selfie stick. He hated that thing, but he had to admit it came in handy sometimes to get some good angles on shots. The photos he was in got more engagement than photos he wasn't in, so though he felt like an ego monster, he had to take cues from his followers. He moved his suitcase and yesterday's clothes into the adjoining room. Even if he decided to fully unpack, he didn't think Mallory had left any drawers empty, having reasonably assumed yesterday that she'd be staying in her room alone. But he could at least move all his belongings out of her sight. He had a feeling he'd be stuck here a little longer, so the least he could do as a decent person was to stay mostly out of her way and allow her to feel comfortable.

He zipped his thick gray sweatshirt over his Henley, then put on his jacket, hat, and scarf, shoving his gloves in his pockets.

Stepping out of the suite, he locked the door behind him. He would have just walked out the front door into the hopefully peaceful cold air, but he should probably check in with Selene first.

He wandered into the bright dining area. There were two mosaic-top tables for four and three tables for two. The two nosy ladies and two of their friends took up the two larger tables. Brenda and a woman whose name he didn't know waved to him as if they were longtime pals, and he nodded at them. Jackie nudged the woman beside her and pointed her chin at Carter, and he realized the story of the screaming mishap had already been eagerly told. All the women were dressed in jeans and garishly bright Christmas sweaters, and Carter couldn't begin to guess if the intention was ironic or genuine. He hoped it was the former; he suspected it was the latter.

Mallory sat alone at a table at the bump-out window. She was writing in a journal, a half-empty glass of orange juice in front of her. Her pen had a bright red fluffball at the top, with a snowman on a coil bouncing in the poof as she wrote. Her chin was in her other hand, and she was frowning—not in anger, merely in concentration.

Carter found himself wondering what she was writing. To-do lists for the day? Content ideas? But something in that concentrating expression told him no, that she was maybe writing personal thoughts. Maybe about how much she loved the holiday season. Maybe about how much of a jerk he was.

He imagined that dopey pen sliding across the page to form "Carter" in loops.

She turned her head slightly to gaze out the window, and her eyes closed as the sun lit up her face.

Carter swallowed.

Then she turned her head the other way, opened her eyes, and caught him staring.

Damn it. And damn it more when she smiled like this was their first date, like she'd been waiting for him, and like he was worth the wait.

"Hey! Selene said it's waffle day," she said, her eyes sparkling.

She didn't invite him to sit with her, not expressly, but it was clear she wouldn't mind if he asked if he could.

Why? He was nothing like her, he'd been barely civil to her, and they were already stuck in an uncomfortable situation.

So why was he contemplating sitting with her and eating waffles?

"Carter." Selene came into the room, carrying plates. She set them down in front of two of the ladies. "Sit wherever you like." She brushed her hands down the front of her apron.

"Oh, I—" He considered for one more moment. Mallory didn't look up. "I'm not much of a breakfast eater."

"How about a to-go cup of coffee, then?"

"Perfect."

"How do you take it?"

"Black."

"Like his mood," Mallory said from the window.

"Generous of you to think it's simply my mood, and therefore fleeting," Carter said. "When in reality, it's my very soul."

"I don't believe that," Mallory said.

"No? Despite all evidence to support it?"

She shrugged one shoulder. "Maybe I see the best in people."

"How far does that get you?"

She opened her mouth for a quick retort, but none emerged. Carter considered he might have hit a nerve. It gave him less satisfaction than he'd have expected.

"Carter, is it?" Jackie said, patting the empty seat beside her. "Come. Sit."

"That's Wendy's seat," Brenda admonished her.

"Do you see Wendy here?" Jackie made a show of turning her head this way and that. "I don't. Because Wendy sleeps until eight, like a fairy-tale princess. Well, she snoozes, she loses, and I win this hunk of man sitting next to me and eating breakfast with me."

"He won't eat," Mallory said. "He's a waffle Grinch."

"Well, aren't you a beautiful girl?" Brenda said. It didn't seem like a question that required an answer, but Mallory lowered her eyes in modest acknowledgment of the sweet compliment. "Isn't she a beautiful girl?" Brenda asked her friends. "All that Christmas-angel hair."

"It's hard to tear my eyes off her hot boyfriend long enough to say for certain," one of the women said. "I'll take your word for it."

Carter opened his mouth but said nothing, and a blush he was sure was as red as the woman's Christmas sweater crept up his neck. He didn't take the offered seat.

"Patrice," Brenda admonished. "You're embarrassing him."

"There's no way I'm saying anything he hasn't already heard." Patrice pulled off her glasses, cleaned them on her hideous sweater that blinked real colored Christmas lights, and slid them back on to look at Carter once again. "I'll grant you that maybe he hasn't heard it from a woman my age."

"He's not my boyfriend," Mallory clarified from across the room.

Jackie raised her brows. "I see," she said, but it wasn't in any way judgmental. "Just a fun night, then?"

"Um." Mortified, Mallory cleared her throat. "No, that's not—"

"Jackie, do you have a polite bone in your body?" Brenda asked.

"Not anymore. I don't have time for that. I call it like I see it. And there's nothing wrong with young, attractive people enjoying themselves."

"I'm sure that's how it looked," Carter cut in. "But I assure you that's not it."

Mallory continued to studiously move her pen across the page, but a new flush on her cheeks indicated she'd heard.

Patrice elbowed her friend in the ribs. "Leave them alone, will you? They've had a rough morning."

"I've had a rough *life*," Jackie countered.

All the women nodded slowly, as if agreeing that mere existence in this world was difficult. Carter didn't have reason this morning to argue for a different perspective.

"There was a reservation mix-up with their room," Selene said, returning with a large pitcher of orange juice, "which I intend to rectify after breakfast. Do you ladies have everything you need for now?"

Carter noticed that Selene positioned herself between the ladies and Mallory. While he was certain the women were well intentioned, he was also certain that Selene didn't want any of her guests subjected to a breakfast interrogation of their sex lives.

There was a chorus of yeses. When Selene slid into the kitchen, Brenda called over, "Hey, lovely, do you knit?"

"Me?" Mallory asked, then smiled. "Knit? No."

Carter wasn't surprised. Based on what he knew about Mallory, she wasn't the sort to sit still long enough to make a scarf.

"Aw, that's too bad. We're a knitting group. We're from all around the country. We met online some years back, and now we get together every December to work on projects. I thought you could join us for some knit-and-chats if you were inclined."

"Sorry. But it sounds really fun, to travel every holiday season."

"It's not the travel that's the fun part, hon. It's the friends." Patrice launched into a story from last Christmas, a complicated tale involving a fruitcake, a hapless waiter, and a half-knitted scarf. Carter was too mentally drained to follow it, and thankfully a man emerged from the kitchen, carrying a paper cup with a lid. He recognized him as the one who'd run to their room with Selene this morning.

"One coffee to go." He held it out to Carter. "Black coffee for a black mood. I'm Owen."

Carter took the cup with one hand and put the other out for a handshake. "Carter."

Owen's grin was warm and genuine. "Morning, girls," he said, and though Carter would never have addressed the older women as girls, they all giggled. Jackie patted Wendy's empty seat again, and Owen slid into it, throwing a wink at Carter as the knitters' attention refocused on an attractive man closer to—if still not quite—their age.

Carter knew he should leave while he had the chance, but he couldn't help taking a sip of hot caffeine. He closed his eyes, allowing the coffee's aroma to travel up his nose into his brain.

"Good?" Selene asked.

"So good that I think this cured me of everything that ever ailed me."

She rubbed his upper arm affectionately, the way a mother would, and he was surprised to find it comforting. "I have a lot to take care of this morning." She glanced at the tables and lifted her chin to greet a latecomer—Wendy, most likely. "I have an inn full of hungry knitters. But in a couple of hours, I'll start calling around to see what I can do to find you a room. You just go enjoy your day."

"Thank you," he said. "I really appreciate that."

"And I appreciate your understanding. There's a lot going on in town today, so have fun. On the table near the front door, you can grab a holiday schedule, which will tell you all the activities."

"I think I have a meeting soon."

Mallory piped up. "*We* have a meeting soon."

"So you work together?"

"Not quite," he said, and when Selene's forehead crinkled in confusion, he realized he didn't know enough about the situation to clarify.

"We'll tell you more later," Mallory said to Selene.

"Please do." Selene left the room.

"I'll see you later?" Mallory said to Carter, and he wondered at the question in her voice, as if it weren't a given that he would see her in *their* suite.

"Yes," he said.

"I'll meet you in my room. Um, our room. The room." She bent over her notebook, and after a moment, her feathery pen was bobbing again.

He took another sip of coffee and left. Might as well take a walk through town and see by daylight what he'd gotten himself into.

★ ★ ★

Mallory had meant to end their conversation with a witty rejoinder, a cheeky grin, a joke he'd snarl at.

There was something so fun about messing with him. Gently messing with him, because Mallory was certain there had to be something serious under the surface that made him so unpleasant. But at the same time, he was a pleasant unpleasant. He wasn't cruel; she knew by the way he'd let down his guard long enough this morning to ask if she was okay after all the screaming. She believed he really wanted her to be okay. And she believed that if she hadn't been, he would have done whatever it took so she would be.

There was a good man under that hard candy shell. Somewhere.

Her phone buzzed on the table, making her glass of orange juice quiver. She picked it up, frowned at the unfamiliar number calling from video chat. She ran her fingers through her blond curls before accepting the call. A woman with a black pixie haircut, blue feathered eyeliner, and a bright grin appeared on the screen.

Mallory knit her eyebrows together at the vision of this ethereal elf apparently calling from Santa's workshop. "Um, hi?"

"Mallory! Trixie from Wanderlove."

Mallory sat up straighter. "Oh … yes! How are you?"

"Wonderful. You're at the Moonrise Inn?"

"I am."

"I know it's not even eight, but I took a chance that you were up, because we didn't get to talk yesterday."

"Yes, I'm sorry about that. I got in late, and I hope Paige let you know that—"

"Yes, she did. Is Carter Scott with you?"

Still annoyed about waking up to Carter this morning—well, not the Carter part, but the surprise part—well, not that she wanted Carter there—whatever—she was tempted to say, *no, why would you ask that?* Instead, she said, "He just stepped out."

"I'd like to talk to both of you."

"Um, okay." Mallory leaned out of her chair, trying to see into the front sitting room. "I'll see if I can catch him."

She muted her end of the call, practically fell out of her chair, put the phone against her thigh so all Trixie could see was darkness, and scrambled to the sitting room. Carter was examining a town schedule from the little pile by the door. "Psst," she whispered urgently.

Carter glanced up at her, then around the room. "Me?"

"Yes." She held up her phone and shook it a little. "Wanderlove."

He squinted. "Is your phone muted?"

"Yes."

"Then why are you whispering?"

"I don't know," Mallory confessed in a normal volume.

He gestured to the blue sofa, and they sat, scooching away from one another when their elbows touched, as if avoiding a hazardous third rail. Mallory put the phone on the coffee table, propping it upright against a cool-blue vase. She quickly realized they'd have to sit very close to both be on screen, so she slid slowly toward him until both of their faces were in full view. She could smell his—shampoo? Aftershave? Sandalwood and cinnamon.

She looked at Carter, and when he nodded, she hit the unmute button. "We're here."

"Hi, Carter! I'm Trixie."

He pulled off his hat and dropped it in his lap and loosened his scarf. "Hello."

"Are you both so excited?"

If her question had been an email and not in person, Mallory was certain there would be several punctuation marks at the end of it, likely several redundant question marks and at least one exclamation point.

"Confused is probably the better word," Carter said, leaning forward with an elbow on the knee farthest from Mallory. "I think I can speak for us both when I say that neither of us was expecting to see one another, not only in the same inn on the same night, but the same room."

"Wait, *what*?" One question mark, three exclamation points.

"Yeah," Carter confirmed. "That's a problem that needs fixing. Not to mention that when we talked this out, we were surprised to learn that this is Wanderlove's doing."

"The same room was not our doing," Trixie said. "Or, it might have been, but it was a mistake. I sincerely apologize."

"Please fix it," Carter said mildly.

Trixie turned from the camera and tapped a message on her laptop, likely an urgent message, judging by the speed of her fingers. "That will be squared away. I'll let the inn know to book you into another room."

"I don't know if—" Mallory said, but stopped when Carter threw her a look, then cut his eyes to where Trixie was still typing. He nodded once, and Mallory understood. Let her deal with it.

"I'm so sorry," Trixie said again. "We have interns here, and—yeah."

Mallory wondered how young the interns had to be when Trixie appeared to be not a day over freshman keg stands, but Carter was right. Let them handle it.

"But while that's straightened out," Trixie said, "let's talk about your TV audition."

"Audition?" Mallory echoed, her uncertainty leaking through her professional smile. "Audition, singular?"

"Yes. As you know, we're auditioning a few travel influencers for the job of hosting the first season of *Wander With Love*."

She paused, apparently waiting for an affirmation, but Mallory didn't think it was necessary. Both she and Carter were here, after all.

"Is this when you tell us why we're both in Seasalter?" Carter asked, and Mallory resisted the urge to flinch at his assertiveness, because honestly, she did want to know what the hell was happening here.

"We want you to audition together!"

Four exclamation points. All in italics.

"Together?" Carter and Mallory asked at the same time, like a cheerless holiday choir.

"For *Wander With Love*, we don't want to simply show beautiful people in beautiful places having fun. Any show can do that. We want to offer solutions to problems that travelers have."

"Uh-huh," Mallory said.

"After some market research on travel trends, we learned that one issue people have with traveling is that their partner doesn't view travel the same way. Many couples are made up of one person who loves to travel, and one person who hates it and only goes to make their partner happy."

Mallory peeked at Carter and heard a very soft, very explicit word emerge from his unmoving lips. She reached over and muted their end of the call, just in case.

"So," Trixie continued, "we thought since we're auditioning influencers anyway, why not use the opportunity this week to collect some content that those travelers can use? Who better to illustrate that kind of odd couple than you two? The sunny angel and the grumpy cave-dweller."

"My brand isn't grumpy cave-dweller," Carter said in a tone that strongly suggested grumpy cave-dweller. Mallory reached over and squeezed his knee in a gesture meant as camaraderie, but she was distracted when his hard quadriceps didn't budge much under her reassuring fingers.

"You're muted," Trixie said.

Mallory unmuted them, but thankfully, Carter didn't have a chance to repeat what he'd said because Trixie rushed on. "Not only will we get to see something a little different from both of you that our company can really use, but it's a chance for you two to show how well you adapt to unpredictable events. Events like a surprise collab!"

Mallory grinned like she loved this seven-exclamation-marks idea, though she couldn't have been more annoyed. Carter Scott was going to cramp her style. What were her followers going to think of him, and what were they going to think of her for collaborating with someone with messaging that was so completely opposite hers?

Smile still on her face, she turned to Carter, who appeared as if his head were about to pop off and fly into space.

And she never would have admitted this to him, but she was in full agreement. This was ridiculous.

"Though I don't have an issue with this idea in general," Mallory said slowly, "I wonder if it will show either of us in our best light. My brand doesn't speak to his audience, and I'm quite sure his brand doesn't speak to mine."

She hoped that both Trixie and Carter interpreted that as diplomatic.

"I get that," Trixie said, "but we're wondering what would happen if you two could combine your strengths to create some fun new messaging. You can each take what you want for your own content, but what you give us will be something fresh and new."

"We just met last night," Carter pointed out. "Under less-than-ideal circumstances, I might add. You—and we—don't even know if Mallory and I get along as friends or coworkers or anything."

But Trixie had clearly taken those classes that teach businesspeople how to overcome objections. "You're creatives. You don't need to love each other as people in real life. We're asking you to try to see how pretty you can make this all look in the airbrushed world of social media. Play pretend. Make it shine and sparkle."

"We can try, but—"

"I think what Carter is trying to say," Mallory cut in, hoping to save this conversation from going in an unproductive direction, "is that we're concerned about what this means for our individual auditions. If we're unable to showcase our own authentic selves because we're creating new Wanderlove messaging, how will you be able to discern what we'll each be like as a possible TV host?"

"We know your individual brands well," Trixie said. "There's no need to convince us with more of the same. We're impressed with what both of you with have done already. This audition is more advanced, because now we want to see how adaptable you are, and how well you take direction while maintaining the essence of what makes each of you so unique and good at what you do."

Mallory glanced at Carter. A little muscle under his earlobe, at the top of his jaw, tightened and released once, twice.

"Are you asking the other candidates to do this?" Carter finally asked. "To work with someone else, audition together?"

"No," Trixie said, leaning toward the camera as if that provided any additional privacy. "You're the only two. Because you're the top two. Don't tell anyone else here that I told you that, but it's the truth."

No one said anything for a minute.

"Can you give us a second, Trixie?" Carter finally asked.

"Sure!" Her relief was palpable, with two exclamation points.

He muted the microphone and turned off the camera.

"What do you think?" Mallory asked.

"I think I'm annoyed as hell."

She had to silently agree. "But if we don't do it?"

"You heard her. She's being really nice about it, but I'm sure refusing means we'll be out of the running. And we'll miss anything that would have come out of the audition content even if we didn't win, like sponsorships."

"It is a good idea," Mallory grudgingly admitted. "Showing a pair of travelers who have different perspectives. It speaks to—"

"It might be a good idea in order to sell winter gear," Carter interrupted. "But trust me, this doesn't work in real life. I don't relish lying to TV viewers and letting them think this opposites-attract thing works out for couples."

He pressed his lips together, as if realizing he'd revealed too much.

"And in your experience, it doesn't?" Mallory probed gently.

She could see the internal struggle on his face—a slight but pained wince, a deep groove between his eyebrows. And after a few moments—"No. It doesn't."

"I get that." She wasn't positive she did, but she drove on. "We're not going to lie about anything, though. We're going to be ourselves, try to play off one another, sell some stuff. We'll show them what works for us and what doesn't, and anyone watching can make their own decisions in their own lives."

"I know. You're right."

"I am right," she confirmed, warming up to her own argument. "And the pros outweigh the cons here, don't they?"

He didn't answer; instead, he gazed out the window again, and his chest heaved with an enormous sigh. Then he reached over and turned their mic and video back on.

"You're back!" Trixie said, her three exclamation points indicating she might have thought there was a chance they wouldn't be.

"Let's try it," Carter said before Mallory could speak, "for twenty-four hours. If we feel like this is working, we'll keep going. If we don't, we'll stop."

Mallory schooled her facial features into passivity, so her surprise wouldn't show on her face. She'd thought they were in agreement, that they were going to present a united front.

Frankly, this wasn't a bad compromise. If they were a disaster, they'd have an out. But it would have been nice to have been tipped off to his thought process.

Trixie was a combination of puzzlement and disappointment, so Mallory rushed to reassure her. "I'm confident we can handle this. Frequent travelers are adaptable by nature. For example, Carter had some car trouble yesterday, and he didn't let it stop him from getting here. Right?"

Carter waited another beat, then cleared his throat. "Yes. Yeah."

Mallory widened her eyes and raised her brows.

"Yeah," he repeated, his lips tight but at least curved up at the corners. "We've probably got this. Just give us a day to make sure."

"Yay!" Trixie shimmied her shoulders a bit, either unable to read the virtual room or not caring what her two content creators thought. "Seasalter has a wonderful Christmas vibe, and we want every nugget of holiday travel cheer documented. They have a ton of town activities to take part in. A holiday TV movie come to life."

"Those are my favorites," Mallory added. "I watch every single one every year."

"Shocker," Carter mumbled.

Mallory tried not to scowl at him. "Only thing missing is the romance."

"Oh!" Trixie lit up even more, if that was possible. "We wouldn't be opposed to you pretending to be a couple, if you think it would make better content."

The noise that emerged from Carter's throat was feral. But soft, so only Mallory was aware. Still, she was seized by the need to reassure Trixie that they were fine; she didn't want to lose this opportunity, even if it was different than she'd planned. She slid her hand toward him, under the camera, spread her fingers, and pressed down in a hold-on-I've-got-this gesture. "I don't think a fake-dating scenario is necessary," she said. "I'd need some serious training with an acting coach to pull off that kind of stunt. I think we can make great content with what we are now: friends with opposite approaches to travel. Right?"

She elbowed Carter in the ribs like she'd been inside-joking with him for a decade. He narrowed his eyes at her.

"Right?" she repeated. "*Riiiight?*" She elbowed him again, then nudged him in the side, pushing her whole body into it. Somewhere in her brain she registered the smell of that spicy aftershave and coffee and something unique to him—something she had no business smelling unless he'd invited her to by voluntarily pulling her body to his. Which he hadn't.

"Right," he finally said.

Trixie laughed. "I was starting to worry for a minute there, but you two are adorable. All right. We sent a box of Wanderlove gear to the inn, which you should get today, and we emailed affiliate links to each of you. Try to use and wear as many of the items as you can. We want Man Cave fans and Sunshine Suitcase fans to all be inspired to run out and purchase last-minute travel items for their significant others. We want your followers to check up on both of you a few times a day. Talk up Seasalter and show how opposites can have a wonderful Christmastime on vacation together."

"But not *together* together," Mallory said. "Just, like, together."

Trixie raised a brow. "I don't want to give you too much guidance. You're the talent. And all your finished content will be considered when we're choosing a TV host. Any questions?"

"The room?" Carter prompted.

"Yes," Trixie said briskly. "We will try to fix the situation, but … if we can't, will you two be okay to share the suite?"

Mallory held up a finger to the Wanderlove rep and muted their sound and video again.

Carter said, "I don't appreciate the way Wanderlove asked if you would be all right with sharing the room with a strange man."

"So we're in agreement, then. You're a strange man."

Carter sighed as if the fate of the world rested in his heroic hands.

"I'm okay," Mallory said.

"I'll take the sofa in the second room, so you can have the bed."

"Whatever."

Another long pause.

Was she okay with this? She was desperate to hold onto this career opportunity. And it wasn't as if she'd never shared a hotel room with a man before, though those few-and-far-between times were mutually desired.

"If we do this," he finally said, "and if at any time, you're uncomfortable in any way, tell me. We'll come up with something."

"I will. We can do this."

"Okay. Yeah. We can do this," he repeated, but Mallory got the feeling he was saying it to himself more than her.

Mallory couldn't help but wonder why Wanderlove would be interested in Man Cave Adventures at all. Instead of the open road and endless possibilities, Carter pointed out all the difficulties travelers faced and promoted finding the comforts of home when far from it.

But maybe that was it. The people who loved travel were easy to sell to; the people for whom travel was an undesirable inevitability were the untapped market for travel items. If Carter

Scott loved a product, his specific fans were likely to trust him, because he felt the way they did about leaving home.

Most travel influencers sold the same message Mallory did; it was merely her aesthetic that made her particularly popular. A collaboration with Carter Scott could only help; next to his gloomy raincloud, her message could shine even brighter.

Carter turned the microphone and video back on. "Trixie, we're a go."

"All right," Trixie said. "Audiences will love you two. Personality, perspective, and presentation. That's what we want to see this week."

The wheels in Mallory's head started frantically spinning. She wanted Wanderlove on her side—and, inexplicably, she needed Carter Scott on her side—in order to keep growing. Keep traveling.

Keep moving.

# CHAPTER FOUR

"Well," Carter said after they disconnected with Trixie. "Today is going to be—fun."

"Why are you making a face?" Mallory asked. "Or is that just your resting man face?"

He sipped his coffee; no need to tell her what he'd been thinking. "I suppose we should make a plan. Your billions of followers and my tens of followers eagerly await us."

"That's not accurate, for either of us. Listen." She softened her voice. "I get it. We're not the same sort of people. We're complete opposites. But that's what led Wanderlove to come up with this collab, and we both need our work to be great."

He nodded warily.

"I had a roommate freshman year of college who was challenging to get along with," she continued. "It was hard to relax at the end of the day with all that tension at home. I didn't need that. Not after growing up with—" She stopped herself, shook her head slightly, and smiled to cover whatever she'd been about to reveal.

Carter couldn't help wondering what she was holding back. He'd assumed Mallory Robson was a best friend to everyone— roommates, children, German shepherd puppies. He realized that at the same time he'd been certain she couldn't be perfect every minute of her life, he'd also been certain that her life couldn't have been too difficult or stressful. That because she didn't outwardly express a jaded attitude, she had no reason to have it at all.

She shifted on the sofa, clearly uncomfortable with saying what little she had. She was curating an image, and she'd cracked that image for a moment.

He understood. After all, he did the same every day.

"We don't need to add to the discomfort that Wanderlove gave us," she said. "I know we're not friends right now. If anything, we're rivals for the TV job that I really, really want and intend to get."

Carter raised a brow.

"But," Mallory added, "I believe we can work together in harmony and mutual respect. And I think it will make our work better. Then, when Wanderlove picks me—"

"Or me."

"—it won't be because one of us fell short."

In spite of himself, Carter found himself wanting to know more about her. But maybe that was her motive—get him to care about her, relax his guard a bit, maybe not put in his best work?

And he would put in his best work. He'd been saving up for so long for his dream home, and the new TV possibility would offer the balance he needed to retreat from this career and create a new life. Even if he didn't get the TV gig, the other sponsorships he might get after this collab with Mallory would push him in the right direction, if a little more slowly.

Nothing else mattered but that home he envisioned while sitting in every cramped plane seat, eating at every quirky restaurant, posing in every selfie op.

Not even Mallory's eyes, softened with vulnerability, mattered as much.

There was a stirring in his chest, matched only by the fluttering in his stomach.

"Um, right," he said, trying to recapture the thread of their conversation.

A small din started to rise in the dining room, indicating the knitters were probably done with breakfast and heading out here. He wasn't in the mood for their Greek chorus after having been blindsided by Trixie, so he edged toward the door and was surprised when it opened from the other side. A brown-uniformed man came in, hefting a large box. He deposited it on the floor and left.

Mallory rushed over to the box and peeked at the label. "Wanderlove!"

The delivery driver walked in with another, even larger box, and placed it next to the first before leaving.

Selene swept into the room, wiping her wet hands on her apron. "What's all this?"

"It's for us," Mallory said, tearing at the flap.

"I have a feeling you two are going to make this week very interesting." Selene winked at Carter and left the room.

Mallory scrabbled at the box with futility, like an overeager kitten, so he pulled his keys from his pocket and sliced the tape open on both packages. Mallory reached into the box and flung out a bunch of packing paper, but she did it with such joy that Carter wondered if this was how she opened brightly wrapped gifts on Christmas morning, face flushed, eyes sparkling with anticipation, long blond hair falling in her face. "One would think you never got free stuff from a sponsor," he said, not so much to be curmudgeonly, but more to erase Christmas-morning Mallory from his imagination.

"Free stuff is always fun, no matter what."

As she yanked out more packing material, Carter noticed his discomfort and tried, like his therapist often suggested, to identify it, to name it. He couldn't. Whatever this was, it was new to him.

"I'm going for a walk in town," he said, replacing the lid on his cooling coffee.

"Oh." She sat back on her heels and regarded him. "I thought we could make a plan for today. What we're going to see, do—"

"We have plenty of time," Carter interrupted. "I'll be back soon."

She paused a moment, like she was trying to figure out what he was thinking, but good luck to her, because he didn't even know what he was thinking. All he knew was that he needed a sharp slap in the face to force him to refocus, and the cold Rhode Island air would be happy to oblige.

"I warn you, if we're collaborating, we won't be skipping one holiday activity in this cute town," Mallory said. "I'm going to Christmas the heck out of this week."

He raised his eyebrows. "Sounds like a threat."

"Only if you consider Christmas spirit a threat."

Did he?

Not a *threat*. Maybe just a … challenge to his well-being. And a reminder that he wasn't where he wanted to be.

Yet.

"Maybe," he just said vaguely, since he had nothing by way of retort, and he turned and let himself out of the inn.

The cold pinched his nose, stung his cheeks, pierced his eardrums. He pulled his hat back over his head and knotted his scarf. It wasn't quite as cold as yesterday, but December in New England wasn't friendly. He looked around the porch, seeing it in daylight for the first time. Two sturdy wicker rocking chairs sat dormant on the porch, and he was sure if he sat on one, the cold seat would pierce his jeans and bite his butt. Fairy lights were strung along the roofline, lit even in daylight.

Christmas was no threat.

Mallory herself, though—she was the threat.

She was talented enough to threaten his chance at the TV job, cheerful enough to threaten his demeanor, and, well, sexy enough to threaten his next seven nights of sleep with dreams of …

Nope. No. Nuh-uh.

No dreams of the woman who could steal his best cash opportunity out from under him. Not dreams of the woman who—even if he could stand her endless, *relentless* good humor—lived for the one thing he hated most: travel. She was not someone he could imagine being with in any real, meaningful way, so he had no business even fantasizing what one night with her could be.

Even though they were stuck together for a week of nights.

He scowled.

"Jingle bells, jingle bells," he sang under his breath, the words less joyful and more annoyed.

Mallory had backed her car into a spot in the lot, so Rudolph's eyes followed Carter to the sidewalk. He wished his own car had googly eyes in its headlights, so he could park it directly in front of Rudolph for a staring contest.

God, he was a jerk.

He loosened his scarf a bit and left his gloves in his pockets. He walked down Oceanview and turned onto Broad Street—a lofty name for a street that was busy with shops on both sides but was physically quite narrow. It was a couple of hours too early for anything to be open, but it was good to scope out the center of Seasalter, get the lay of the land to see what he'd want to document later.

This town was a red-and-green yuletide fever dream, even this early in the morning. The shops and restaurants weren't open yet, but the lights were on inside each building, and proprietors were moving about their premises, sweeping and straightening and prepping for opening. Everyone who noticed him peering inside waved at him with cheerfulness and without squinting hesitation. It didn't matter that they didn't know who he was—yet. They all shared this town, this time of year. He might feel like an outsider, but he wasn't considered one.

The main focus of Man Cave Adventures was finding little spots of comfort, of home away from home. Carter had begun the account after a breakup that was instigated by his last serious girlfriend, Leah, after dragging him on a long vacation and realizing that they weren't "compatible" when she discovered he preferred sitting in pubs watching European football, relaxing in hotel lobbies, reading books, and eating food he already had a palate for. He realized he couldn't be the only man out there who hated to travel but was obligated to for one reason or another, so for Man Cave Adventures, he went to new places and instead of panoramic views or historical landmarks, he showed his followers where the most comfortable bathrooms were, where you could smoke a soothing cigar, where you could get a good burger, where the softest armchairs were to play games on your phone.

Turned out, he had a bigger audience than he'd thought he'd have, and he continued to gain followers, many of whom were not men. Reagan told him it had more to do with his face than his content, but he wasn't sure whether to take his little sister seriously when she said things like that.

Carter passed Sea Reads, a bookstore with a large picture window and a tree decorated with colorful bookmarks hanging from ribbons. The real estate office featured in its window a menorah made of branches of local beach driftwood and lit with LED candles. Blue Ocean Fitness's window was painted with a buff Santa in a tank top, holding a barbell over his head, white snowflakes falling all around him. Taco Tuesday's window was covered in burrito wrappers and adorned with strings of red lights shaped like chili peppers.

The coziness of Man Cave Adventures was exactly all this.

Mallory—hell, even Trixie—didn't quite get it. He just preferred the comforts of home, and he sought them out wherever he went. He wasn't sure how he'd judge Seasalter at the end of this week, but his first impression was ... hopeful.

He sipped from his half-filled coffee cup, scowling that it had gotten cold before it had adequately caffeinated him. As he tossed it in a brightly painted sidewalk trash can, he noticed the shop he was in front of was already open when someone walked out carrying a steaming cup and a white paper bag that smelled suspiciously like fresh doughnuts. Painted across the picture window in gold-edged pink letters were the words *Jasmine Pink's Tea Shoppe.*

Tea?

It wasn't coffee, but he wasn't picky about the form of his morning drug.

He stepped into a doll's house of human proportions. Elegant bistro tables and comfortable armchairs. Cream-and-rose wallpaper etched with gold. A gleaming blond hardwood floor.

But it was the scent in the air that stopped Carter in his tracks. He inhaled once, deeply, then parted his lips to try to taste the air.

The woman behind the counter turned, and Carter was struck first by her agelessness, then at her amused, soft smile.

"Ah, a first-timer. I'm Delilah. You're ... lost?"

Her voice was somehow simultaneously gravelly and light. It was an older voice, though, carved by about eighty years of time.

"'Not all who wander are lost,'" he tried, quoting Tolkien.

"Ah, but not all who wander truly wish to. They're searching for their warm seat by an eternal fire."

"How—" *did you figure me out so quickly?* He cleared his throat. "How did you make that up on the spot? Are you a poet?"

"Not a poet. Just an observer."

"Carter," he said, and would have reached for her hand, but she opted for a kind of regal nod of acknowledgment. He tried to return it, but suspected he looked less like royalty and more like a fool. "What's—what do I smell?"

"What do you think it is?"

"Licorice."

She tilted her head slightly, regarding him as a curious cat would. "Licorice is a memory for you."

"Home," he said, startling himself with his answer.

"Tell me more," she said quietly.

He struggled to find words.

"Close your eyes. What do you remember?"

He obeyed, and in a moment, the images flooded his mind. "I used to eat licorice candy with my father in the summertime. He always said licorice is an acquired taste, to be savored slowly, so we sat quietly and ate it together. We moved around a lot, so I don't have a lot of childhood memories that feel like home, but those licorice moments were grounded, peaceful. Like … what home would feel like. What home should feel like."

He popped his eyes open and glanced around, hoping no one had walked in and heard him going on and on about licorice like some kind of sentimental sap. But there was no one.

"That's lovely," Delilah said. "And you're right. It's licorice. I could tell you had an attachment to it."

Carter wasn't sure how to respond.

"And now," Delilah said, "it's tea time. Are you ready for your prescription, Carter?"

"My—what?"

"How it works here is, you tell me how you're feeling or what you want, and I'll prescribe a tea for you."

"Oh," he said. "Um, well, I want to go home, if you want to hear the truth."

Delilah nodded. She appeared to be waiting for him to elaborate, but on that subject, he preferred not to. "As for how I'm feeling?" he said instead. "I woke up screaming this morning, so I had a bit of a headache to start, but it's subsided."

Delilah pursed her lips. "Nightmares?"

"Eh, no. It's a long story."

"I won't drag it out of you." Delilah stepped back and studied him longer than a regular person would call polite. He resisted the urge to squirm under her scrutiny. Then she put out a hand. "May I?" He nodded even though he had no idea what she intended, and she plucked a long, golden hair off his jacket.

She held it between them for a moment, amusement creeping over her face.

He tried not to imagine the face framed by all that golden hair.

He'd see her soon enough, since they were stuck working together. For at least twenty-four hours.

Popping open a trash can with a foot pedal, Delilah dropped the airy strand of hair in, then sanitized her hands with a dispenser on the wall. "Bergamot," she finally said. "With lemongrass. Sit and I'll bring it to you."

"Do you have a menu?" he asked. "I'm not sure I—"

"No menu. I know what you need. Unless you need to tell me about any allergies?"

Carter shook his head. He realized too late that his dumb mouth was hanging open.

"Sit," she repeated. "I'll bring it to you. Doughnuts?"

Good, she used the plural. "Yes, please."

She waved him off and moved behind the counter.

Carter chose a small table in the corner, and when he sat, he let out a long breath and allowed his shoulders to relax. This was how he knew he'd found a place to tell his followers about. The gingerbread-man garland on the fireplace, the elaborately red-and-green sprinkled doughnuts in the case up front, and the sparkling stars of the votive candle holders on each table gave it that holiday feel, and the warm service and atmosphere gave it the Man Cave Adventures stamp of approval.

It was far cutesier and quainter than his usual haunts, but that was what made it unique. He pulled out his notebook to jot down his observations and thoughts. He'd written a paragraph when Delilah approached with a tea tray. He'd expected a cup, maybe a saucer. She explained everything she brought: a beautiful pot in a Victorian floral print, a tea strainer to catch the loose tea leaves, a little timer to steep it for the right amount of time. He also got a cloth napkin in the same print as the pot, as well as lemon, milk, sugar, and honey. And a plate with two small doughnuts.

This wasn't a caffeine fix; this was a ritual.

"Bergamot is for anxiety. Frustration." She took the lid off the pot, gesturing for him to lean over and absorb the fresh scent. "Lemongrass is uplifting and bright. A pinch of cardamom to add some depth and to soothe your physical self."

"What's with this town?" Carter asked. "This place, where somehow, you've managed to feed both my stomach and my ... well, my soul. Um, that's weird. Don't tell anyone I said that."

Delilah pressed her lips together, her eyes sparkling.

"And I'm staying at the Moonrise Inn, where ... All I know is that I walked in there last night and the—the *energy* of that place calmed me. I need to stop talking. I sound like a woo-woo lunatic."

He paused, worried that Delilah would take offense, but she merely smiled at him like he was a particularly charming boy whom she was tasked to keep an eye on.

"You know," Carter added, "I'm staying in an inn full of ladies in a knitting group. I have a sense this is their kind of café. I'll send them over."

"No need. The Crafty Ladies are my friends. Every year, we meet in a new location for the holidays, and I convinced them to come here this year and stay at Selene's inn."

"Good choice."

"Do you knit?"

"Me?" Carter snorted. "No."

"That's too bad. Well, perhaps I'll see you at the inn tonight."

She patted his shoulder and left to greet a trio of men who'd walked in—a trio, Carter noticed, that would look at home in a sports bar with beers. Ex-athletes? They sat at a white-painted bistro table that was far too tiny for them; Carter doubted they could all lean in at once and put their elbows on the table. But Delilah welcomed them as longtime friends, and they quietly conferred. Probably about their "prescriptions."

Carter took a few pictures of the room, the table in front of him, the fireplace. Then he pulled out his phone and opened his notes app to write a caption.

His thumbs hovered over the tiny keyboard for a full minute, another, and another before he put his phone down. With his content, his aim was to provide not just the description of a location, but the prevailing emotion that accompanied it. He chose places that provided the comforts of "home" to followers who valued comfort and peace over adventure and sightseeing, but something about this tea shop ... the Moonrise Inn ... Seasalter.

It all seemed like a home.

He'd gone to grade school in Germany and to high school in Japan. He'd attended Diwali celebrations in New Delhi and hiked in South Africa's Drakensberg Mountains. By the time he'd landed in D.C. for college, he'd been tired. More tired than an eighteen-year-old should be.

Since then, he'd traveled lighter for his blog, but he also searched for the place where he might finally, finally plant roots for the rest of his life to grow, sure and steady. There was beauty everywhere he went, so it wasn't aesthetics he was weighing; it was a—feeling.

He hadn't found it yet but was certain he'd know it when he did.

This little oceanside town he'd barely seen couldn't be it.

Yet—

Despite the stress caused by the Wanderlove snafu, and despite his car trouble, and despite the unseasonable bitter cold, the cords of his neck were relaxed, and his shoulders weren't hovering up by his earlobes.

*This is silly. Inns are supposed to be homey, and a tea shop isn't a rock concert. Of course it's peaceful here. It doesn't mean Seasalter is the place.*

He shook his head, maybe a little bit more vigorously than he should; Jasmine Pink's patrons might wonder why he was acting like a cat shaking off water. There was too much happening in his brain: his work assignment, another Christmas without permanence or traditions, and Mallory.

# CHAPTER FIVE

Mallory sat cross-legged on the floor of her—their—room, staring at two beautiful pictures on social media. The first was an armchair with pink-striped upholstery and elaborately carved armrests seated near a fireplace, and a small tea table in front of it held a delicate teacup and saucer, and a pink teapot.

*Most of you are coffee drinkers,* the Man Cave Adventures caption began, *and you know I love mine, but let's face it: Coffee is the to-go drink of America. Coffee is a Styrofoam cup in the car while you're late for work, or an offering at a work conference to keep you awake and alert, or a drink to share with a tentative first date while you're fielding uncomfortable questions about how long you've been on that app looking for a match. I confess I rarely enjoy a cup of tea; it's not my thing. But this tea, and this shop—they're different.*

Mallory lifted her head and looked toward the window, surprised. It was on brand for Carter, but there was something more. Wanderlove was watching him now, but his words didn't strike her as contrived. The caption struck Mallory as real, heartfelt.

She turned her attention to the other photo: a tabletop with a hand-painted pot of tea, a doughnut with a bite out of it, and a small book folded open to show a half-finished sudoku puzzle.

Carter Scott made his sevens with that little European strike-through in the center.

The corner of Mallory's lip quirked up. How very prim and proper. She realized she would have guessed that Carter scrawled numbers and letters in barely legible caveman hieroglyphics.

*I'm man enough to not be intimidated by a little pink, and Jasmine Pink's Tea Shop in Seasalter is very, very pink*, the caption read. *The owner, Delilah, greets you like a new old friend and "prescribes" a tea for you—yes, you read that right. You're invited to sit for as long as you like—no, as long as you need. I'm spending the morning here, eating homemade doughnut after doughnut, and a group of men around my age seem prepared to stay here and talk for hours. They are the sort of men who you'd see at any bowling alley or ax-throwing bar, but they're drinking tea and chatting in this dollhouse of an establishment in that confident way people have when they feel at ease. They love it here, and so do I. I allowed Delilah to make me a cup of tea after she insinuated it would cure what ails me. And she looked at me like she knew exactly what ailed me. Unnerving ... but familiar and welcomed.*

Mallory clicked away from the app, and when the phone screen went dark, she drew her knees up to her chest.

Carter Scott was ... sentimental. And a little sappy. And a lot interesting.

Why did he try so hard not to appear so in real life? Why did he walk around with a permanent just-ate-a-lemon look on his face?

She scrolled through his account—not for the first time, but for the first time since she'd met Carter in the flesh. His pictures were colorful, interesting to look at, and even the pink tea shop somehow matched his brand's message of comfort and home wherever one went.

Then she browsed his comments.

Lots of people liked him.

And why not? After all, despite herself, it was possible she even did.

No. She dropped her forehead, closing her eyes and letting her kneecaps massage her eye sockets. No, she didn't. She couldn't.

He was not like her. In any way. He was different, intriguing, interesting to observe and to contemplate, but she couldn't allow herself to entertain any real thoughts about his eyes, his jaw, his hands.

She remained in place for a few minutes, listening to herself breathe. Finally, she pushed herself off the floor and left her—their—room.

Selene walked into the sitting room, drying her hands with a dish towel. "There you are!" she said. "I'm so sorry. I really tried, but the closest hotel room available right now is in Providence. The nightly rate is very high, which I'm sure your company would pay since this is their mistake, but it is a bit of a drive to do daily if you want to stay connected to what's happening here."

Mallory nodded. "We should have told you not to waste your time. I'm sorry. We will make it work. Our job is to cover this charming small town on social media together, so I don't think riding in from the city every day would help me any. You can ask Carter, but I have a feeling he'll say the same."

"Can you manage?"

"We're both adults," Mallory said, but realized that answer could mean one thing or the other. She refused to think of Carter in the context of *the other*. "Wanderlove made an honest mistake. We'll roll with it."

"I'm sure you will. You have a good head on those shoulders. I can tell."

"It shouldn't be hard to make some engaging posts and videos. It was a little awkward when Wanderlove asked us if we'd consider pretending to be a couple to sell their stuff."

"Well," Selene said, "they are a big business. Here they've hired two lovely and talented people, who happen to be complete opposites. What wonderful business it would be for them if you fell in love."

Mallory put up both hands. "Whoa, whoa," she said. "Don't bring the L word into this."

"Hm. You don't believe in love?"

Had anyone ever asked her such a probing question? Not lately, but she didn't want to be rude. Selene sounded genuinely interested. Mallory could try to answer. "Sure, I do. It's not that. It's just—not for me. Well …" Mallory paused, gazing at the little happy-moon night-light plugged into the wall. "If I were to be with someone, it would need to be someone like me. Someone who loves to travel. Not someone who'd rather be at home and would rather I be at home. Like you said, Carter and I are complete opposites."

"Maybe a Christmas in Seasalter can show you that you have more similarities than differences."

Mallory cocked her head. "Maybe you're a matchmaker."

Selene laughed. "In September, two people met here and fell in love. It's not unheard of."

"Have you met Carter? He's like if Ebenezer Scrooge and Oscar the Grouch had a baby."

"Perhaps on the outside."

"You think he's different on the inside?"

"Do you always present yourself outwardly exactly as you are on the inside?"

Mallory winced. This woman was insightful; uncomfortably so. "Did I read that Moonrise only opened this year?" she asked, only to change the subject.

"Yes, I opened over Labor Day weekend." Selene's eyes suddenly darkened a bit and her face grew … sad.

"Are—are you all right?"

"Oh," Selene said. "I'm sorry. I ..."

Mallory led her to the sofa, guided her to sit, then sat beside her, trying to think of what a good friend might say. "You look as though you had a very upsetting thought."

Selene sighed. "I did. But it wouldn't be professional to—"

"It's okay," Mallory said. "Tell me."

Selene's shoulders sagged and caved in a bit, as if protecting her heart. "I just heard myself say I opened the inn in September. *I.* But I've always said 'we.' This is ... my husband died last year, and I always thought of this inn as ours, even though he wasn't here to see it open. I didn't expect to change 'we' to 'I.' Or, I did, but not ... so soon."

"Oh, Selene," Mallory said. "I'm so sorry for your loss." She hugged the woman briefly, rubbing her hand on her shoulder blade before releasing her.

"Thank you," Selene said, and stared into the space in front of her for about ten seconds before she blinked and crumpled the dish towel in her hands. "What's your plan today?"

"I'm going to find Carter, and we'll work on some content for Wanderlove," Mallory said, and a flash of Carter's face across her mind made her frown.

Selene cocked her head. "You don't want to?"

"We're auditioning for a TV show. Maybe I'm a little nervous."

"I suppose the freedom of travel is a little lost when you have a company calling the shots."

"Yes, that's it, I think. I always travel solo. So I have freedom to do what I want, see what I want, eat what I want. I haven't been told what to do since—well, since I was in high school and lived at home."

"Where is home?"

"I grew up in New Hampshire. Not much to see there."

"I'm sure people not from New England would find plenty of interest there. Mountains, nature, historic sites."

"Hm," Mallory mused. "I stared at the same yard, the same trees, the same everything for my whole childhood. My family didn't go anywhere."

"They didn't like to travel?"

"There wasn't much money," Mallory clarified. "Raising me and my two older brothers didn't leave my parents with much left over."

Her mother had reminded Mallory and her brothers several times a year of her sacrifices, but at Christmas, she must have felt it the most, because it was a nearly constant refrain. Somehow Dad had attuned his ears to not hear it; it was part of being in love with her, Mallory supposed. And maybe some guilt. But while icing cookies, while hanging ornaments, while carefully printing her letter to Santa, Mallory always wanted to cover her ears to block out her mother's laments.

"It's true lots of families don't have the means to travel," Selene said now. "But it seems you've made up for lost time. I perused Sunshine in a Suitcase this afternoon while I was on hold with hotels and inns, and it's easy to see how much you love seeing the world."

Mallory nodded slowly, feeling her mouth freeze into the ever-sunny smile she was known for. She did love to travel, and she did love to see the world, and most of all, she loved that as long as she kept moving, she wouldn't be as unsatisfied as her mother was for so many years; she wouldn't waste her youth on settling down.

Once you settled down, it could be years before you got off the ground again. If you ever did.

"Are you going back to New Hampshire for Christmas Eve?" Selene asked.

"No. My parents are in Bali."

Selene raised her perfectly shaped brows. "Nice."

"They saved a little money here and there over the years. And now that my brothers and I are adults, they've been traveling."

And they were always gone at Christmas, because that was when her mother had suffered the pain of her small life the most. Neither her brothers nor Mallory were bothered by not seeing their parents for the holidays. Her brothers had their own families now, George in California and Jared in Chicago, and Mallory— she had to keep moving.

"Are you all right?" Selene asked. "Pardon me for throwing your observation back at you, but you look as though you had a very upsetting thought. That particular smile, pretty as it is, doesn't fool me."

"It wasn't an upsetting thought. It was actually a reaffirming thought."

"What are you reaffirming?"

Mallory stood. "That I'm doing exactly what I'm meant to be doing. And now I need to get some work done."

"Bundle up." Selene got to her feet also, wrapping her long navy cardigan tighter around her. "It's very winter out there. And, Mallory?"

"Yeah?"

"I'm glad you're here." Her gaze passed over the room. "This inn seems to—host the people who need to be here. For one reason or another." Selene's eyes twinkled, as if she knew more than she was letting on. Then a little flash hit the corner of Mallory's eye, and she snapped her gaze to the wall. "What was that?"

"What?"

"Did that little full-moon night-light thingy just go on and off really quickly?"

"If that's what you saw."

"Did you see it?"

Selene shook her head, winked, shook out the dish towel, and headed into the dining room.

Mallory stared at the night-light plugged into the wall for a few minutes, examining its mirthful face, before she finally shrugged and went to her room for her jacket.

*Their* room.

★ ★ ★

When she pushed into Jasmine Pink's, she spotted Carter right away, reading a book she didn't remember him leaving the inn with. He didn't glance up to see who'd come in, engrossed in the story. She noticed the shelf behind him, neatly stacked with used books, and guessed he'd helped himself.

She approached his table and slid into the seat opposite him, placing the large, sporty Wanderlove duffel bag at her feet. He did look up then, and though he didn't quite hiss at her or anything, he didn't seem thrilled to see her. He slid a clean napkin between the pages of the book to hold his place.

"I would have called," Mallory said, "if I'd had your number. We should probably exchange that info."

"Probably." He made no move for his phone.

"Do you have everything you need to get some work done? Selfie stick? Lip balm?"

"You sound like you have a plan."

"I do. We do." She nudged the duffel bag an inch toward him with her foot.

Rather than open the bag, he continued to gaze at her.

"Sorry," she said. "Should have assumed I'm dealing with someone who hates surprises."

"I don't hate all surprises," Carter said. "If someone ran in here and gave me a winning lottery ticket as a gift, I'd love that. It depends on the surprise."

"Good." She smiled brightly. "Now, keep that fun open mind."

"Now I know I'll hate it. Weren't you wearing a pink jacket yesterday?"

"Yes. This one was in the Wanderlove box. There was one for you too."

"Gray's not your color."

She wasn't even a bit insulted. "Agreed. Gray isn't anyone's color because it's not even a color. It's a storm cloud. On second thought, maybe it's your color."

She bent over, unzipped the bag, and half-revealed one of four ice-skate blades. The twinkle lights over the fireplace shimmered in the fresh, unused steel.

"That's a nope," Carter said, standing and pushing his arms into his sleeves.

"Carter. You promised to try this for twenty-four hours."

He opened his mouth, but whatever objection he was about to voice froze when she added quietly, "Please."

His chest rose and fell with an exasperated breath. "I did," he confirmed. "Let's go."

As they left, he waved the book at the shop lady, who nodded back at him.

# CHAPTER SIX

As they left the tea shop, Carter slid his fingers under the strap of the duffel bag and removed it from Mallory's shoulder. He had to do it carefully, lest he yank on her long blond tresses.

"Oh, you don't have to—"

"I know I don't have to," he said. "And part of me wants to let you stagger under the weight of it since this is your big idea for the morning. But I have manners."

"Could have fooled me, caveman."

He winced. "How about that's not my new nickname?"

"It is until you prove otherwise."

He supposed it was fair of her to say, judging by the Man Cave name and the fact that she was meeting him at a difficult time of year for him. "I finished the *New York Times* crossword earlier today. I'm no anthropologist, but I don't think a caveman can do that."

"You did not. You did a sudoku."

"I did both." He hefted the bag over his shoulder. There would be no comfortable way to carry this without the heavy skates banging against his thigh, but better his than hers. "Do you know where we're going?"

"Yes, there's an outdoor rink set up in the town square."

"Of course there is."

"A little farther down Broad Street."

They walked in silence for a few minutes, and though he was sure Mallory wouldn't expect him to break the silence, he did. "If you knew I did a sudoku, then you looked at my account online."

"I did."

"And?"

"And what?"

"You strike me as someone who enjoys offering her opinions, so I assume you have some."

She grinned. "Aw, you're asking me what I think of your work."

He didn't respond. Did she voice every thought that slid through her mind, or did she ever let the subtlety of a moment be just that?

"You take really nice photos," she said. "I mean, that tea shop is so pretty that it would be hard to take a bad picture in there, but all your photos are—enticing."

Carter didn't give a lot of thought to any particular individual seeing his photos; in his mind, he posted to a big blob of people. If he overthought it, he might fall prey to fear about putting his work out in the world and being judged. So it surprised him that he caught himself wondering which of his posts Mallory Robson liked best. Her opinion of him, or his talent or lack thereof, wasn't relevant.

Music reached his ears, slightly scratchy and tinny through an outdoor speaker. A small town green came into view, where a temporary, oval-shaped ice rink had been set up. Its walls were around waist height, so he couldn't see skated feet, just a sea of colored knit hats with furry pompoms, and scarves billowing out like superhero capes. The skaters were moving counter-clockwise, except for three or four older-teenage boys dodging and weaving around the others with the skill of hockey players. A few girls were in the center of the ice, twirling in circles, trying little jumps, clutching each other, laughing.

In this idyllic holiday scene, no one was tumbling to the ice, ass over tin cup, and sliding into a wall.

Mallory picked up her pace, then flipped her hair over her shoulder and peered back at him as they moved over the frozen grass. Through the speakers mounted on two poles, Paul McCartney was simply having a wonderful Christmastime.

Carter decided to get ahead of this. After all, they were equals in this endeavor. "How about I take some video of you putting on your skates, then of you skating around the rink a bit."

"What?" Mallory found a spot on a bench and sat, unlacing her plaid boots. "That's a terrible idea. That puts you completely behind the scenes."

"That's okay. The skating can be your thing."

"You don't want to skate?"

"No, I'm not really—"

She pulled off a boot and pointed it at him. "I see what's going on here. You can't skate."

"No," he admitted. "I can't. But that's okay. We can—"

"This is perfect. Put the skates on."

"I didn't bring my tripod. I wasn't expecting you to meet me."

"I brought mine."

He knelt and reached around in the duffel, his fingers finding the tripod in an outer pocket. He opened it. "If you want, I can lace up your skates for you, and we'll both be in the video."

"Better idea: You sit, and I'll lace up your skates. We'll do a voiceover later about how this is your first time."

"No."

"Carter. We promised we'd give this our best for twenty-four hours."

"My best does not involve the emergency room."

"Listen," she said, tugging on his sleeve until he sat beside her. "I know it's uncomfortable to try something new. But we're being asked to show the audience how opposites can travel together.

We can show how I love to do something active, and you don't, but that compromise is possible. You try it for a short time, and if you like it, we can keep skating, and if you don't, we can relax with hot chocolate and enjoy the atmosphere."

Carter glared at the black skates at his feet. "They couldn't even give me cool hockey skates? Those are figure skates."

"They have better ankle support, which, if you're a beginner, is best."

She slid a dark-blue-and-green plaid scarf out from the bag. "May I?" Before waiting for an answer, she unwound his old, tattered scarf from his neck and wrapped the new one around him, tucking it into his jacket collar. The skin of her fingers grazed his bare collarbone, and warmth filled his chest. Either this was a magic scarf or—

"Where are your gloves?" he asked.

"In my pocket. I need my fingers to lace up."

He stood and set the tripod up a few feet away, hoping a child running on blades wouldn't knock it over.

Mallory had already put on her blades and stood. She gestured to the bench, and he sat, and she crouched in front of him. He kicked off his sneakers.

"Foot," she said, gesturing.

He lifted his leg, and she said nothing for a minute. "What is this?"

"You don't like them?" He turned his foot this way and that, like Cinderella admiring her footwear. Except he was admiring his Homer Simpson socks.

She laughed, tossing her wild mane. "No, I don't like them; I *love* them. I feel like you just let me in on a big secret."

"Socks are underrated. Why do most people just wear plain socks? Boring. Even if no one sees them but me, I need expressive socks."

"I'm the same way with stamps. It's the same price to buy a book of fancy stamps as it is to buy standard stamps with flags or something, so I always ask at the post office what kind of stamps they have before I buy a book. If I have to pay excise tax, I might as well slap a Tweety Bird stamp or a Yellowstone National Park stamp on it. More fun."

They grinned at one another for a moment, before Carter realized he'd been distracted from ice skating. He let the smile fall off his face but Mallory, seemingly unfazed, kept hers on. She patted her knee, and he rested one heel on it, trying not to drop too much weight on her leg. He pulled the little remote from his pocket and started the video.

She pushed the skate onto his foot. He watched her fingers nimbly maneuver the black laces around the hooks, pausing once or twice to tug the laces taut. She finished it with a double-knotted bow, and gestured for his other foot.

"How about for this one," she said, "you smile at me, like you're anticipating fun?"

"I'm not. I don't want to fool the public into thinking I love this idea."

"At least, try not to look so terrified. Look at all those little kids. They can all do it."

"I'm not sure why you think that watching six-year-olds competently skating would add to my confidence rather than deplete it."

"It's going to be fun."

"For you."

"Yes," she said, tying another bow, then lining up their shoes under the bench. "You're good. Walk around, make sure they're not too tight."

"How?"

"Just stand up."

He stood and, unused to the balance on two blades, pitched forward. Luckily, Mallory stood at the same time, and he landed in the puff of her jacket, her arms safely around him. He didn't want to lean against her like this, his mouth so close to her ear. A little jingle-bell earring he hadn't noticed before tinkled. He blew her hair out of his mouth.

"I've got you," she said softly, and he suddenly wanted that melodic voice to follow him everywhere, always reassuring him.

He didn't want to push against her to stand upright for fear of knocking her backward, but she did it herself, hands on his shoulders. "Not too bad for a first-timer. I'll get the phone."

Realizing he'd been filming this entire time, he clicked stop on the remote as she dismantled the tripod. "I have an idea," she said, clunking back to him on her blades. She put his phone in his jacket's chest pocket; the top half stuck out. "Perfect! This is going to be your skating cam. We'll hit record and get a first-timer-on-ice perspective."

"I don't think—"

"If it's terrible, we don't have to use it. But let's try." She put her gloves on as the wind bit down on both his cheeks.

"I don't suppose you brought a hat."

"You suppose correctly." She ran her fingers through her waves, adding a little height, then shook it out. "But, like you, I have a Wanderlove scarf." She twisted the purple material around her neck. "There we go. Warm *and* cute. It's even got a little pocket in it for a key or a hair tie. Let's go."

She took his arm, and somehow, he walked to the opening in the wall that led to the rink. People got on and off slowly, except for the few who didn't quite have speed control—those people flew off the ice onto the rubber mat, laughing, gripping the wall.

"Stay here," Mallory told him. "I haven't skated since last Christmas, so I'm going to do a lap or two, get my legs under me, then come back for you."

"Take your time. And trust me, I've never meant those words more."

Mallory stuck her tongue out between two slickly glossed pink lips and glided away.

Her ankles wobbled the slightest bit, but a mere second later, she was confidently moving across the ice, navigating the short end of the rink by crossing her right foot over left, right over left, until she was on the long side.

A lot of people stood at the wall like he did—mothers, husbands, teens—watching the skaters with expressions that ranged from fond to trepidatious. His face was likely a textbook version of the latter, but a string in his heart sprang loose, begging to be pulled tight. To be able to watch with that fondness for someone you loved enjoying themselves on this frigid holiday morning—he'd never admit this out loud to another human, or even barely to himself, but that was what he wanted.

He *didn't* dislike Christmas, or any other holiday. What he disliked was not having his own home to celebrate in, building his own yearly traditions of food and gifts and decorations and joy.

With someone who wanted the same ...

He kicked the thought out of the playground of his brain as Mallory sailed in front of him. She opened her arms wide, as if inviting an embrace, and when she zoomed right past and he realized her open hug was for the world in general, he was embarrassed at almost lifting his own arms to her, to bring her in.

Mallory Robson was a lover of all places, all people, all experiences.

Not the girl he might one day find, the one who'd want to intertwine her roots with his.

About three feet in front of Mallory, a little boy flopped to the ice, sliding into the wall. Mallory turned on a metaphorical dime and followed him. She scooped her hands under his armpits, set him on his feet, and whispered something into his ear that relaxed his face from near tears to near giggles. She waited until he was on his way again before resuming her own circumnavigation of the rink.

Her legs, encased in those black leggings, were strong, carrying her with zero effort. She didn't even need to watch her feet; instead, she lifted her chin, appearing delighted at the colored lights strung in the bare branches all around them. She came around the final turn and caught Carter's eye, gesturing *come here* with both hands.

He resisted shaking his head like a petulant kindergartner. Instead, his grip on the wall grew tighter.

Skaters slowed near the opening, stumbling on and off. Mallory turned both feet and scraped to a stop, a bit of ice flying. "Did you take some video?"

"Um," he said, unwilling to tell her he'd been too busy watching her with his own eyeballs to actually use his phone.

"Aw, you're really nervous," she said softly. "It's okay. Did you see that kid fall?"

"Yeah."

"I asked him if it was fun when he fell, and he realized it was, just sliding around on his butt."

"A few things," Carter said. "The first and most important one being, that kid is a lot lower to the ground than I am."

"What are you, six foot?"

"Six one."

"You're even taller on blades."

"You're not helping."

"Listen," she said, stepping onto the rubber mat and standing beside him. She wrapped her gloved hands around the top of the wall, next to his own leather-gloved fingers. "Just try going around once. One time. If you like it and you're feeling good about it, we can go around again. If you don't like it, we're done. I'm not going to force you to keep doing something you hate."

"Even if it makes good video?"

"It's not good video for anyone if you're frightened or you're truly miserable. In that case, we'll erase it and shoot something else later. It's only good video if you succeed and it's a positive experience."

He studied her face, but he read zero disingenuousness.

"Or," she said, "you can take the skates off right now, and we can say the hell with it. You can pose right here with them for a pic, and then we can say forget it. But—"

"But what?"

"But what if you end up liking it? What if it ends up being a holiday tradition?"

*What if?*

"I hate this," he said.

"That's the spirit."

They awkwardly stepped to the opening. "This is the hardest part," Mallory said, "even when you're a decent skater, because everyone is coming on and off here. Let's keep holding the wall when there's ice under you."

Carter looked down at the chopped-up, uneven ice where so many blades started and stopped. He put a boot out, then the other, gripping the wall—which was difficult considering it was only waist height.

Mallory skated on his outside. "Give me your hand."

"That's not possible."

"One hand. Keep the other on the wall."

A girl of about four, holding her mother's hand, humiliated him by passing him without a care. He stuck out his own hand, and Mallory grasped it. "Don't let go."

"I won't. I promise."

He stood still, one hand on the wall and one hand in Mallory's. After a few moments, she said, "Good balancing. Now, let's move a bit."

He slid a skate forward.

"Pick your foot up and place it down, then the other. Like you'd walk on a moving sidewalk at the airport."

He nodded, and regretted it since it messed with his vertigo. He was already on the ice now, and he couldn't turn back and go against the group flow. He'd end up taking at least one person down.

Mallory swooped ahead of him and took his other hand, moving backward easily. "Follow me."

Carter tried but couldn't quite push his feet forward easily without feeling like he was going to fly out of control.

"Hi!" he heard, and suddenly there was a group of high school girls surrounding him.

"Is this your boyfriend's first time on skates?" one girl asked Mallory, pushing her glasses up the bridge of her nose.

"Yes," Mallory said.

"He's kind of tall," another girl said, with the confidence of a future Model Congress participant. "Do you want us to help you get him around?"

Somewhere in his mind, Carter realized they were talking about him rather than to him, but it was hard to stand up for himself when he could barely, like, stand.

"Carter?" Mallory asked. "Is that okay?"

The girls all looked at him, and whatever they saw in his face must have made up their minds. Mallory released his hands and moved aside. Two girls replaced her, each taking one of his hands. Two flanked him, each sliding an arm around his coat, and he felt two hands on the small of his back.

"Wait!" Mallory said. She slid the phone out of his front pocket, turned the video on, and stuck it back in. "Skater cam."

Jingly piano notes came from the speakers, and Bruce Springsteen warned all that they'd better be good for goodness's sake.

A girl with a wool head scarf taming her curly red hair said, "One, two, three!"

They tugged, and pushed, and guided, and Carter skated.

CHAPTER SEVEN

It was fortunate that Mallory hadn't known the kind of hot-chocolate buffet that awaited them; otherwise, she might have allowed Carter to talk her out of ice skating.

After they'd changed back into their shoes and shoved the barely used skates back into the bag, they ambled about thirty feet away from the rink to long tables set up as a hot-chocolate bar. Cups of steaming liquid in hand, Seasalter residents and visitors each worked their way down a line of toppings, from whipped cream to nonpareils to butterscotch chips to red-and-green sprinkles. The final selection was a festive bucket of candy canes, meant to hook on the cup, or to perhaps serve to stir the toppings in.

Mallory loved a buffet, especially this frothy-sweet one. So many options. No need to choose only one.

Carter insisted on paying for two large cups. While she opted for a bit of every topping, he went for only whipped cream—though he did spray on an impressive two-inch mound of it. A white picnic table was being vacated by a family, and Mallory rushed to get dibs on it. Carter planted himself across from her, warming his hands on his paper cup.

"This is an experience," Mallory said, spooning some chips out of her whipped cream.

"It is. Though the option of adding rum or amaretto would have been appreciated."

"What? It's barely lunchtime."

"Time of day is irrelevant when I just risked life and limb out there."

"Maybe not life"—Mallory licked her spoon—"though yeah, definitely limb. But you had fun, right?"

"I had fun not breaking any bones, yeah."

"Oh, stop. You barely even tripped. I even saw you smile at the end."

He hadn't smiled; he'd grinned from ear to ear.

"Those girls were cute," he said. "It was hard not to smile at them when they seemed so proud of themselves for dragging a clumsy ox all the way around the rink once."

"Mark my words, the reason those girls even bothered is because they thought *you* were cute."

"Get out of here," he said. She watched, fascinated, as he used his candy cane to dig a hole in his whipped-cream pile to drink through. He sipped and came away with whipped cream on his nose.

Mallory resisted the urge to brush it away. "Nuh-uh. I'm right about this. Girls that age—they wouldn't give a boy the time of day unless they were interested in flirting."

"Boy? I haven't been a boy for years."

"I can't picture you as a boy anyhow. I kind of thought you sprang from the womb as a fully formed Grinch."

She expected him to respond to her half-insults with his half-pained expression, but he didn't. He laughed. The sound of it startled her, but in a good way, like she'd been mining in a dark cave for jewels and finally yanked one free.

In that moment, she was a high school girl, and he was the cutest boy she'd ever met.

After he stopped laughing, they drank in silence for a while, avoiding each other's gaze. At least, she was avoiding it, though she couldn't say why.

"Hard to believe the ocean is right there, a few streets away," she said eventually, gesturing behind him. "It's so cold, I can't remember ever being warm. But it was only about two and a half months ago."

"Same. And in the summer, I struggle to recall how it can get so frigid."

"What's your favorite thing about each season?"

"Are you ever at a loss for small talk?"

She ignored his quip; she happened to be excellent at small talk. "I'll go first. Summer: parasailing. Or exploring a new city and finding the best ice cream. What about you?"

"Summer's easy. Drinking lemonade while rocking in a porch swing and counting fireflies."

"Ah, good one. Autumn? I like a good heated workout class."

"Giving out candy to trick-or-treaters on Halloween," he said.

"Huh. You don't leave your light off and hide behind the couch?"

"Nope. I'm the type to hand out full-size candy bars."

"Didn't see that one coming," Mallory admitted. "Okay, winter. It might be ice skating."

"Hard to believe."

"But I love holiday window shopping. Especially in a new city. Some stores have the most elaborate windows. How about you? I bet it's not Christmas."

"It's close. The day after Christmas."

"What? Why?" She unwrapped her candy cane and dunked it into her hot chocolate. "That's the boringest. Everything is over on December twenty-sixth."

"It's not over," Carter said. "It's the day to really examine and enjoy your gifts, to open them and put them together or try them on or whatever. Also eating leftovers and going out to spend gift cards."

"Hm. I guess you have a point. What's left? Spring. Picnics. Eating outside is the best."

"Eating in general is the best. But I'd have to say … spring cleaning."

"Are you insane?" she asked. "You *like* spring cleaning?"

"Have you noticed that I don't judge what *you* like best about each season, but you make me explain mine?"

Mallory shrugged one shoulder, sliding the candy cane out of the hot chocolate and into her mouth. "That's fair," she said around it. "But I still need to know what you like about spring cleaning."

"Opening windows to let in the breeze. Ridding everything of the winter blues: curtains, rugs. A fresh beginning."

Mallory nodded slowly. "Do you realize that all your favorite seasonal activities can be done at home?"

His eyes grew distant for a moment, then refocused on his cup. "Although no one's asked me to list them before, I guess I do realize it."

"So your Man Cave Adventures isn't a schtick. That's really you. You are happiest at home."

"I think I would be."

"Would be?"

Carter leaned back, as though trying to create some space where he'd accidentally allowed some intimacy to creep in. "I don't quite have the home I want right now. Yet."

She inched forward, closing the space, realizing she wanted to know more. But instead of asking for specifics, she waited to see if he would come to her. She let the silence expand but never took her eyes off his face. Finally, his eyes met hers.

"My parents are United States diplomats," he said. "From the time I was a little kid, we moved. A lot. For a while, it was every year. By the time I got to high school, they managed to keep it to every two years or so. For stability." He snorted.

"Wow, that's—"

"Exotic and adventurous?"

Mallory didn't want to confirm those words as the first two that did pop up in her mind, yes. Because they didn't sound the same coming from his mouth as they would from hers.

"My mom and dad are really good at their jobs," he said. "And they never went anywhere without me and my sister. Everything they experienced, we did—food, culture, art, politics."

"Your family is close?"

"Ironically, even without a home base, we are. I was very privileged."

He used the tip of his candy cane to circle the edges of his cup, allowing the melting whipped cream to fall into the cup rather than slide down along the outside of it.

"You started this by saying you don't have the home you want yet."

"I don't. I have a great apartment in Jersey City, where I live full time, but it's not—" He cut himself off.

"I think I understand," Mallory said.

"How could you?"

She drew her chin back, insulted.

"I'm sorry," he said quickly. "I—I suppose I don't run into too many people who get it. And you, well—"

"I *really* wouldn't get it, what with my suitcase full of sunshine and all."

He answered in the affirmative with lifted eyebrows and cocked chin.

"It's true, I don't get your desire to stay put," she said. "For me, that would be—" She shuddered. "But what I do get is wanting to make a much different choice than your parents made. And I get not having any guidance on how to do it, since they didn't model it for you."

"Don't tell me you didn't travel as a child. You?"

Too late, Mallory found herself flailing in the deep end of the conversation pool. She preferred the shallow end, where talk was fun, light, relaxing. Noncommittal.

"Hey," Carter said quietly. "Is it none of my business? Because—"

She instantly felt bad for not sharing after he'd shared with her—after she'd *encouraged* him to share with her. "My family never traveled anywhere," she said. "And not because—well, let's just say my mother was born with the soul of a wanderer. She went everywhere when she was single: India, Galapagos, Australia."

She paused, and Carter said, "Did something happen?"

"Life. Normal life happened. She met dad, got married. After she had children, my father insisted we not move every six months like she used to, that we stay in one place. For stability," she said, also snorting at her repetition of Carter's word. "Mom couldn't help reminding us often that we were the reason she was—grounded. She refused to take us on short vacations because she said they would make her feel worse, make her long for when she could travel for weeks, months, and never come home. A seven-day trip to Disney World would have been more torturous for her than going nowhere. So ... we went nowhere."

She realized Carter had been studying her as she spoke, his own face softening a bit. "Nowhere?"

Having never recounted this story before, she didn't have the words, so she spoke slowly. "I didn't leave New Hampshire until I was eighteen," she said. "And I didn't get on a plane until I graduated college. You know, I wanted to go to camp when I was a kid, and my dad tried to help me convince Mom to send me. I'm still unsure why he was on my side in this debate, but Mom said absolutely not, because she didn't want me to start to love visiting new places. All that would happen, she said, was that I would have my heart broken when I got married and had kids, and I would need to be tethered."

Carter winced. "That's mean."

Mallory shook her head. "No, she—she really wanted what was best for me, I think, and—"

"No," he interrupted. "I don't know your family, and I'm sure there was more going on behind the scenes than you could understand as a child, but limiting you when she had the means not to wasn't fair. And frankly, you don't need to get married if you don't want to. You don't need to have children to be happy. But she wasn't allowing you to entertain any visions other than her own about what your life could entail. That was not fair."

She was about to tell him not to be angry at her mother on her behalf but stopped. Her mother had done all she knew how to make sure her kids didn't make the same mistake she did, and Mallory had never really allowed herself to feel angry about missing out on experiences she could have had at a young age, or angry about the guilt her mother planted in her children for stunting her own happiness. Carter's reaction was quick and honest, and Mallory didn't mind using his anger as a surrogate for her own.

"Anyway," Mallory said, "it turned out well for her in the end. After my brothers and I grew up and left home, she and my father began traveling and have never stopped. Once in a while, I go to them wherever they are. This summer it was Nova Scotia. She's happy. He's happy that she's happy. I don't know how either of them put up with each other during our childhood, but they miraculously worked it out."

"And you're on the road forever?"

"Hopefully," she said, grinning. "I'm still growing my business, and it's expensive to travel. I do have an apartment in D.C., but one day that will only be where I get mail and keep my furniture. I want to be out there, to see as much as I can."

"And will you get married? Risk being … grounded?"

"I don't know," she said honestly. "Maybe if I find the right man. But the right man has to be like me."

"Restless?"

"I'm not restless. I'm—I'm trying to have what you had. Cultural and culinary experiences. World perspective."

"And to look beautiful doing it, I suppose."

"Is that a compliment? Did Carter Scott just compliment me?"

"Like you need my compliments." He brushed imaginary hair off each shoulder. "Yes, I'm a natural blonde," he said in a high-pitched voice. "Do you love my angelic hair?"

"That's not my voice!"

He laughed. "You argue that's not your voice, but not that I'm wrong about what that voice is saying." He pushed his voice up several octaves again. "I look so hot without a hat! Even though I'm freezing, obviously I'm hot."

Mallory pitched her napkin at him. Then she hit him in the chin with a nonpareil. "No, don't attack me!" he shrieked. "Don't hate me because I'm beautiful!"

Though Mallory was prepared to tease him, goad him, even encourage him, she wasn't prepared for what to do when Carter Scott called her beautiful.

He was making fun of her, sure, but—

It lit a little ember inside her that sparked to life, and she forgot about the cold. He was laughing. And she was beautiful.

As quickly as it all happened, it stopped. Carter ceased laughing, furrowed his brow as if confused by his own display of emotion, and slurped the last of his whipped-cream-laden drink.

*Carter Scott, please don't make me like you. Not like that.*

"We'd better get back," she said, standing. "We have work to do."

He nodded and stood also, hoisting the equipment bag over his shoulder. "Lead the way."

They walked in silence down Broad Street, toward the Moonrise Inn, but Mallory didn't mind the quiet. She hadn't expected to learn so much about another person or to be so open with him about her ambitions and about her life growing up, and maybe it was best to let a little silence spread.

"I'm going to stop here." Carter tilted his chin at the bookstore, Sea Reads. "I'll meet you back at Moonrise."

"I'll wait for you."

"You might regret it. I take my time browsing books."

"That's okay," she said.

The bookstore employee, busy chatting with another customer, nodded at them when they walked in, and Mallory sank gratefully into a large armchair near the picture window.

She tried not to be obvious about watching Carter examine books on the front table, opening one or two to read the first page. It stood to reason that he was a read-by-a-roaring-fire type, homebody to the core.

It also occurred to her, as her mind replayed all Carter's favorite things about the seasons—porch lemonade and spring cleaning—that with his upbringing, he might never have done any of them, and that instead of beloved memories, they were his most fervent dreams for his future seasons.

## CHAPTER EIGHT

Selene's head popped up from her folded arms when her cell phone buzzed. She'd collapsed with frustration onto her desk only a moment prior, racking her brain for who to call next, but maybe this was an inn or a B&B or a hotel calling her back.

She snatched up her phone. Owen.

A call from Owen never failed to slip a smile onto her face, but stress tightened it a bit. "Hey, there."

"Hey, back."

Maybe it was the fact that misery loved company, and she was listening for it, but she noticed a tension in his tone. "Everything okay?"

He chuckled. "You're frighteningly perceptive. Sure you're not a witch? A clairvoyant?"

If she had been, what would she have done if she'd foreseen having to open and run the Moonrise Inn alone? "Anything's possible, but I sincerely doubt it."

"First tell me what's wrong on your end."

"Maybe you're the witch."

"We men witches prefer the term warlock."

"L-O-L," she enunciated. "I just feel terrible for Carter and Mallory, since we had that room mix-up today."

"I thought they assured you it wasn't your fault."

"It wasn't, not officially, but they're under my roof, and they're kids in their twenties, and I feel responsible for them."

"You're very kind."

"I'm trying to convince myself that my worry is out of kindness and not out of wanting to get a bad online review," Selene admitted. "I think it's mostly the former and a tiny bit the latter."

"No vacancies anywhere, huh?"

"It's Christmas in Seasalter. This town is a little slice of sugarplum pie during the holidays, and though I can't complain—it booked Moonrise solid—it also means every other place is sold out."

"Mallory and Carter are in one of your suites. They can probably manage."

"Yes, but …" Selene put Owen on speakerphone, sat back in her high-backed rolling chair, and rubbed her eyes. "It's awkward for them."

"Or … maybe it isn't."

"What do you mean?"

"I mean," he said, and she could hear the smile in his voice now, "that I saw them for a brief time, and yes, they were shouting and confused, but … I sensed something between them. Especially at breakfast this morning. That mutual dislike was definitely covering something else, for both of them. Didn't you notice?"

"Owen Cardiff. Are you an amateur matchmaker?"

"I have zero to do with anything that's happening. But I don't mind saying I'm pretty good at clocking romantic attraction."

Selene's mouth suddenly felt like she'd swallowed a plastic baggie full of Seasalter Beach sand. She tried to lick her lips and was grateful Owen couldn't see her. Was it possible he'd noticed something with her?

He was sweet, generous, smart, and, yes, very handsome. She'd caught herself watching him when he wasn't looking at her, tracing the lines of his broad shoulders, following the inverted V of his body to his waist.

It was not "romantic attraction." It was—appreciation. Which was not illegal, not even for a fifty-year-old widow. Artists appreciated. People with working eyeballs appreciated.

The silence reminded her that it was her turn to speak. "You might be right—about Carter and Mallory," she clarified, if only for herself. "But it's not my place to give them anything other than somewhere to be comfortable for the night."

"They'll understand, and they'll adapt," Owen said. "If it seems to either you or Mallory that Carter has nefarious intentions, I'll be happy to dropkick him into the ocean. But so far, I have a good feeling about him."

"Well, thank you for offering your heroics. They're noted for the future. Meanwhile, I don't have anyone left to call."

"I know the feeling," Owen told her. "I suddenly find myself in a similar leaking rowboat."

"What do you mean?"

He sighed. "My landlord told me this morning that he has to quickly sell the house. I'm a tenant-at-will, so he gave me notice."

Selene blinked. "That's—that's terrible. In two weeks, it's Christmas."

"He was apologetic. I knew this wasn't a permanent situation, but I was hoping to stay at least another year."

A wave of guilt washed over Selene, sitting in the house that was once supposed to belong to Owen. After his stepmother had sold it to her and Dan, Owen had remained in a rental house in town, waiting out the yearlong contract he'd made with Selene. If the Moonrise Inn wasn't profitable in a year, he'd buy back the house so she could start over elsewhere.

Now Owen was being displaced, with his family's former home hosting out-of-town guests and an owner who was learning the job as she went. And it was only recently that her reluctance to do so had faded, replaced with confidence that she might be able to pull it off.

"I'm so sorry," she said, and if he realized she was saying it for what she'd unwittingly done and not simply for the circumstance he'd found himself in, he didn't acknowledge it.

"I've been calling all over town also," he said instead, "hoping to find something right away, because I'm uncomfortable living there while the house is being shown to prospective buyers. I've been searching for rentals, even short-term rentals. But there's nothing available until January first."

"There has to be a solution. Let me think."

"I didn't really call for you to come up with the answer. I just needed to vent."

"Are you done venting?"

He paused. "Yeah."

"Okay, so now it's time to find a solution."

"No, really, you've got your own—"

"I used to be an advice columnist. I told you that, right?"

"You did."

"And so, it's my nature to solve others' problems."

"That's why you were trying to find a room for Carter and/ or Mallory."

"Yes. That was a bust. I'm not a fan of failure, so I'm twice as motivated to help you now."

"I won't say no again," he said. "You've already called every nearby hotel, so we know a room isn't available for me."

"I even called ones that weren't quite nearby. So, we have a few options. Mallory and Carter need to be in Seasalter for assignment, but you don't." Selene pushed the words out, without time to admit to herself that she hated them. "You could try Providence for an apartment. Or even Boston."

"Then I won't …" His voice trailed off.

"Won't what?"

"I won't be in Seasalter."

No, he wouldn't, but Selene refused to see that as a problem for herself. This wasn't about her. "Beggars can't be choosers, Owen, and though I wouldn't quite put you at beggar status yet, you're not at chooser status either."

"You're right, of course, but I don't think a short-term rental would be possible in those cities. Short term is more likely in a smaller vacation town. And even then, short rental is more a summer thing."

"Good point." Selene chewed on a fingernail, immediately remembered her DIY manicure, and dropped her peach-tipped fingers into her lap. "You can look in those cities for a yearlong lease."

"My clients are here."

"You're an accountant," she pointed out. "You've said to me that you love it because you can work at home."

"But clients still drop off and pick up paperwork, and I have relationships with them."

"Is that an insurmountable issue?"

"No, most clients will probably keep me, but ..."

Selene waited a beat. "But what?"

"But nothing. I need to stop being a crybaby. Not being near the house for a while is no big deal."

*The house* meant the Moonrise Inn. She understood. He'd grown up here, and though he didn't live here, being able to spend time here was something he clearly enjoyed, because he was here often. When he was here, he was invaluable to her as a friend and as a helper.

For his loyalty and care, the house owed him.

*She* owed him, despite his always waving away her countless offers to pay him for deliveries or minor carpentry. *What are friends for?* he never got tired of asking. *I know how to fix this loose board, and you have enough to do. I'll do it. No big deal.*

Once, in September, when their acquaintanceship hadn't yet grown into friendship, she'd asked him why he wouldn't let her fend for herself, since according to their agreement, he'd gain the house if she couldn't profit.

*That wouldn't be right*, he'd said.

Now, she needed to do right by him. Even if it was—

"I know what we're going to do," she said. "I know where you can stay."

"What? Where?"

"Here."

Owen said nothing for a moment. Then, "I don't follow. Aren't you all booked up until after New Year's?"

"The guest rooms on the first and second floor are, yes. And I live on the third floor myself, but there is a room up on my floor that I don't use. It's on the east side."

"I know it," he said. "With the dormer window. It's my old bedroom."

"So you know it's small. And you know that it has no bathroom, so you'll need to use the hallway one on the second floor."

"Why don't you book it for guests?"

"It's tiny," she said, "and Dan and I disagreed about it. He was certain it would be perfect for some guests, especially in winter. Maybe guests who want privacy."

"A writer," Owen said. "An artist. Or someone who wants a silent, meditative retreat."

"That's what Dan said." Nearly word for word, in fact. "But I didn't love someone having to pass by our living space to get to that room and being so close to us."

"Understandable."

"But it's you," she said. "And it's an emergency. I think it would be all right for a while."

Would it? Because as she was saying it, Selene's pulse began to speed up a bit. It would be Owen, close to her space. Trusting him was not even a question.

What didn't she trust? Herself?

That was insanity. And maybe loneliness. And—

Owen must have sensed her sudden reticence, because he said softly, "If Dan were here—"

"If Dan were here, he would insist," she said, certain it was true. "He'd of course say it's not renovated because he hadn't talked me into it yet. But he'd have been the first to offer it to a friend in need. Of course," she added, "once you left, he'd say, 'See? It was fine, right? Now let's renovate it and list it on our site as a room for guests.'"

"Every time we talk about Dan, I'm certain we would have been friends."

"No question," Selene said. "Dan loved people, and you're … you're good people, Owen. As long as you don't mind that you could cross the room in two giant steps, you're welcome to stay there for as long as you need it. There's a bed and a desk, so you could do your work there, or if you need to spread out, you can scoot over to the public library. And, as you likely know, you'll have the room in the house with the best view of the ocean. Even though the window is the size of a porthole."

"You don't need to convince me of anything except that it's all right with you. You haven't had much time to think on it before offering."

"What's to think about? Are you going to trash the place like an entitled rock star?"

"I might."

Selene smiled. "You never trashed a hotel room in your life. You're not the type."

"Don't underestimate me. In my twenties, I did some very stupid things. Admittedly, that wasn't one of them."

"Now I'm curious about young, stupid Owen."

"Young, stupid Owen isn't worth discussing, I assure you. He wasn't worthy of Selene Bellamy."

*But you are now?* Selene was tempted to ask. She didn't. She knew he was worthy of any woman who wanted him.

He shouldn't be wasting his time hanging around her, or he wouldn't find that woman.

Selene realized that she'd hate that woman when he found her and was mortified at herself for that.

"I mean it," he said now. "At least think about it overnight."

"Don't make me beg you to move in, Owen. Seriously."

"I promise to make myself useful."

"You already do. Find a storage space for your furniture and bring what you'll need until New Year's."

"Thank you, Selene," he said in a husky voice that sent a shiver down her spine and pooled in her belly.

*Is this okay?*

The window to her left was adorned with short, gauzy yellow curtains, and as she glanced at them, they lifted as if from a breeze.

But the window was sealed shut against the winter wind.

"Yes," she said.

# CHAPTER NINE

Back at the Moonrise Inn, the Crafty Ladies had taken over the main room with an intimidating flurry of colorful yarn balls, pink cocktails, plates of gingerbread men—no, Carter noticed, gingerbread women—and popcorn. Delilah from the tea shop waggled her fingers at Carter as he and Mallory walked in, alerting the other women to look up from their projects.

"Hi, Mallory. Hi, Carter," Selene said, setting her needlework on her lap and starting to stand. "Is there anything you need?"

"We're fine. Don't get up," Carter said. "Really. We have some work to get done, and we'll go to our—er, the room to do it."

Jackie chuckled, and Patrice elbowed her. "What?" Jackie protested. "He said they're going into the room to 'do it.' "

"You have the sense of humor of a thirteen-year-old boy, Jackie," Brenda informed her.

"Carter and Mallory, meet Wendy and Beth Ann," Patrice said.

Mallory smiled at all of them, though, Carter noticed, she was starting to fidget a bit. She was probably exhausted from the long day, what with all the screaming in the morning and skating in the afternoon.

Meanwhile, this was a bit like being in a room full of nosy aunts, and though his own mother was never a crafter or sewer or gossiper, he didn't hate it.

"What are you making?" Carter said, his eyes locked on Brenda's fingers. She wasn't even looking down as she spun magic.

"I'm making a shawl for my goddaughter," she said. "She has a sort of goth style, so I'm using this black yarn with deep purple and silver in it. See?"

"How do you know what to do?" he asked.

"It's second nature at this point, hon. I have a pattern, but I'm improvising here and there. Using some different stitches for texture."

All the knitters began to explain their projects to Carter, who found himself surprisingly, genuinely interested. It didn't escape his notice, however, when Mallory edged silently out of the room and up the stairs. As Beth Ann showed him a complicated pattern for a sweater, Selene left the room and returned with a pile of napkins, which she dropped on the coffee table beside the snacks. "Carter! Are you joining us?"

"Are you a knitter too?"

"No, but I do crochet, and these ladies were sweet enough to consider that acceptable for entry to their club for the week." She lifted a golden half-crocheted pile of yarn off the floor and sat herself easily on the hardwood, crossing her legs.

"I don't know how to do any of this," Carter said, gesturing vaguely at the room.

"Have a seat, and we'll teach you," Wendy said, pointing at the floor next to Selene. "I have extra needles, and as you can see, there's plenty of yarn to go around."

"Oh, I—"

"Stop protesting before you even start, my love," Jackie said. "Sit and learn a skill that you'll use forever."

"It's the best," Patrice said. "I didn't think I could learn it, but once I did, I realized it was a nice, cozy hobby I could turn to any time."

"Plus, think of all the chicks who would love to date a man who knits," Jackie said. "You could knit together and make each other all kinds of adorable presents."

It was appealing—in a Man Cave kind of way, of course. Holing up with a hobby was on brand, and he was never much of a gamer.

"I'll do it," he said, and the ladies cheered.

"We've never had any testosterone in this group," Beth Ann said thoughtfully. "It's a nice addition."

"I have to get some work done first," Carter said, remembering Mallory in the room and the whole reason he was even in town. "Will you be knitting after dinner?"

"We'll be knitting all week," Delilah assured him. "Go do what you have to do."

Jackie chuckled.

"What now?" Brenda asked.

"Go do *who* you have to do—"

"Grow *up*, Jackie," Wendy admonished.

"No, thanks," Jackie said, winking at Carter, who shook his head.

"Jackie," he said, "Your mind is in the gutter."

"*Yeah*, it is." Her hands began working the yarn furiously. "You think knitting is all old ladies think about? We'll talk later."

"What did I get myself into?" he asked, and all the women laughed.

* * *

Carter climbed the steps, knocked softly on the room door, then cracked it. "It's me."

"Enter!"

Mallory was sprawled across the now-made bed, writing in a notebook. "It's your room too," she said without looking up. "You don't need to knock."

"If it's all the same to you, I will. Because I'm polite."

"Since when?"

"Since I'm sharing a room."

"Selene couldn't find a replacement room."

"I figured. I'll take the sofa in the other room tonight."

She scrambled to a sitting position. She'd kicked off her plaid boots, and they lay beside the bed.

"Rooming with me is already starting to turn you into a slob." He chin-pointed at her shoes. "Just look at this mess."

"I'll have you know I squelched the urge to fold your clothes and organize them in a drawer by color."

"But then you realized you hogged all the drawers?"

"I cleared one for you. The top one over there."

He slid the deep drawer open. Indeed, it was empty. "Oh. Um, thanks."

"I'm a great roommate."

"You're certainly a humble one."

She twisted her lips. "You're welcome."

"Thank you," he said, chastised. God, he *was* a caveman. When had he gotten this way? "I'm going to learn to knit," he blurted, for some reason needing her to see him in a brighter light. "Tonight."

"Oh," she said, clearly taken aback. "Good luck. I don't think I could do it."

"Why not?"

"I'm too … fidgety for a hobby like that."

That was a fact. Mallory was always in motion, and even when she sat in one place, like now, her gaze darted around the room constantly—at the door, at the sunny window, at him.

"I reviewed my video from today," she said, "and we need to look at yours too. I'm working on a voiceover script we can use after we edit and splice the videos together. The park was pretty around the rink, and I got some still pics of that to add, and the thematic focus should be that it's your first time on the ice."

"Why do we have to—"

"Because," she interrupted, clearly having anticipated his protest, "you looked a little nervous, then really proud of yourself, then really happy piling whipped cream on your hot chocolate. You proved that someone could make their traveling companion happy by compromising and trying something new. It's a great video for Wanderlove's skates. It's all exactly what they wanted, and whether you really enjoyed yourself or not, you *appeared* to." She nodded as she added, "And that's what the socials are about, right? Showing the best experiences. Aspirational moments."

Everything in him wanted to argue, but he couldn't. She was right. "Can I see your script?"

She beamed. "Yes." She moved to the center of the bed and patted the spot next to her, then turned her attention back to her notebook.

Carter hesitated.

Ice skating was not what he'd expected this week. Mallory twirling a lock of blond cloud around her finger as she bit the end of a pen and read her notes was not what he'd expected this week. Sitting on a bed with her and working together was not what he'd expected, ever.

Mallory peered up. "What's wrong?"

"Nothing." Everything. Nothing.

"You promised to give it a twenty-four-hour chance."

"Yes, I did."

"It's only been—" Mallory shook her arm so her sleeve rolled away from her wrist, allowing her to look at an imaginary watch.

"Point taken. Shove over," he said.

"I did shove over. How much room do you need?"

More than this, he wanted to say. But he sat beside her.

"Take your shoes off," she said.

"I won't put my feet on the bed."

"I don't care about that. I care that you're comfortable."

He glanced at her, but her eyes were on her phone as she pulled up her video from earlier. She held out the phone, leaned close enough that her shoulder rested on his upper arm, and hit play.

Typically, Carter's content was comprised of either selfie photos or video with his looking directly in the camera as he spoke. But in her video, he could study his own smiling profile. He squinted; yes, that was him smiling, and even open-mouthed smiling at one point. He suspected that was when he had asked the girl pushing his lower back to slow down a bit. He'd been nervous to crash and slide, but that fear was overpowered by the way it felt to float with these determined, young ice princesses. His arms were outspread but not in search of something to grip onto—rather, he appeared to embrace the experience, to be welcoming it into his open chest. As he came around the corner, he looked straight into the camera, straight at Mallory, and he now saw himself release a surprise huff of air, air that vaporized into smoke in front of his face.

"Look at that," Mallory breathed softly, and he did.

* * *

Carter and Mallory spent about an hour cutting the videos and splicing them together with a voiceover that she wrote. He'd tweaked it a bit but only to be able to say he'd contributed, because it would have been fine without his meddling.

"It's not easy to come out of your cave, to try something new," Mallory said in the video over the fairylike, jingle-bell music they'd chosen. "But sometimes, when you do, you find a smile you didn't know was in you."

They added a bit of Carter-cam too, so the viewer wobbles in his point of view as he moves slowly toward a cheering and clapping Mallory.

"It feels like coming home—to yourself," Carter's voiceover added.

A photo of their festive hot-chocolate mugs overlaid with sparkling snowflakes closed the video, along with their affiliate links to the Wanderlove scarves and skates.

"Let's skate again tomorrow!" Mallory's joyful voice said over the final image.

"Nope," his grouchy voice answered.

"Please?"

"Never again."

The video faded out with their bickering.

Watching it all through one last time, Carter tried not to grin. It was good. It was funny, and it was endearing, and it was holiday-spirited. And somehow, it was true to both of them, opposites though they were.

"Ready?" she asked, flopping back on the pillow and holding her phone aloft. "I'm posting it to Wanderlove and tagging both of us."

"Wait. It's—" he started, feeling like too much of an idiot to continue.

"It's what?"

"I'm sort of the star of the video," he said. "Are you sure you want to take this angle? When you—you are the star everywhere you go?"

She dropped her hands and studied his face. "No, I'm not."

"You know you are."

She stared at the ceiling as she considered a moment, then shook her head. "I think it's great. It captures both of our messages. And if it makes you feel better, when we go out tonight, we can focus on me somehow."

"It's best that way. People want to see you. Your cheerfulness, your enthusiasm for everything. Your hair. You're the whole package, on your own."

"If that's true," she countered, "Wanderlove wouldn't have wanted us to work together. I can't do it all. Wanderlove recognized I needed your rain to parade on."

"You are quite the parade."

"I'm surprised," she said. "Honestly. You're good at what you do for your audience, but I wasn't convinced we'd be able to work together, that our styles could merge into anything interesting. But they do. We can."

"How about the first video of you lacing up my skates? Can we get anything from that?"

"Oh, right. Let's cut some still shots from it and use one or two. Meanwhile … one, two, three, video posted."

Carter swung his legs over the side of the bed, stood, and stretched. His legs were a little sore from earlier, and he was disappointed in himself, because even if he'd never skated before, he'd only done one full rotation of the rink. Not nearly enough to justify soreness. He was possibly the unmanliest man who ever manned.

Speaking of unmanly, he was a fan of afternoon naps, and he could really use one now, but with Mallory hogging one side of the bed, hair spread all over the pillow, there was no hope of sleeping here.

A mini xylophone began playing "Jingle Bells," and Mallory gave a start, nearly dropping her phone before glancing at it. "Excuse me, I have a call."

"That's your ringtone?"

"For December, it is."

He rolled his eyes but not as hard as he could have. "I'll leave," he said, heaving himself off the bed and heading to the door. With a little wave, he stepped into the hallway and traipsed down the stairs.

"Here he is!" Brenda called. "Ready to join us, cutie?"

It was a room of warmth and smiles and comfort. There was only one answer Carter could give to that. "Only if I can sit next to Jackie."

Jackie beamed and nudged Beth Ann's thigh with her own. "You heard the man. Go sit in the rocker."

Beth Ann pursed her lips in a smirk and shook her head.

Delilah indicated one of several baskets littering the floor. "Pick a color."

Carter rummaged around, lifting and moving soft balls of yarn in a rainbow of colors. It was soothing to touch and look at, and he didn't realized he'd been lingering until Brenda knelt beside him. "Can't decide?"

He shrugged, and she reached in, pulling out a fat ball of smoky gray. "This almost looks like a little cat," she said, and he chuckled and took it.

Jackie dropped her own project in a tote by her feet. "Let's start with an easy slipknot."

# CHAPTER TEN

Paige's face filled Mallory's phone screen, her unnaturally red hair in a fishtail braid hanging over one shoulder. "Hey, Sunshine boss! I saw your post. You're working *with* Man Cave man? How did that happen? Why did you agree? How did you get him to agree?"

Mallory gave Paige the abridged version of how the collaboration came about, with Paige alternately shaking her head and dropping her jaw in open-mouthed surprise.

She did leave out the fact that they were not only in the same hotel, but the same room. Paige wouldn't get the wrong idea if Mallory explained it, but she didn't want to explain. She wanted to keep the little details to herself.

Because they weren't important, of course. Because she didn't want her assistant to worry.

"Tell me," Paige said, leaning forward. "Are you driving him insane with your endless cheer?"

"It's not just me," Mallory pointed out. "It's two weeks to Christmas. He's surrounded here with Christmas good will. And he's even smiled a few times."

"I saw! It's in the video! I can't believe you pulled it off."

"It was surprisingly simple. I had to convince him to get on skates, but once I succeeded, he secretly had a blast and pretended he didn't."

"Interesting."

Mallory sat up on the bed and ran a hand through her hair, catching her fingers in a tangle. She extricated them and flopped back down. "It seems to be a personality thing for Carter. Be grouchy, have fun, then make like it wasn't fun at all."

"So his grumpy shtick is an act?"

"No, not quite. I think he's … complicated." Carter's face floated unbidden into her mind, his full lips pressed together in a straight line, his blue eyes holding discomfort. "There's a lot simmering under that good-looking surface. He wants …" A place to call home. But she didn't want to betray him by sharing that with Paige, so she allowed her verbal musing to drift into silence.

Paige sat back in her chair, pulled in her chin, and raised one eyebrow. "Now, that's even more interesting."

"What?"

"What?" Paige mimicked. "I think you kind of like him."

"Of course I do. I like everyone." It was true, but only basically. Mallory could find something to like about nearly everyone she met. But when it came to digging deeper, she—well, she didn't do that.

Friends—and more-than-friends—were attachments. Attachments were traps.

Paige was her closest person to a friend, but Mallory kept their conversations about work and the people they'd met in the course of work. Now, Paige's suspicious tone, and the way she was scouring Mallory's face for hints of what lay beneath, made Mallory's skin itch. "Everyone," she repeated, remembering the conversation with Carter over hot chocolate, when they'd shared more than she'd expected to hear or intended to say.

Lips pursed, Paige shook her head. "I'm not even into guys, and I can objectively call him very handsome. No one could blame you for being attracted to—"

"I'm not attracted to Carter Scott. Stop it. He doesn't want anything I want."

"If he wants you, and you want him—"

Something in Mallory's chest went ping, and she resisted the urge to press her hand to her sternum. "I've said five words to you about him, total. How could you even surmise that he wants me?"

"The video, silly. It's so obvious that you kind-of maybe-like sort-of like each other. There are sparks."

"We're supposed to be appealing to traveling couples. It's the assignment."

"*Very* sparkly sparks."

"Paige—" She didn't want to chastise her industrious and capable assistant. But she'd already opened herself up in conversation with both Selene and Carter today. Her thoughts and memories and feelings were used to being under lock and key.

"Okay," Paige said, but her sudden backing off didn't seem genuine. "If you say so."

"I want to win this TV gig."

Paige shook her head like a cat shaking off droplets of water. "Right. That's why I called. You don't just want to win, Mallory. You have to."

"What are you talking about?"

"Nirvana Airlines announced today that they're selling an unlimited travel pass."

Mallory shot straight up. "Unlimited?"

"Yes. You can go everywhere the airline goes for a single one-time price. The pass is good for five years. There are some travel-day restrictions, of course, but you don't care about that."

"No, I don't. How much?"

Paige named a figure that was light years away from Mallory's budget. But with the TV gig money in her account, she could afford it. No more tight budgeting to afford her tickets, flying at the worst times, getting the worst seats. She'd be able to go anywhere at any time, and the money she earned could go toward other ways to build her business.

She wouldn't even need a home base. She could put everything in a storage unit and—go.

Nothing would tie her down.

Not even—

"—Carter Scott," Paige said.

"I'm sorry, what?"

"I said, I think your only competition for the TV show is Carter Scott. And you're working with him, not against him. How will Wanderlove choose between you?"

Mallory remembered Carter Scott telling Trixie they'd give it twenty-four hours. "Should I tell them it's not working?"

"No way. I hate to tell you this, but that video is adorable, and it's getting a ton of traction already. Keep doing what you're doing. Show you can work with anyone, even him. They'll *have* to choose you in the end. It's Wanderlove, not Wanderbarelylike. They want someone who wants to be out there in the world with an open mind and a love for exploration. That's you."

"But the pass—"

"The pass is on sale for sixty days," Paige said. "If they pick you, you'll be able to get it."

"The TV show, the Nirvana pass ..." Mallory took a deep breath. "Suddenly, I have opportunities."

"You've worked hard. You deserve a big break. This is it. Make the best content you can. You're off to a great start."

Mallory couldn't respond. This was everything she ever wanted, all within reach. Finally.

Her mother was right when she'd said, *Don't let anyone—any man—hold you back.*

She would call her mother right now and tell her. If she did that kind of thing.

"You're the best, Paige."

"I don't know. You have a weird look on your face. I'm worried I put unnecessary pressure on you. Maybe I should have waited to tell you."

"No. You did the right thing," Mallory said, sliding off the bed onto her butt on the floor and putting her shoes on.

"Where are you going?"

"To find Carter and talk about what we're going to do tonight. This little town is a perfect holiday-card scene. We can find something great to use."

"Good luck. And hey—"

"What?" Mallory tied her boot with a double knot.

"He's cute. Really cute."

"He is." She hopped to her feet and stomped one foot, then the other. "And he's good at this work, but you're right—he doesn't love it like I do."

"I'm trying to say—"

"I know what you're trying to say," Mallory gazed at Paige for a moment. "But please don't."

★ ★ ★

After running out to get a bagel sandwich and returning for a nap, Mallory awoke to the purplish sky of late-afternoon winter twilight.

Carter had to still be here at the inn, because he'd left in his socks and his shoes were still on the floor beside the bed. She bounced down the stairs and stopped short when she heard laughing.

Warm laughter. Friend laughter. Family laughter.

Her limbs froze for a moment, and she reminded herself that she wasn't stuck here. She could jump in her Bug and drive off at any time. She was choosing to stay. She could leave if she wanted to.

The irony didn't escape Mallory that she was unafraid to travel alone anywhere in the world but feared walking into a cozy room full of sweet older women.

She breathed deeply once, twice, then rounded the corner into the front room. The knitters' fingers were dancing rapidly over their projects as enthusiastic cross-conversations went on. Owen had arrived and was sitting cross-legged on the floor beside Selene, and when she said something that made two women giggle, Mallory noticed the flush in his cheeks when he gazed at her.

Oh, those were *very* sparkly sparks, as Paige would have said.

But Carter couldn't have been looking at Mallory in the video the way Owen was looking at Selene now. Mallory would have noticed.

Or would she? Selene was an extremely smart woman, yet she was oblivious, and when she glanced at Owen, he averted that adoring gaze quickly enough that she likely missed it.

Mallory cut her eyes to Carter, but he was paying attention to the long needles in his own hands, working them slowly under Jackie's tutelage. She took the yarn and needles from his hands, demonstrated, and handed them back to him, and after he worked on it another moment, she patted his arm.

"Mallory!" Selene said. "Come join us."

"I don't know how to—" She shrugged one shoulder.

"Neither do I," Owen said. "I'm here for the food and drinks and company."

"The company" was what was uncomfortable.

Not anyone specifically; they seemed to all be kind people, fun people. But it was the sitting and chatting that unnerved her.

She wasn't sure what was etched on her face, but whatever it was prompted Selene to say, "Oh, Mallory doesn't want to hang out with us old folks."

"Hey!" Owen protested. "You and I are Generation X. We don't get *old*. We get vintage."

"Well, we're old," Brenda said, circling her hand to indicate her friends. "But we're proud of it. It took a lot to get to an age of not giving a shit. I'm enjoying it."

Mallory grinned in spite of herself.

"Speaking of enjoying," Delilah said, "are you two kids going to Clash of the Carols? It starts in about an hour."

"It's on our list to check out, but we don't know what Clash of the Carols is," Carter said, holding his work up for Jackie's nod of approval.

"It's a cross between karaoke and *American Idol*," Selene said. "With Christmas songs, of course. It's packed every year. Practically the whole town turns out for it."

"That sounds like my worst holiday nightmare, if I'm honest," Carter said.

Secretly, Mallory agreed, but she wanted to lock in Carter as her partner for the week, so they needed to finish their twenty-four-hour trial day strong. She had twice as much riding on this Wanderlove thing as she had this morning, and she wouldn't quit until she won. "Of course we're going," she said. "Watching goofy contestants mangle songs sounds like a good time to me."

"It's at the high school," Delilah said. "On Broad Street, about three blocks past the gazebo. Dress warm."

"But I'm just getting the hang of these stitches," Carter mumbled.

Jackie gently took the needles and yarn from him. "We'll continue this tomorrow. Go have fun with a beautiful girl."

Mallory's face got hot.

"I'm already having fun with a room full of them," Carter argued, and all the women said, "Awww."

Wow. Carter Scott charming a room.

"Get out of here," Wendy said, shooing him away with a hand holding a half-full martini glass.

He stood slowly, reluctantly, and when Mallory waved goodbye to the room and headed upstairs, she heard him behind her. They went into their room, which was fully dark now, and Mallory turned on two soft lamps before going to the dresser to find an even warmer sweater if they were going to walk outside a bit. "We should probably grab dinner."

"Tacos?" he immediately suggested, kneeling and pawing through his disaster of a suitcase. "I met two guys last night who own Taco Tuesday in town."

"Great," she said. "Tacos will be quick, so we can get a good seat at Clash of the Carols."

"A good seat might be the one farthest from the stage."

"You are such a Scrooge."

"Tell me I'm wrong."

She turned her back and lifted a cream-colored sweater with little white sewn-on beads. Maybe it wasn't warmer. But it was cuter. She grabbed dark-blue jeans, then cut across the room to the bathroom, went in, and closed the door.

"I knew it!" Carter called. "You agree."

"Selene said tons of people go," she called back, quickly changing her top. "So it can't be that bad." She went to the mirror, shook out her hair, and slicked on some cherry-red gloss, sliding the tube into her pocket for later.

"Maybe Seasalter is full of rubberneckers who can't resist staring at a horrifying pileup."

"Oh, st—" The word died in Mallory's mouth as she opened the door to a shirtless Carter.

His back was to her—his smooth, sculpted back. In the soft golden light, shadows played across the planes of his skin.

He shook out a sweatshirt, and the movement rippled across his shoulders. His jeans, though cinched with a belt, hung low enough to give her a view of his tapered waist, and if she wanted to—

She didn't.

She *didn't* want to.

Though it was December in New England, her mouth was suddenly dry desert sand. He tugged the sweatshirt over his head, the loose hood falling over his upper back, and she tore her gaze away from him and walked into his field of vision. "Um ... tacos, you said?"

"If that's okay with you."

"It is," she said quickly.

She pushed her feet into a pair of brown faux-shearling boots and yanked her jacket on.

"Are you okay?" he asked. "I can leave the room if you need solo time."

Mallory would forever have solo time. She'd make sure of it. She'd only answer to herself; go where the wind blew her Nirvana plane.

"I'm good!" she said, wrinkling her nose in that way that one of her old boyfriends called cute and cheerful. She struggled with her zipper halfway up, as it snagged in the nylon.

Carter stepped in front of her, and when she dropped her hands, he worked the zipper calmly until it freed and he pulled it up.

She tried not to look up at him, and she didn't know why. "Thanks. There's a jacket for you too, in that box. It's not an exciting color, but it's really warm."

"I should probably wear it." He rummaged through the cardboard box. "How did you get this all up the stairs?"

"Owen helped me while you were at the tea shop earlier. He's a good guy."

"I agree. Are he and Selene a … thing?"

"Listen to you." Mallory giggled. "A couple of hours of knitting, and you're suddenly the gossip grapevine's main leaf."

"Yapping is all they do. I was starting to get emotionally invested in what Beth Ann's neighbors are going to do about the person watering their lawn on the even day when they're supposed to do it on odd days."

"Riveting."

"It strangely is," Carter said. "I found myself giving advice on a non-confrontational approach."

"Anyway, I don't think Selene and Owen are *together* together, but there's something there for sure."

"There is. I caught her looking at him when he wasn't paying attention."

"Oh!" Mallory said, grabbing his arm as he pulled the tags off his new red Wanderlove jacket. "I caught *him* looking at *her* when *she* wasn't paying attention!"

"My jacket's a better color than yours. Okay, let's roll."

She threw her phone, notebook, fold-up tripod, and mic into a corduroy tote and zipped it up. Then she grabbed her new scarf, gloves, and—

"Wear a hat. It's cold out."

"I don't have one."

"You're going to be freezing. What's wrong with you?"

"Nothing," she said, shaking out her mane like a headstrong pony.

"Do you have earmuffs? Earmuffs are cute."

"They are, but I left them at home by mistake. Let's go."

Carter muttered something under his breath as they locked the room and headed downstairs. "Have fun!" the ladies and Owen called as they left the inn.

# CHAPTER ELEVEN

Carter tugged the hat over his skull and scowled at the blond waves in front of him. At the bottom of the porch stairs, Mallory fell into step beside him.

Through the cold, they walked quickly and companionably.

If he were forced to define the relationship he now had with Mallory Robson, it would be impossible. He alternated between comfort and extreme awkwardness in her presence. She was so—there. An exuberant, crackling ball of hot energy. He wondered what soothed her. Maybe nothing. Maybe a wild shooting star like her couldn't ever go dormant.

"Do you hear the ocean?" she asked. "A reminder of summer."

They were friends now, he supposed, but cautious friends. She'd caught him flat-footed more than once, and he wanted to do the same to her, just as an equalizer. He decided to try an unexpected question.

As they rounded left onto Broad Street, he put it out there. "What's your secret identity?"

She laughed. "What? You ask that as if assuming I have one, assuming we all have one."

"I think you do, same as me."

"Explain," she said, pulling her scarf over her mouth.

"Your day job. I'm a graphic designer and website creator."

"Oh!" Her voice was muffled under her scarf. "I didn't know that."

"Well, that's my real-income job. I don't post about it on the travel socials."

She walked along a bit, and he thought he'd bored her, or maybe she'd forgotten he'd asked her a question, but she finally asked, "Are you good at it?"

"I am. I love it, really."

"You do?"

He let out a single huff of a laugh. "Why would I do something I hate?"

"You hate traveling."

"True," he said, "but I do like helping people like me find ways to travel more easily and comfortably."

"Can I see your design work?"

"Sure, I'll show some stuff to you later." A little glow of pride that ignited somewhere in his chest. He pointed at the Taco Tuesday sign. "We're here."

He jogged two steps ahead of her to open the door for her, and when they walked in, they were greeted with, "Heeeeey, Carter!"

Mallory side-eyed him. "Pretty popular for a guy who hasn't been here a full day."

"I met these guys last night when I had dinner."

One man came around the counter and gave Carter a hug with back slaps, and the other waved a spatula from the open kitchen. "Hey, man!"

"Mallory, meet Kyle. That's Darryl in the back."

"Girlfriend?" Kyle asked, tipping his baseball cap.

"No, just girl," Mallory said. "I mean, just friend."

"We're collaborating on a work project," Carter explained.

"I got it. How are you liking Selene's place?" Kyle asked.

"We love it." Carter wouldn't mention the room mix-up to anyone, partly to protect Selene's business because it wasn't her fault, and partly so no one would speculate in any salacious way about Mallory. "It's a beautiful house."

"Selene's a real nice lady," Kyle said, leaning on the counter with both elbows. "Classy. Pretty, too, for a … an older woman."

Carter and Mallory perused the menu and put in their orders for tacos. Carter glanced around. "Slow night?"

"Everyone's headed to Clash of the Carols," Darryl called over the sound of sauteing ground beef. He moved the crumbles across the grill with a spatula and shook some seasoning on it.

"Everyone?" Mallory laughed. "Like the whole town?"

"Of course." Darryl slid the meat off the grill and set out taco shells. "It's tradition."

Carter couldn't help loving Seasalter. A little town with traditions, a celestial inn, a magical tea house, a picturesque gazebo, and friendly residents. Had he seen a lot of towns like this one, all over the world? Yes. Was he feeling a strange, thin filament of attachment starting to form here? Also yes.

He glanced at Mallory, who was gathering napkins and forks at the little wooden station. She wasn't part of Seasalter, he had to remind himself, even though his experience of her was simultaneous with his experience of this setting.

"Remember when I told you that thing about my cousin?" Kyle asked. "I decided to call him and talk to him, the way you suggested, and we had a great conversation, man. He promised to do more research, and I promised to help him with it. That really helped, talking to you guys."

Carter grinned, remembering that after a couple of drinks last night, Kyle had unloaded his anxiety about his cousin's new "business venture" onto him and Darryl. They'd agreed it sounded like a pyramid scheme, and they'd helped Kyle get the courage to kindly confront his cousin. "I'm so happy to hear it. Any time."

Kyle took the plates of tacos from Darryl and pushed them across to Carter. "Sorry to say it, man, but we're closing in twenty. Darry here is going to murder 'Frosty the Snowman' on the mic, and I need to be present."

"No, I'm not!" Darryl called from the back. "I don't sing."

"One year you will," Kyle called back.

"We'll eat fast," Mallory assured him, and she and Carter sat at a small table by the front window.

"These look great," Carter said. "And I haven't forgotten that you didn't yet answer my question."

"What question?" Mallory said, and tore a taco in two with one bite.

"Your secret identity."

"I don't know what you're talking about."

"You do," he said, chewing and swallowing. "Sunshine in a Suitcase has really impressive numbers. But I suspect you're not making a full living with it yet. How are you paying for airfares and for your bills?"

"You know," Mallory said, "you're not very good at small talk."

"Oh."

"But you are very good at big talk. I admit … I did not expect that from you. I was under the impression that you were a surly guy, but here you are, making friends all over the place, from taco guys to lady knitters. Actual *friends*—you helped Kyle with something last night, and the knitters were sincerely sorry to see you leave for dinner. You're good at that."

"You say that like you're not." But now that he thought about it, she had left the room when the ladies were showing Carter their sewing projects. She was mostly quiet with Kyle and Darryl just now. And though she was Little Miss Enthusiastic when she'd first met Carter, in those first-impression moments, but she'd reeled it back quite a bit, even seeming a bit nervous while they drank hot chocolate—and now.

He thought they were connecting, but when they did, she seemed spooked by it.

Still, he gently pressed, hoping she'd understand he could be a friend.

*A friend, huh?*

He ignored his own brain.

"I'm not," she said. "And I'm not sure I should tell you that, just like I'm not sure why I should tell you what my secret identity is."

"I put my life in your hands today. I risked my well-being to create content with you. I trusted you. You can trust me."

"Wasn't trying something new its own reward?"

He took another thoughtful bite of his taco, nodding. "In this instance, it was. And in admitting that to you, I've once again trusted you with something. Now you owe me twice."

"I take issue with your accounting, but sure. I give in." Mallory put her taco down and looked him in the eye. "I work for ChicShop."

"Wait, is that—" He grinned. "Is that the TV channel where people shop from home?"

"Yeah." She dipped her head so her hair fell around her face.

"You're on TV?"

"No, of course not. Those hosts are professionals. I work from home and answer calls to take orders from customers."

Carter sat back in his seat, extending his legs. "I did not see that coming." When the toe of his boot touched her calf, he yanked it away like she was a live wire.

She lifted her chin and shook her hair back over her shoulders. "It's good money," she defended, even though he didn't think he'd insulted it. "The channel is twenty-four seven and we're taking calls at all hours, so my shifts are flexible. I can plan the working hours around travel. And it's familiar to me, in a way."

"What way?" He reached for another chip but realized he'd finished the ones on his plate. Mallory noticed and dropped a few from her plate onto his. "Thanks."

"I watched it all the time when I was a kid."

"Why? I assume you didn't have a credit card."

She half-smiled. "No. But …"

He waited a beat before prompting, "But …?"

"There was something about it. The hosts were all so—happy. Happy to be telling you about a toaster oven or a pearl ring or a Pilates machine. They were happy to talk to callers. And the callers were so excited to talk to them on the air."

"Did you ever call them?"

"No, but it was nice to turn the channel on in my room after school and do my homework while listening to a smiley woman talking about all the benefits of a carpet steamer. And if I glanced up, she was always looking right at me. She never minded being at home with me."

Carter remembered what Mallory had told him about her mother, who'd considered herself a prisoner at home, and his heart cracked a little.

Mallory crumpled up her taco paper. "We need to go. And I don't know why I told you all that."

"Because I asked you."

"If you tell anyone I work for ChicShop, I'll call you a liar." She smiled as she said it, but Carter detected a current of trepidation under her lightness.

"I won't, but as far as secrets go, it's hardly a dark one. And I still think they should put you on TV."

She scoffed, piling her discarded napkins onto her plate. "I can't sell anything."

"You convinced me to get on ice skates. Ask my sister, and she'll tell you she's tried a number of times, and I always said no to her."

Mallory narrowed her eyes at him, but rather than suspicion, it appeared as if she were trying to discern the truth of his words.

"I'd buy anything you sold," he said.

No. No, he didn't say that. He thought it. But he'd come dangerously close to saying it.

He shouldn't have thought it. Mallory Robson was not a woman—was not *the* woman—for him.

Carter popped out of his seat, took their plates to the trash, and held the door open for her to sweep through.

* * *

When they arrived at Seasalter High, there weren't many people in the lobby, but after they bought tickets and entered the auditorium, Carter realized that it was because nearly all the seats were already full. It did look like the whole town. The curtains on the stage were closed, and red and green spotlights danced across the thick fabric.

They found two seats together on the aisle about halfway down. Mallory instantly cheered upon seeing the giant decorated tree in the corner of the stage, in front of the curtain. "This is fun, right? I've never been to something like this before, karaoke with Christmas carols. And everyone's kind of buzzing. It's contagious."

"Oh," he said, patting his pockets. "I took off my gloves to buy the tickets, and I left them on the table in the lobby."

"Go get them."

He slid out of their row and slow-jogged back to the lobby. He spied his gloves on the table where he left them and noticed people filling out white index cards and throwing them into a slot on a huge wooden box. Some kind of raffle. He wrote his name on one card and Mallory's on the other, secure in his assumption that Mallory would be delighted if she won anything in a drawing.

Making his way back to his seat, he glanced around. Owen waved from a side section. Selene wasn't with him, but Carter would be willing to bet the empty seat beside him was likely hers, and she'd dashed to the ladies' room.

A woman with long wavy hair and glasses bounded up the stairs of the stage, a blond woman at her heels. "Hello, Seasalter!" the woman said into the mic, pulling it off the stand, "and welcome to Clash of the Carols!"

The auditorium went bananas. Carter couldn't help grinning. This was so cheesy and ridiculous. So small town.

"I'm Ana Capuano, a graduate of this bastion of education, and this is my bestie, Lacey Adams, who is also a Seasalter High grad, but more importantly, our brightest Broadway star."

The thunderclap of applause startled Carter for a second, but he joined it. Evidently, this whole crowd knew Lacey, who curtseyed and blew kisses in an easy, well-practiced manner.

"Lacey will be a judge tonight," Ana continued, "along with myself and Joel Brennan, Seasalter High's principal and theater coach. Thank you all for coming, and as you know, tonight's proceeds go to the high school's music and theater program. Okay, Seasalter, you know the rules, but I'm obligated to provide them anyway. If we pick your name out of the box, you're up."

A man in khakis and a fleece jacket carried a box to the stage and deposited it on the corner.

A wooden box.

*Oh*, no.

Carter swiped a hand down the side of his face. Yeah, he'd just put his name and Mallory's in that box. Should he tell her?

He glanced at her; her eyes sparkled as she took in the scene before her.

Nah, he'd keep his blunder to himself. This theater was packed. There was practically zero chance that either of them would be picked. And what was the worst that would happen if she got picked? She'd go up there, toss her blond waves, sing "Santa Baby" or something equally adorable, and probably go home with the grand prize.

And if he got picked, he'd deal with it. It would be his own fault for not asking someone what the box was for.

Ana and Lacey finished with the rules, and Lacey elegantly descended the steps and took her seat at the small table in front of the stage.

Mallory leaned over and murmured to Carter, "A Broadway star is judging? They seem to be taking karaoke a bit seriously."

He nodded, distracted by her cotton-candy scent. He parted his lips a bit so as not to inhale more of it and scramble his brain.

The man with the box opened it, rummaged, drew a name, and handed it to Ana.

"Jessica Reynolds!" she called, and the far right of the theater erupted in shrieks. A teenage girl shot up to the stage, all smiles, and consulted with Ana, and a moment later, the first notes of Mariah Carey's ubiquitous holiday song rang out.

Mallory looked as startled as Carter felt when Jessica began to sing. Her voice was a heralding angel. They listened for a few lines before Mallory leaned into him again. "Wow. This is practically professional. No wonder the whole town comes."

"I definitely underestimated this," he whispered back, fighting a little feeling of unease. There had to be three hundred people here; no way was he going to be chosen.

Jessica finished with a flourish of her hand, and the audience cheered loudly.

Two more contestants were called to sing. As an older man sang a hymn in a deep baritone, Mallory said, "Unfortunately, I don't think we're going to get to shoot much here with you and me. We'll have to find something afterward, maybe in the center of town, with lights?"

"I think you're right."

The man on stage drew a name and strode to the microphone. "Mallory Robson!"

Carter froze. He forced his eyeballs to roll to the left. Mallory's mouth was hanging open. "What?" she finally whispered.

"Mallory Robson?" the man called again.

Unfamiliar with her name, the residents of Seasalter glanced around the theater, trying to pick her out.

Mallory grasped Carter's arm and squeezed it, hard. "How is this possible? I don't remember giving our names when we bought tickets."

"Mall—" Carter began, but Mallory released him, took off her jacket, stepped into the aisle, and walked slowly toward the stage. When the audience saw her approach, they clapped encouragingly.

She was going to kill him when he told her how this happened. Meanwhile, he opened her tote, pulled out the tripod, and set it up in the aisle, zooming in on the microphone stand. He hit record. And waited.

# CHAPTER TWELVE

Mallory was confident in front of a handheld camera. She could tune her image, adjust the lighting, do several takes until she hit the right one.

Mallory was not confident now, on a stage, in front of a far-larger crowd than a Christmas-carol event warranted. She was not confident she even remembered any Christmas songs all the way through. And she was absolutely, one hundred percent not confident that she wouldn't faint dead away on the spot.

Because she couldn't sing.

She was a terrible singer. She couldn't carry a tune at all.

Her hand shook as Ana took it, leading her to center stage. Then Ana bent close to ask, "What song would you like to—"

A loud horn rang out, making Mallory jump, and everyone began to cheer.

"Oh!" Ana said into the microphone. "Mallory, it sounds like it's time for one of our special challenges."

Mallory shook her head in confusion.

"Instead of selecting a song yourself, you get to spin the wheel for a song."

The man who'd picked her name pushed a large, elaborately tinseled wheel onto the stage, and the cheering got louder.

"If you can get through the challenge, you'll get an immediate prize," Ana said, then softly, she added, "Don't worry, everyone wins the challenge, even if they don't do well."

"Spin! Spin! Spin!" the audience began to chant.

*Oh, God, I can't do this.*

She walked to the wheel as if in a dream, grabbed the edge of the wheel, and spun it as hard as she could without reading the individual items.

Her brain rush was a deafening ocean wave. The wheel slowed and slowed until it stopped. Mallory squinted.

"Your challenge is"—Ana lifted on tiptoes to see—" 'Silent Night.' But … in German!"

Everyone clapped, as if she were in some insane dystopian nightmare.

"What?" Mallory found her voice, but it didn't sound like hers. "I don't speak German," she said into the microphone.

"Ah. That's the challenge," Ana said. "The lyrics will be on the screen stage left, so you can sing them phonetically." She pulled the microphone off the stand and handed it to Mallory before she left the stage.

Mallory looked out at the dark silence. She wondered if everyone in this auditorium could see her knees knocking together. It wasn't that she couldn't sing well; she couldn't sing at *all*. She sang alone in her car—never, ever in front of even one person, let alone however many were here.

The first notes played, and she opened her mouth, but realized she didn't know the words, so she turned toward the screen. Was the first word pronounced still-ee or still? Or steel?

"Um," she said into the microphone, and tears sprang to her eyes. "I—"

A gentle, warm hand on her shoulder.

She spun, surprised, and Carter was on stage with her. He said into the microphone, "Could we start over, please?" Then, to Mallory, "It's okay. I've got this."

The music cut. The first chords played again, and he turned to face the huge room.

*"Stille nacht, heilige nacht,*
*Alles schläft; einsam wacht ..."*
Carter was singing.

His voice was soothing but strong and sure. He wasn't even looking at the words on the screen.

Mallory couldn't simply stand here like an idiot after he'd rescued her. So she took a deep breath, channeled ten years of ballet classes, pulled her boots off, and danced.

*Chaîné* turns into a *tour jeté*, a pirouette, an arabesque. Luckily, her jeans had stretch, and spins were easy in her socks. She danced at Carter's right, then at his left.

Carter sang all three verses, giving Mallory time to relax into movement and improvise. As he sang the last words more slowly, she circled to his left and bowed in a deep *révérence*.

Silence.

Then, applause. Loud applause. Fervent applause.

She stood, and Carter turned to her, handing her the microphone.

He smiled.

Mallory leaped into his arms, wrapped her legs around him, and hung on.

She'd assumed he'd catch her, and he did. Her mouth next to his ear, she said, "You can *sing*."

"I can."

"You know German!"

"I do."

She hugged him harder with arms and legs. "You saved me."

She felt his deep breath, and his heart hammering against hers. "I guess I did."

★ ★ ★

"*You* put my name in?"

"It was a mistake. I thought it was for a raffle, not for—"

"Agh!" Back at their seats, house lights up, event over, Mallory stood and pushed her arms into her jacket. She shook her head as she zipped up.

"I'm really sorry, I—" Carter tried.

"Great job," a woman said to them as she passed. "You two are adorable."

"Thanks!" Mallory smiled brightly, and as the woman walked away, she scowled at Carter again. "I can't believe you got me into that mess."

"It was—okay, though. I think."

"You two were wonderful!" another woman gushed as she passed their row with two kids in tow.

"Thank you so much!" Mallory said again, as sweet as a sugarplum. "Yeah, it turned out okay," she muttered to Carter without the enthusiasm she'd had onstage for him saving her. She hadn't known then that she was standing in the spotlight because of him. At least, he'd told her the truth. And he had saved her. "You recorded it, right?" she asked gruffly.

"I hit record right before I ran up."

"As long as we edit out the part where I'm standing there in a panic with my mouth hanging open, catching flies."

"Hey!" Owen said, pausing at their seats. "You had the crowd entranced, both of you."

Selene was behind him. "Carter, what a voice. You gave me chills. Mallory, you simply sparkled."

"I wasn't—I wasn't prepared for that," Mallory said, her smile breaking just a bit.

"You'd never have known," Selene assured her with a warm smile. "You complemented one another beautifully. Two shining stars. We'll see you back home."

They melted into the wave of people headed to the double doors. Mallory folded the tripod, her movements a little less jerky and annoyed. Selene had a motherly way about her; her compliments made Mallory feel genuinely seen. Sighing, she put a hand on Carter's arm. "Thank you again," she said quietly. "You are really, really talented. And you got to share it with the town."

"The judges went with Jessica, though, for the grand prize," Carter said, play-pouting.

"A Mariah Carey song is always a crowd favorite. You had no chance against that."

"At least we got the challenge prize." He held up a heavy wicker basket full of Christmas candy, fancy tea, fuzzy socks, and other stocking stuffers.

"What's this 'we'? You're the one who sang."

"Everyone coming up to us says *we* were great. That was a team effort. Your dancing was really, really—" He hesitated, glancing down, meeting her eyes with his. "You were perfect."

Mallory had taken anatomy in college. She'd learned all about the autonomic nervous system, how one's heart beat without one's willing it, quietly keeping one alive. But right now, her heart suddenly demanded to make itself known, to let her know it was there, it was keeping her alive, it was beating hard and pumping her blood through her veins and rushing it through her ears and pooling it into her belly and below.

She was alive.

He reached for her jacket zipper and slid it down a couple of inches, then brushed her hair back with both hands and zipped it back up. "Your hair was, um, caught."

But he didn't straighten up right away. They shared one breath. Two.

"Carter!"

Mallory started as Kyle held up his hand for Carter's high five, telling them how terrific they both were on stage.

As they moved away, Mallory stepped into the aisle. "Work awaits. Let's get this scripted, edited, and posted."

Carter nodded and followed.

★ ★ ★

After they got back to the inn and finished their work—posting a video which, Mallory had to confess, was quite charming—it was close to midnight. They both fell back on the pillows, exhausted.

"I'll take the pullout in the other room," Mallory said without turning her head, staring at the ceiling.

"No way. Take the bed."

"I insist. The room is smaller. The bed is smaller. I'm smaller. I'm fine with it. It's pretty in there."

"This bed is really comfortable."

"I can sleep anywhere," she said. "I once slept so soundly on a train from Rome to Florence that someone stole my bag lunch right off the little table in front of me. Just swiped it and ran."

"But—"

"Please," Mallory said. "Let me do it."

"I will on one condition—that we switch tomorrow night."

Mallory pretended to think it over, but her mind was on the fact that he said tomorrow. "You're convinced? Trial period over? You want to work together the rest of the week?"

"Yes," he said.

"I'm glad I talked you into it."

"You didn't have to. Your work is excellent. I'm—I'm learning a lot from collaborating with you."

She turned her head to him, but his eyes stayed fixed on the swirls in the paint above the bed. "Me too." She cleared her throat. "Have you checked our first post?"

"No."

"Let's look. And maybe we can even like and respond to some comments."

He threw an arm dramatically over his face. "No. I'm tired. I tried out for the U.S. Olympic skating team today, and performed on Seasalter's Got Talent tonight. It's enough for one day."

"Five minutes," Mallory cajoled. "Just a little engagement so people know we care."

"Five minutes," he agreed.

She rolled to her back again and, side by side, both of them held their phones over their faces.

"That's more likes on one post than I've gotten cumulatively in a month," he muttered.

"It's good!" she said. "Is your follower count up?"

"Considerably."

"Mine too, which means we're getting some crossover fans. You're welcome."

"Thanks."

They scrolled in silence for a few moments.

"Mallory," he said. "The—the comments."

"What?"

"Some are ..."

"Unkind?"

"That's a kind way to put it."

She scrolled away from the performance metrics and started reading comments on her account. "Here are some fun ones. *What? You're in a collab with Cave Man Carter Scott?* Heh, she called you Cave Man. Another comment: *Hey, you and Carter*

*Scott? I didn't know you were* ... Oh, no, we're not doing that." she said quickly. She skimmed down. "Well, most of these people are either encouraging me to hook up with you or asking me if you're as grouchy as you seem. I'm neither commenting nor confirming."

Carter's expression was a storm cloud, darkening by the second.

"What's wrong now?" she asked brightly. "Wanderlove is going to be really pleased with all this."

"Um," he said haltingly. "Some of my followers are saying ... not nice things."

"About me, I suppose?"

"Y-yes."

"Let me guess." She cleared her throat. "I'm ugly, I'm too thin, I'm too fat, I'm too happy, I'm secretly miserable, my hair is Photoshopped, my nose is Photoshopped, my teeth are Photoshopped. And Elle Woods would punch me in the face for being too cheerful and pink. Stuff like that?"

He looked up, baffled. His fingers were white, gripping his phone. "Among other, more vulgar comments, yes."

She shook her head and waved her hand. "Ignore them. Don't engage."

"I'm not engaging. I'm blocking these bastards."

Mallory could almost hear the smallest crack cross her heart at the idea of Carter defending her. "Don't bother. You'll never get them all."

He punched his phone keys, scowling and mumbling, until she put her hand over his. "Stop."

The muscles in his hand, stiff with anger, released a bit under her touch. His skin was soft—softer than she'd have guessed. If she were guessing things about him. Which she wasn't.

"I'm appreciative of your trying to protect me." Mallory let out a long breath. "But you're not going to shut up all the trolls. It's a waste of time. I have plenty on my account too. Paige blocks the worst of them, but people are going to say what they're going to say."

"Doesn't it bother you? Doesn't it … hurt?"

"Not particularly. I know who I am. It's a very small price to pay to get to do what I do. Don't you get trolls?"

"Sure. But not like this. Not that personal. Not that shallow and cruel."

"Yeah, well …" She trailed off. He seemed to be learning in real time what it was like to be a woman on the internet. There was no softening it. There was merely learning to live with it.

"I'm sorry," he said, turning his head this time, and she mirrored it.

"For what?"

"For the time that I thought you were—too bright. Too shiny. Sort of insufferably cutesy."

Mallory snorted.

"I thought you were an image you created, something to impress the world," he said. "But you're real. Genuine."

Swallowing hard, Mallory tilted her head at the ceiling again.

It was mostly easy to squelch the feeling that she was a fraud. No one knew her, not really. She didn't let anyone in to see the clouds that were often beneath the sunshine. But Carter thinking she was genuinely enthusiastic every second of every day? That filled her with guilt.

Because, she realized, he was a man who craved a home, a family, a community, tradition. He needed connection.

She'd read once that humans needed connection as a basic requirement for survival. But she'd gotten this far, and she'd seen so much, without creating ties.

And as she lay here beside Carter—a little bit too comfortable—she sensed the golden strands of an invisible tether reaching out from her chest, trying to attach itself to …

She rolled off the bed and onto the floor with a thud.

"What was that?" Carter asked, peering over the edge. "What's wrong with you? Are you okay?"

The cold slap of the hardwood floor on her shoulder and hip broke the spell. Broke the connection. "I'm fine. I'm going to bed."

"Did I say something wrong?"

"Nope." She scrambled to her feet, took three strides to the dresser, and pulled out her pajamas, then headed to the smaller room in the suite, pushing out Carter's suitcase as she did.

The windows in this room were pretty, and there was an extra TV, which Mallory appreciated. She found sheets, pillows, and blankets in the closet, and she opened the sofa bed without effort. She made up the bed, changed her clothes, and knocked softly on the door between her and Carter.

"Come in!"

"I need the bath—"

Carter was on the floor, riffling through that mess of a suitcase, wearing only a pair of gray sweatpants. His torso and feet were bare. He'd turned on the fireplace; certainly the sudden warmth in her face was from that.

"Don't knock," he said. "Come in to use the bathroom any time. I promise to sleep decently tonight." He swept a hand downward, as if implying that his sweatpants made anything about him decent.

She opened her mouth, but the only words that she had on her tongue were words she couldn't say. *Carter Scott is not for you. Carter Scott is for a woman who wants to bake pies and change curtains with the seasons and volunteer on the town's planning committee. Not a woman who wants—needs—that unlimited Nirvana Airlines pass. Who needs the sky.*

"Yes," she said stiffly. "Thanks for that." She went into the bathroom and splashed cold water on her face for what felt like ten minutes.

Ministrations complete, she walked slowly back into the bedroom, where Carter was now propped up in bed with a book. She grabbed a pair of socks from her top drawer and stood there for a moment, the socks dangling from her hand. "Um, good night."

"Good night, Mallory."

She paused for a half-second, long enough for him to glance up from the book and cock an eyebrow at her, before she went back into her room and closed the door.

★ ★ ★

Mallory noticed two things when she woke up around two thirty in the morning.

First, the night-light glowing in the far corner of the room. It was a full moon with encircling stars, and it glowed golden, though Mallory was certain she hadn't seen it before she'd gone to sleep. She'd been distracted and tired, though.

The second and more crucial thing was that she was cold. Really cold.

She tossed off the blankets and wrapped her arms around herself. She went over to the old-fashioned coil radiator against the wall and put her hand on it. Nothing. Glancing at the thermostat on the wall, she gasped at the temperature and turned it all the way past eighty. Tapping an impatient foot on the floor, she waited, but the radiator didn't kick on.

These beautiful old houses sometimes had issues with heat. She recalled a *pensione* she'd stayed at in Rome in which she'd awakened with no heat, and where the receptionist had shrugged at her when she went down to ask them about it.

Mallory was certain Selene wouldn't shrug her off, but she didn't want to wake her in the middle of the night, not when she likely rose at dawn to prepare breakfast for everyone.

Wondering if Carter had no heat either, Mallory creaked open the door gingerly.

It was as if she'd walked into a sauna. The fireplace was snapping and throwing off heat, and the baseboards were clicking in that way they did when the warmth was coming through. Mallory's shoulders relaxed. Maybe she could lie on the floor in here.

Or—

She peered over at the bed. Carter was on the side of the bed he'd used last night, and his leg was hanging off the edge.

Plenty of room.

She wouldn't stay long, and she wouldn't wake him up. Last night, he hadn't even realized he was sharing a bed, so he was a heavy sleeper. And the bed was king-sized; she'd be nowhere near him.

Watching his sleeping form, she tiptoed to the bed. He didn't stir, even when she lifted the comforter on the opposite side and slid in.

Yesssssss. So much better.

She'd warm up for a while, then go back to the other room, wrap herself up, and hope she'd absorbed enough heat to fall back asleep comfortably.

She burrowed deep into the pillow, pulling the blanket over her shoulders and lying as still as humanly possible.

Every muscle in her body softened, melting into the mattress. She was only inches from Carter, and he had no idea. This was definitely an invasion of his privacy, and she should not be here.

After a few moments, her breathing matched the rhythm of his, and the heat of his body dissolved her consciousness.

★ ★ ★

When narrow strips of sunlight slid into the room around the curtains, Carter was already awake and unmoving, watching her sleep.

He wondered when it happened—if it had been when she helped him with his car, or held out her arms to assist him off the ice, or told him about her mother, or when he had awakened to find her right here. But it had happened. He was feeling something he feared he wouldn't be able to unfeel.

When she began to wake slowly, languorously, he forced himself to let his eyelids drop and feign deeper breathing. He felt her pause, likely remembering where she was. A moment later, she slid out of bed and tiptoe-ran into the other room. The door closed between them with a whisper.

# CHAPTER THIRTEEN

When she saw her daughter's number flash on the phone, Selene turned off the sink, briskly dried her hands on a dish towel, and clicked Accept. Her still-damp finger slipped on the button, and she cursed under her breath before hitting it again. She could count on one hand the number of times her daughter had called from college since September, and though Luna had a good head on her shoulders and Selene didn't worry about her ability to navigate everyday life on campus, she couldn't help the hurt in her chest. "Luna."

"Hi." Even though Luna had initiated the conversation, the one syllable was sulky, as if she'd been interrupted from doing anything more interesting than talking to her mother.

Without a question or a dialogue opening, Selene found herself lost for words. "Everything going okay?"

"Why wouldn't it be?"

"No reason." Selene tried to keep her voice light, breezy. "All done with finals?"

"Yes."

"Which one was the hardest?"

"God, Mom, I don't want to talk about that. And anyway, what makes you think any of them were hard?"

"Good point." Selene fell onto the sofa in the sitting room, which was unoccupied by guests at the moment. "Which one was the easiest?"

"Mm," Luna said, and paused long enough for Selene to think an answer wasn't forthcoming before she finally said, "Calculus."

"Calculus was the *easiest*?" Selene laughed. "Wow."

"Anthropology was the hardest."

Selene smiled at this grudgingly offered scrap of information. Psychology had been her own favorite, and the knowledge had served her well as an advice columnist. She wouldn't have thought it would come in handy as an inn owner, but it was interesting how many guests talked to her about what was happening in their lives, as though they needed to not only unburden their bodies and minds on vacation, but also their souls.

Of course, all the psychology in the world couldn't help her relationship with Luna these days. But one thing she *did* know not to do was say all this to Luna now.

Though she did need to approach a subject that would be prickly. "You're coming home soon? The dorms won't be open over winter break."

"I don't know," Luna said, her tone implying that she did know. "I might stay with Bex. Her parents don't live far."

"I have no issue with you staying in Arizona, visiting Bex's folks over the break, but I'd really like it if you were here for Christmas."

"Will the place be closed?"

By "place," Luna meant "inn," and Selene's heart broke a little at the impersonal word her daughter chose to describe the house she'd so lovingly helped her dad renovate and decorate. She'd dug in her heels when Selene had to eventually open to try to recoup the investment. Without her father, the inn was no longer meaningful for her, or perhaps it broke her heart, and when Selene listened to her pleas but did what was necessary anyway, the fabric between mother and daughter had ripped down the center.

Selene didn't want to pressure her daughter, but she longed to have her back.

"No, Luna," she said as gently as she could. "The inn is booked out for weeks, which is a good thing, as I'm using it to pay bills."

"I suppose you mean tuition."

"That's not what I was saying directly, but yes, that is one of the bills."

"I can't believe you'd hold that over my head."

"I'm not." Selene fought to keep her voice even, unruffled. "Your father would have wanted you to attend your chosen college without issue. Your scholarship money has been crucial, and that's your accomplishment and contribution, and I appreciate it. I'm doing what I can on my end."

"So if you closed the inn, we wouldn't have money for school?"

"If I closed the inn, I'd find the money some other way. But I do have the inn, and that's my job." *Twenty-four seven*, she wanted to add, but that would be playing into the fight Luna seemed to want to engage in.

"If I came for Christmas, I'd have to live in a hotel, is what you're saying."

"When the three of us decided together to open an inn, you knew we'd take the third floor to live in. That's where you lived before you left, and I opened Moonrise. So yes, that's where you'd stay now. It's not unlike being in an apartment with other people in the same building. Except here, I give them breakfast and straighten their rooms."

"You haven't hired anyone to help you clean or cook or anything?" her daughter asked, as if she were a business consultant and Selene was a desperate client, and Selene silently counted back from five to one.

"No, Luna, because that would be an additional expense. I'm hoping to be able to hire someone for spring, because this is quite a bit of work. But, you know, a lot of it is enjoyable work.

I have a group of knitters staying this week, and you would get a kick out of them. It's like *Golden Girls* meets … well, knitting, I guess. They've decided to teach someone else staying here how to knit, and it's adorable because he's in his late twenties or so, and he loves it, and it's like they've adopted him."

"Hm," Luna said, and this time, the sound had a hint of curiosity.

"He's an influencer online. And there's another influencer staying here, a woman."

"Do you mean a content creator, Mom?"

"Yes, I guess that's what I mean." Selene suspected that she wasn't supposed to tell people who was staying at the inn, but Luna was her daughter, and this was her inn too, and it was her home, whether she liked it or not. "Her name is Mallory. Sunshine—"

"—in a Suitcase? Yeah, I follow her. I haven't been online much lately with finals. I like her, though. Is she nice in real life?"

"Very sweet. She's certainly doing a great job on social media of making Seasalter look like a premier destination."

"Well, at Christmas, I guess it is. And … in the summer, with the beach. And … in fall, for the leaves." Luna snorted. "It's hard to see it as a vacation place because I lived there. But Dad—"

She stopped. Selene didn't want to push but couldn't help prompting, "Dad …?"

"Dad thought it was, that's all." She grew distant again. "I have to go."

"Christmas?" Selene asked, hating herself for not being the kind of mother who could demand her daughter's presence and get it. She and Dan had raised Luna to think for herself.

"I'll think about it," came the vague reply.

"Good. I'm glad you called. I love you."

"Bye."

Selene hung up and stared at the dark phone screen for a while.

*"That girl is her father's daughter. She always will be."*

*"She loves us equally, my moon goddess."*

*"I'm sure she does, but she's obsessed with having your attention."*

*"You both have it. Forever."*

Forever hadn't lasted as long as Selene and Luna had counted on, though. And there were some days when Selene missed her daughter more than Dan. Dan couldn't help what happened. But Luna's absence was a decision, one that Selene found more and more difficult to accept.

Selene realized she'd not mentioned Owen to Luna, and that he was temporarily staying at the inn while looking for a new place. Not just at the inn, but on the third floor. She hadn't mentioned Owen to Luna at all, in fact, during their rare phone calls, even though she and Owen had been friends for nearly four months, and he spent a fair amount of time at the Moonrise Inn—and with Selene.

She hadn't meant to keep Owen a secret—there was no secret about friendship, after all. Her infrequent phone calls with her daughter were mostly surface-deep, and she never thought about much during their conversations except how to keep her on the phone as long as possible.

Well, Dan had wanted to rent that room out despite Selene's disagreement. Luna would understand that, especially if she mentioned that Owen's family used to own this house.

*You know, don't you, that mentioning a man to Luna will not have a positive outcome? A man friend will be a threat to her, to her father's memory.*

Yes, Luna would think that, despite the fact that there was nothing between Selene and Owen except companionship. But since Selene had opened Moonrise three months ago, Luna was determined to see her mother as a wrongdoer. So much so that she wasn't even coming home for the holiday anyway.

Selene was, however, determined to be a constant for Luna, a moon that shone through every night, there whenever Luna chose to acknowledge it.

And so, as she got up to take clean towels out of the dryer, Selene refused to acknowledge the unbidden thought of Owen's green, green eyes.

# CHAPTER FOURTEEN

Trixie from Wanderlove called before breakfast, many-ex-clamation-points thrilled with Mallory and Carter's collaborative content and even more thrilled that they planned to keep it coming for the remainder of the week. They went to the breakfast room together, though Mallory widened her eyes when he sat.

"Oh? Breakfast today?"

Carter was sorely tempted to inform her that his eating with her this morning was not nearly the craziest thing that happened in the last few hours—her getting into his bed was. Instead, he silently raised his eyebrows. "I'm hungry."

She tucked her hair behind one ear and shook out her napkin. It was casual, unselfconscious, as if they started every day together.

They'd beaten the Crafty Ladies to breakfast today, and the room was peaceful for now. Selene smiled as she poured coffee for Carter and brought Mallory a glass of pink grapefruit juice. He wondered if Selene knew Mallory liked grapefruit, or that she liked pink. Either way, it earned Selene a large grin from Mallory. "Omelets today?" Selene said and they nodded, so off she went to the kitchen.

He shifted his eyes back to Mallory and realized that he wanted to be looking at her every moment she was near. And as he studied her lips—her upper lip was a bit fuller than her lower lip, like a baby doll's—and her dark eyelashes, he realized something else.

He kind of had it bad for this woman. After *two* days. After two days of encouraging each other and rescuing each other and working with each other and talking to each other—and, apparently, sleeping beside each other.

This was not good. It was great for his influencer account; not great for his overall well-being.

Mallory was a bird, or maybe even a flying squirrel, adorable and goofy and unique. He was a turtle, needing to haul his safety and security around with him everywhere he went. In the wild, turtles and flying squirrels weren't buddies; they weren't symbiotic.

He'd just confirmed to Wanderlove this morning that everything was fine. And it was fine. Surely he could last the week without—yeah, without.

"How'd you sleep?" he asked, unable to help himself even as he was thinking that being near her was trouble.

"Funny you asked." She gulped her juice. "The heat in my room went out last night completely. It was subzero. Well, you know, low enough."

"Oh?" He brought his cup to his mouth to hide his smile, watching her over the rim. "Sounds uncomfortable."

"I, um, managed. But this morning, it was back on. And it was really, really warm in the room, like it had been going all night. The radiator was too hot to touch."

She didn't sound like she was fibbing, though she was clearly leaving out how she'd coped with the chill. Carter noticed his disappointment, but what did he expect? That Mallory would want to be closer to him? Him, the man on the planet most opposite what she wanted in life?

If he dared to hope so, he was an idiot of epic proportion.

"It was as if I'd dreamed the whole thing. But I remember the cold. And the night-light …"

"The night-light?"

"Never mind."

He didn't pry. "What's on the docket today?"

"A cookie contest, wreath decorating, and a pet parade."

Selene brought their omelets out, plated with fresh fruit. Mallory's face lit up. "This looks wonderful. Thank you."

Selene patted Mallory's shoulder affectionately and went back to the kitchen.

Carter tried not to notice the thin, lacy, black bra strap that now peeked from the neckline of Mallory's blue ribbed sweater. "Uh, I vote for wreaths and pets. Hopefully there are no more athletic feats any time soon."

"That's what skating one time around the rink was for you?" Mallory asked, sprinkling pepper on her eggs. "An athletic feat?"

"The closest thing to it that I ever get."

"Get out of here. I suppose your muscled torso is genetic?"

"What do you know about my muscled torso?"

Her ears went a bit pink, which he found gratifying. "I saw you last night."

"Ah." He cut his omelet and forked in a mouthful, savoring both the cheese and her discomfort before swallowing. "I do go to the gym. But I don't consider that athletics. It's basic maintenance."

"If you say so."

They ate the rest of their breakfast quietly, the clinking of their silverware the only sound.

Though his follower count had increased significantly overnight, this collaboration would have the most immediate benefit for Mallory, Carter thought. Her social media account was much larger, and he sensed that Wanderlove had possibly made him a prop for her. They would choose her for the TV show in the end, wouldn't they? And if that were the case, why had he just agreed to keep doing this? Well, some progress was better than no progress, and there was the slightest chance they'd see something in him, something that would get him the show and the money and the down payment for his own house. He could retire from traveling, work from home, and start creating memories—in a place like Seasalter.

Maybe even with a woman like—

Mallory shoveled in her last bite and tossed her napkin on the table. "Let's get a move on. Those wreaths aren't going to glitter themselves."

Ordinarily, this would have prompted a comment from him like, where would he put a wreath? But he *would* have a house. He could save it. Maybe next Christmas, he'd be hanging it on his own front door. A new tradition.

Mallory stood from the table and stretched her arms overhead, revealing a sliver of soft skin over the waistband of her jeans. He didn't want to brush his fingertips against it. He definitely didn't want to touch his lips to it.

Nope.

He gulped the rest of his coffee as Mallory left the room, and Selene came out with a to-go cup for him. "In case that wasn't enough."

"You're the best," he said sincerely.

She turned him by his shoulders toward the door. "The Crafty Ladies told you: Don't keep a beautiful woman waiting."

Carter nodded, though he was certain that particular beautiful woman would never sit and wait for anyone.

* * *

He and Mallory returned to the inn with two decked-out wreaths—his was decidedly more amateurish than hers—and laughing over the Christmas Pet Parade, won by his favorite, a grouchy-looking hairless cat dressed as an elf. Afterward, he'd asked the owner if he could pet the cat and was surprised to find its skin was as soft as velvet, with a cozy personality to match as it licked his fingers and snuggled into the crook of his elbow.

That made two creatures he was quickly smitten with in the last couple of days.

He and Mallory worked for a while together in the room, editing video and creating posts. The video of Mallory opening the glitter with an unexpected pop was a good one—and she still had silver sparkles in her hair and on her Wanderlove jacket and scarf. She'd also snapped a photo of him cradling the cat, which was endearing even to him. When they uploaded the content, they'd looked at each other, and each made hasty excuses—her, a walk down to the beach and to find a snack; and him, the Crafty Ladies, who had just been getting under way when they'd returned.

Now he was sitting with the older women in the soothing blue room, practicing a garter stitch over and over. Each row of stitches was like another reinforcement of confidence. A candle in the corner burned, throwing the scent of pine over the scent of Christmas cookies from the oven. "They're from a refrigerated can," Selene confided to the room. "I didn't have a lot of time today. But I did ice and sprinkle them, which I suppose is something."

"Who cares?" Jackie asked, grabbing one and taking a bite. "Why are women expected to do everything? You're running this whole inn. You think we'd have an issue if you didn't serve us cookies baked from scratch? Either way, they're delicious."

"You men," Brenda said, and when no one responded, Carter lifted his head from his stitches and found them all waiting on him to comment.

"Me?" he asked. "I don't speak for men. I can barely speak for myself."

"All that time we spent fighting for women's rights in the '70s," Beth Ann said, "and there are still men who think women should be taking care of them instead of taking responsibility for themselves. Some of them young men, too. How is this happening?"

The women nodded.

"I assure you, it's present company excluded," Carter said. "I have zero ground to stand on and talk about women's rights, but my parents were both diplomats, and my mother never baked a cookie in her life. And my family didn't notice or care."

"That pretty Mallory isn't your girlfriend?" Wendy asked, pushing her reading glasses up her nose, never taking her eyes off her yarn.

He returned his close attention to his work. "No."

"Do you have a girlfriend?"

"No."

"What are you waiting for?"

He threw up his hands, then pulled them right back so he didn't drop his rows of stitches on the floor. "What's the rush?"

"I think," Selene said, working with only one needle, "Wendy means what kind of woman are you waiting for?"

"Oh. That's … that's personal."

No one said anything for a long minute. He squirmed in his seat. "I guess … I guess I'm waiting for a woman who's smart. And funny. And attractive … and she knows it. Who has a goal and goes after it every day. Who …" He trailed off. *Who wants a home. With me.* "You know. The usual. Blah blah blah."

"You were doing fine until that last part," Patrice said.

The front door opened, blowing the winter inside, along with Owen. "Ladies," he said, scuffing his hiking boots on the mat before stepping in. "And Carter."

"I'm fine being lumped in with 'ladies,' " Carter said.

"This cold snap, I'm telling you," Owen said, leaning against the door and not making a move to take off his jacket. "Selene, did you notice that house three doors down on Oceanview is for sale? The little red one?"

"Is that so?" she asked.

"Yeah, it's real cute. I saw Roman Montgomery putting the sign up today. There's an open house tomorrow."

Carter's ears pricked up. He did like this town. It was a possibility he'd have the money soon. Wouldn't hurt to take a little peek, right? Looking wasn't committing.

"Are you finally ready to commit?" Jackie asked in his ear.

He quickly turned his head. "What?"

"Are you ready to pick a project? You've been practicing for a while. There are a few different things you can create with a garter stitch, and we can help you. What do you want to make?"

Carter didn't have to think about it long. Jackie lifted a brow at his yarn color choice, but for once, she said nothing.

# CHAPTER FIFTEEN

That night, after burgers and fries at the Town Diner and an evening gift-wrapping lesson at Town Hall, Mallory and Carter landed, exhausted, in their room. Carter flopped on the bed face down, and Mallory kind of wished he hadn't so she could. Though they'd been sharing the bed space to work, it was starting to feel a bit—crowded.

Intimate.

She fell into the chair near the desk instead, kicking her shoes across the room and stretching her legs out in front of her.

"I'm not sure I can keep up this holly-jolly pace," Carter said into the mattress.

"Festive fatigue?"

"Something like that."

"You never really told me why you don't like Christmas."

Carter rolled over, toeing off his own shoes and putting his hands behind his head. "I don't remember saying I don't like Christmas."

"You glare at my reindeer car in the lot every time we pass it, like it's your worst enemy."

"It's goofy."

"It's a vibe I got from you at first. Though it's definitely faded. Maybe you're changing your mind."

She watched his chest rise and fall as he sighed. "I don't hate the holidays at all," he said. "What I hate is that it's a time of—well, belonging. Everyone has the traditions of their family, their community, and I don't have that. When I got used to the traditions of one part of the world, my family moved to another. Then, at Cornell, I was a holiday orphan, going to a different friend's home each year. They were great, don't get me wrong, but everyone is a part of something this time of year, and I'm not. So I don't love the feeling." He rolled over once again and propped himself on his elbows. "Even tonight. It was kind of fun learning how to curl ribbons and use fabric wrapping. But I haven't had anyone to give a gift to in a long time. My sister is in California, my parents are in Switzerland. Hopefully I can remember how to do everything for the Christmas I'm finally—"

He paused for a long time. "Finally what?" she asked.

"Home."

A little pain bloomed in the center of Mallory's sternum. She ignored it, lifting a leg to examine her sock. "I don't have anyone to give a gift to this year either."

"How can that be?"

"My parents are in Bali. My older brother is in Florida, and my younger brother is in Michigan, and they're not big gift-givers anyway."

"You seem like you'd have a big group of girlfriends. Lifelong friends. Like the knitters. And you meet lots of people on your travels, right?"

"No. Well, yes, but …" How to explain that no one she met really lasted? She'd encountered many fun, unusual, cool people who she would have been friends with if she'd planned on staying wherever they were.

She had the meeting-people part down, just not the friends part.

When she still didn't say anything, she heard Carter turn his head. His eyes were surely on her face, and she didn't want to meet his gaze because he might see in the depth of hers that she was mostly alone.

Thousands of followers but no real friends.

Paige was the closest to one, but one day they wouldn't work together anymore, so a friendship wouldn't last.

Uncomfortable, Mallory did what she always did. She smiled. "Be careful, Carter Scott. We might become friends and have to get each other gifts next Christmas."

Then she did look at him, and he seemed about to say something, so she jumped out of her chair. "It's late. What are we doing tomorrow?"

Carter used the flat of one hand to push himself up to sitting. "Um, yeah. I don't know."

"I'll look in our big Wanderlove box for clues."

"If there are skis in there, you can forget it."

Mallory pulled the box from the corner into the middle of the floor. "Skis wouldn't fit in here. And what have you got against skiing, anyway?"

"Literally everything. It combines two things I despise. Snow and falling down."

"You don't like snow?"

"Here we go."

"No, it's fine," she said in a voice that implied it wasn't fine.

"I don't mind it out *there*," he said, gesturing at the window. "I just don't like being out there with it."

"Yeah, yeah." She rummaged around and located a couple of sets of long underwear, which she wished she'd seen earlier. "Wait," she said, pulling out two plastic bag and reading the labels. "Why would they send us bathing suits?"

"Maybe they thought the Moonrise Inn has a pool?" He bounced off the bed and grabbed his jacket off the floor, taking the Seasalter town holiday schedule from the side pocket. He scanned it a moment. "Ohhhh."

"What?"

"No, nothing."

"What?"

"You wouldn't be interested."

She stood and tried to grab the paper from his hand, but he held it over her head. "There's nothing in the morning," he said.

"You're a big liar." She jumped to reach his hand, but he was too tall, so she tickled his armpit. He gasped and lowered his arm to block her, and she tore the schedule from his hand. "Ha!"

"I'm only trying to save both of us."

She scanned the schedule, found tomorrow's date, and gasped. "A Penguin Plunge?"

He nodded.

"At nine a.m. Well." She went back to the box and tossed him the pine-green swim trunks. "We'd better get to sleep."

"You're kidding, right? You don't want to run into the ocean."

She shook out her own tomato-red one-piece racerback suit. Nice. "No, I don't want to do that. We're doing it for the content, baby. And hey, we skated and sang on stage for the content, too, and we both survived, and you even had fun."

"Try as I might," he said, removing his suit from the plastic and frowning at it, "I can't see the upside to running into the ocean in what's likely to be twenty-degree air. If we're lucky. Our suits are Christmas colors, red and green."

"You'll be easy to find in the surf, then." She had even more trepidation about this than he did, but Sunshine in a Suitcase tried it all. "Don't think about it. We're going to do it, come right back, and take hot showers."

"I hate this."

She chuckled. She did too, but he was luckier than her—his brand allowed him to publicly dislike discomfort. Hers only allowed her to embrace it.

"We'll need sweats to put on over our suits," he said.

"Oh. I only brought—"

"Super-cute clothes?"

"Well. Yes."

"Don't worry, I always bring plenty of comfort clothes when I travel. You can borrow some of mine."

She wondered if his clothes had that same woody scent about them that his skin always had. Then she wondered what he would look like emerging from the sea, shaking salt water from his hair and smoothing it back with both hands, his chest glistening, a trail of water sliding into his navel, his eyes sparkling as he smiled openly.

When she realized that in this daydream, he was moving in slow motion, she yanked herself out of it. "I'm going to sleep now," she announced.

"Take the bed tonight," he said, collecting a pair of sweatpants from his drawer. Oh, so he did put something in the drawer she'd left open for him.

"No—"

"Take it," he insisted. "You said it got cold in the other room, and I don't get cold easily. I'll be fine. You can stay in here with the fireplace, and I had no problem with the heat last night like you say you did."

Was it her imagination, or did he very, very slightly emphasize the word "say"? Did he not believe her. Or—oh, God—did he know she was in bed with him last night?

No, no way. He'd been dead asleep.

"Sure," she said, because it was useless to argue; if she slept in the warm room, she wouldn't be driven to take embarrassing action again. "I'll set the alarm."

"Ugh, I hate alarms." He walked to the door between the rooms, then stopped. "Hey, can I say something?"

She dropped her arms to her sides, her suit dangling against her thigh. "Sounds serious."

"You're the most adventurous person I've ever met, so far be it from me to encourage you to step out of your comfort zone, but—" He hesitated, studying her face, but whatever he saw there must have encouraged him to go on. "There are potential friends everywhere. Letting yourself choose a few would be okay. You wouldn't need to change who you are. It's okay to let people in."

Heat rushed up her neck, but she stopped herself from retorting with a smart remark, or from making a joke out of it. He seemed to be speaking from somewhere deep, and she didn't want to say he was wrong.

She didn't know if he was, anyway. She hadn't really tried in a long time to make and keep relationships. One-night stands and friendship flings, she knew how to do. Maintain something long term? Her mom had drilled it in her to avoid it if she wanted to live a full life.

But wouldn't most people agree that a full life included friends, family, and someone to love?

"Thanks," she mumbled.

He gave her a little awkward salute and disappeared into the other room, closing the door between them.

* * *

A couple of hours later, Mallory awoke to the door whispering open. She blinked a moment to get her bearings, and realized Carter was in the room, likely to use the bathroom. But he stopped in the middle of the room and didn't move for a couple of minutes. Was he a sleepwalker?

"Carter?" she said in a voice hoarse from sleep.

He cursed quietly. "I'm sorry, I didn't mean to wake you."

"Is the room too cold?"

"No, it's too hot. It's like boiling hot in there. Even in here with the fireplace, it's like ten degrees cooler. I tried to turn the radiator off, and I can't."

"It's fine," she said. "Sleep in here."

He didn't say anything for a moment. She almost took it back, but it was too late, so she doubled down. "Sleep in the bed if it's better for you. This bed is the size of a freight barge, so I won't touch you, if that's what you're afraid of."

"That's not what I'm afraid of," he said quietly.

Mallory's heart thudded so loudly in the silent room that she was certain he could hear it. "You need to sleep so you can be alert for our ice expedition in a few hours. What if you get a cramp in the ocean?"

"Insomnia doesn't cause cramps."

"Oh? Do you know that for a fact, doctor? Are you willing to take that chance?"

He started to walk to the bed.

"Don't roll your eyes at me."

"How did you know I rolled my eyes?" he asked. "Do you have cat night vision?"

"No. I could feel your eye roll."

She was sleeping on the side she'd slept on the last two nights. When he sat, she slid a bit toward him, so she righted herself as he stretched out. "You're sure this is okay?" he asked.

"I offered."

He slid under the sheets and blankets, but left one leg out, probably still warm.

She wanted—to talk? No, she wanted to reach out and touch his arm, or his hair, or his lips. She wanted to tell him all the things she hid, all the things she was afraid of. All the things one would reveal to a lover.

But she wouldn't. She couldn't.

*Carter Scott is not the man for you.*

But what man was?

Maybe no one. But definitely not him.

*It doesn't have to mean anything if you—*

"Mallory?"

She swallowed. "Yeah?"

"There was no night-light when I went to sleep. And when I woke up sweating, there it was, on."

"I told you!" She propped herself up on an elbow. "Remember, I said—"

"You did. This place is … interesting."

"Magical, maybe."

"You said it, not me." His eyes were dark, but they caught an ember of the firelight, sparkling as he looked at her. He opened his mouth as if to say something more, then rolled over so his back was to her. "Good night."

Lying back down, she turned in the opposite direction, hyperaware of his body only inches from hers. "Good night," she mouthed without sound.

# CHAPTER SIXTEEN

When Carter and Mallory crossed the boardwalk and descended onto the sand, the crowd of excited people renewed Carter's spirit a bit. People were squealing, hugging, slapping each other on the back like they hadn't seen each other in years when they probably all saw one another yesterday at the pet parade or the wreath decorating. Many small tents were set up with blankets and towels piled up. Carter wondered if he and Mallory would be woefully unprepared with only a few towels, supplemented by Selene. She'd also handed them to-go cups as they walked out and gave them some last-minute tips: Deep breathing when they went in the water was helpful, and only stay in for a couple of minutes total. He'd thanked her, thinking, *What have I gotten myself into?*

But now that they were here, with music playing over speakers and the smell of coffee mingling in the air with the salt of the ocean, he realized he felt grounded. Calm.

"You guys!" A woman ran over to them like they were her best friends and hugged Mallory, then him, and it wasn't until she pulled away that he recognized her.

"Ana, right?" he asked.

"Yes! You two were the absolute stars of the show this year." She pushed her glasses up the bridge of her nose. "Even though that other girl won, people are still talking about you two and your adorable performance. You'll have to come back next year and emcee."

"Oh, we won't—" Mallory started but Ana waved over a man in a burgundy hooded sweatshirt and navy sweatpants.

"This is my boyfriend, Roman Montgomery."

"Nice to meet you." Roman shook their hands with an easy grin, and Carter remembered where he'd heard his name.

"You're the real estate agent?"

"That's me. Can I entice you to live in our little town?"

"I heard there's a house for sale on Oceanview, by the Moonrise Inn."

"Sure is. Swing by this afternoon to the open house. It's my favorite listing right now, really nice inside."

"Will do."

Mallory glanced at him, confused.

"Are you two at the Moonrise Inn?" Ana asked. "It's so romantic. And so magical. Have you noticed?"

" 'Magic' is the word we used last night, in fact," Mallory told her.

"We fell in love there," Ana said, taking Roman's arm.

He kissed her cheek. "I fell in love with her in high school, but she didn't know it. She fell in love with me at the inn ten years later."

Mallory put a hand on her heart. "I love that."

"Enjoy it," Ana said with a wink.

"Oh, we're not a couple," Mallory clarified.

Ana narrowed her eyes and cocked her head playfully, as if she didn't believe a word of it. "You'd better be careful, then. That place will get you."

A couple of whistles blew, and a man in an inflatable penguin costume with a bullhorn shouted, "Welcome to the twenty-third annual Seasalter Penguin Plunge!"

Everyone cheered, including Mallory and Carter.

"Every year, we gather two weeks before Christmas in honor and respect for the ocean, which gifts us with its eternal presence."

Mallory pulled a scrunchie out of her pocket and twisted and piled her hair on top of her head, securing it with the bright purple elastic.

"Do you have a tent?" Roman asked, and when Carter shook his head, Roman led Mallory and Carter to their tent, inviting them to put their towels and clothes in. They tossed the towels in.

"I'm not stripping down until the absolute last second," Mallory said, dropping to her knees to pull out her waterproof sport camera. "Good thing I keep all my equipment in one bag because I never thought I'd need this in December in New England." She hung it around her neck.

"Not sure what I would have done without you," he told her honestly.

"Probably slept in."

"True."

The announcer was thanking a couple of sponsors and volunteers, and Mallory took a step closer to Carter so that her arm was touching his. She shivered against him, and he wrapped an arm around her shoulders. Even through both their heavy shirts, he was aware of her body and its warmth. To distract himself, he asked, "You couldn't wear a hat?"

"We're going swimming."

"This is not swimming. This is running in, screaming, and running out."

The whistle blew again, and people began throwing off their clothes and racing to the water.

"This is it," Carter said, shucking off his sneakers and sweatpants. He yanked his top layer off to reveal a long-sleeved black rash guard.

When he turned, the sight of Mallory Robson in a bright-red bathing suit was nearly too much for his soul to bear. Her shoulders and chest were sprinkled with a night sky of freckles, and it was really, really cold, so her—

Nope, he wasn't going to look.

But he didn't need to fight his primal urges long, because she suddenly broke into a run, kicking up sand and calling back to him, "First one in is the first one who gets a hot shower!"

He took off after her, ate the space between them in four long strides, then scooped her into his arms. She shrieked, and he shrieked when his feet hit the water. He didn't stop until he was waist deep. "Ready?"

"Yes!"

He set her on her feet, and, suddenly half submerged, she yelped. "It's cold!"

"Yes," he said, his teeth chattering.

"It's so cold!"

He backed up a few feet and splashed her, and she splashed back. They slapped the water at each other. She began taking pictures and video of him, of both of them. After a minute or so, he motioned for her to give him the camera, and she began to dance around in the water, her movements exaggerated. She kicked an arc of water over her own head, and he snapped as many pics as he could in a row so later, they could pick out the best one. Then he lowered the camera and watched her.

How could someone who embodied so much joy be so alone? How could she hold herself back from sharing this joy with someone else?

She stilled and stared over his shoulder, then pointed. "There!"

Roman knelt in the sea, holding a little box out to Ana, who was crying. She took the ring, put it on, and Roman caught her in his arms, spinning her around.

Mallory stepped beside Carter as he watched. "Wow," he breathed. "Look at that."

Everyone cheered for the happy couple, and people started back to the sand.

"Selene warned us not to hang out in the water too long," Carter said.

"We're going to freeze."

"We'll go fast."

They rushed out of the water, sand caking onto their wet feet as they headed for the tent. Carter grabbed her sweatshirt, put it on her, and rubbed her shoulders vigorously for a moment before holding out the pants. She held his shoulder for balance as she stepped into them. He threw a towel over her like a cape and wrapped it around her body. "Are you okay?"

"Yes. Put your clothes on!"

"There's something women don't say to me every day."

"Ha ha. You didn't have to help me first."

"Yes, I did," he said, and put his clothes on before sitting half in the tent and wiping his feet with a towel until he could put his sneakers on.

When he stood, Mallory was hugging Ana and congratulating her. Carter shook Roman's hand and gave him a half hug. "Congrats, man."

"Aw, thanks. Will you still be doing the open house after this big event?"

"Yeah, I have to work, but we're celebrating tonight."

Carter and Mallory fast-walked across the sand, up and over the boardwalk, and down the street, and kicked off their sneakers on the porch before they flew into the front door of the Moonrise Inn.

"How was it?" the Crafty Ladies asked as they passed through on the way to the stairs.

"Cold!" they both said, pounding up the steps and into their room.

Once inside, they paced the room, back and forth, their arms around themselves.

"How do I get warm?" Carter asked, his teeth chattering. "How do I get warm?"

"A shower," Mallory said, her voice shaky with her own shivering.

"Are you sure? What if the shock of the temperature difference makes my heart explode?"

"Oh, crap. I don't know. Look it up online."

"I don't think I can make my fingers work yet."

"We need to get out of these suits."

"Roger that."

She darted into the bathroom, and he heard her throwing off her clothes. He stripped down in the center of the room.

"Warm shower!" she called from the bathroom. "Not hot. I just looked it up."

"Okay, you go first."

While she showered, he turned on the fireplace, and when she came out wrapped in a white robe, he darted past her without even admiring the skin that showed between the lapels of her robe, and sluiced his body with warm water. It was a while before he stopped shaking. He dried himself briskly, wrapped the towel around his waist, and emerged.

Mallory hadn't changed; she sat in her robe in front of the fireplace, so he sat on the rug beside her, stretching out his bare legs and crossing his feet at the ankles.

They remained there in silence for a long while.

By now, he knew she wasn't one for sitting still in one place for very long, and it was gratifying that she chose to do it with him.

"Are you hungry?" he asked finally.

"Sort of, but my stomach is still too cold to eat."

"Though I suspect that's a medical impossibility, I feel the same."

She shifted her feet out from under her and leaned back on both elbows as if basking in the sun. "Ana and Roman getting engaged was really sweet to see."

He nodded.

"Did you say you're looking at a house?"

"Window-shopping a house," he clarified.

"You must window-shop often. You really want that dream house."

"I haven't yet looked at houses for sale. I haven't wanted to before, because I worry about getting attached to a place before I can afford it."

She twisted her mouth to the side, as if trying to work something out. "But you can afford it now? Ah ... the TV show. You think you'll win?"

"There's an outside chance, but it's more that this place, this town—it tries really hard to hook a guy in."

"And you're letting it."

"I've lived a lot of places, but there's something about Seasalter."

"You think this is the place?"

"Maybe," he said. "Maybe."

She nodded slowly. "I think if I were that sort of person, I might agree. The town is lovely and has everything you could want. The beach is right there. The people we've met are kind. If I were the sort to settle down, I could see the appeal."

"Do you really believe you're not the sort to settle down? Or do you just not want to settle down now?"

She sighed. "Anyone can change, I suppose. But I'm planning my life based on how I am now."

"What if fate came together and presented the perfect opportunity for you to buy a house, have a relationship, and travel wherever you want a few times a year? Wouldn't that be the best of both worlds?"

Sitting up, Mallory glared at him. "Why are you asking me if I'd compromise? What would your compromise look like?"

"Like that, I think. A house, a relationship, and traveling a few times a year, which is a few times more than I'd want to, probably. But I would, if she wanted to."

"Why are you talking compromises at all? Don't you want to find a woman who wants what you want?"

"I'm finding," he said, staring into the fire so hard that his eyes started to tear, "that what I want doesn't always come in the package I expect."

"What does that m—"

He turned his head and looked her in the eyes. He shouldn't say it. And he almost didn't say it.

But if he didn't, he'd regret it every day and night.

As his brain and his libido wrestled, his turmoil must have shown on his face. Mallory's brow furrowed.

His brain collapsed in defeat.

"You, Mallory. Right now, I want you."

Her jaw dropped open. But she didn't recoil in horror or slap him across the face, so he pressed on.

"Yeah," he said. "So that happened. And I'm sorry, and I promise that if you're not feeling it, I can move forward professionally with you and never mention it again. But I feel it's a disservice to both of us for me to try to ignore this—this thing."

The three of them sat together silently: him, her, and the thing. Her chest rose and fell a little more heavily underneath her robe, and her skin was flushed—either from his confession or the fireplace.

"I—can't change," she finally said. "As much as I want … I can't change who I am. I don't want to."

He hadn't expected the shred of his heart, like it was in a garlic press. He hadn't realized his heart was even involved. She electrified his skin, she made him hard, she made him want to laugh. But the crush of his most vital internal organ was not something he was ready for.

"But," she added, and stopped.

Carter watched her face carefully. She licked her upper lip, then tried to brush a lock of hair from her face, but it was damp from perspiration and stuck to her cheek. She lifted her hand again, but he beat her to it, moving it gently off her face and tucking it behind her delicate ear. Not wanting to release her, he wound his fingers in those golden strands, cupping her jaw.

"But?" he prompted softly. He hardened under his towel, and he didn't bother to try to press his other hand over it or hide it. At the moment, he didn't care if she saw what she did to him.

"But there's something here," she confirmed. "There's something here that's—physical, and if you want to, I want to."

"Do you mean—"

"Yes."

Was he disappointed? Yes. He was ashamed of his disappointment, because he'd known since the moment they met that they weren't compatible, that their goals for their lives were completely opposite. He wished she felt the emotional connection that he somehow did and not simply the desire that darkened her eyes.

But she wanted to be free. And he wanted to be the kind of man who could nobly say that if he couldn't have her completely, he couldn't have her at all, and leave her alone.

*Say no.*

*Let her go.*

*Let her go.*

But he was not that strong. He would devour the crumbs she was tossing him, even if the onetime memory of how she tasted was all he'd ever have of Mallory Robson.

Closing the few inches that separated their lips, he kissed her.

# CHAPTER SEVENTEEN

Mallory parted her lips, groaning into Carter's hot, hungry mouth as he deepened the kiss. His fingers tangled and twisted through the strands of her air-drying hair, and the unfamiliar moan that emerged from her own throat turned her on. He made a similar sound before easing her onto her back and moving his lips to her ear, the column of her neck, her collarbone. She wondered if he could hear, or even see, her heart beating hard and insistently inside her. Lifting both arms, she trailed her palms down both his shoulders and pressed on against his chest. She tweaked one nipple, and he gasped, playfully slapping her hand away, so of course she had to do it again, and a third time. He caught both her wrists and stopped her, then reached down and untied her thick terry belt.

Carter peeled her robe apart, one side at a time, leaving it open under and around her like Christmas wrapping paper. It was daytime, but the room was dim with the drapes pulled, and the firelight shone on his skin, much like it was probably shining on hers. He pulled back to take in the sight of her entire body, and she squirmed a bit. Despite her confidence in her own appearance, it was difficult to be so … naked, and not immediately worry about flaws. Carter didn't leave her much time to consider it, though, before he opened the towel around his hips and tossed it out of view. His length was impressive, but before she could decide what—of many things—she could do next, he began to explore every inch of her skin with his hands and mouth and tongue. His cock dragged across her body as he did, and every time it skimmed below her belly, she gasped and arched her back, opening her knees a bit wider.

The heat from the fireplace dried the kisses he left on her body, one by one, and when he finally crawled toward the wet juncture between her thighs, she sat up and tugged at his hard thigh and hip, directing him to straddle her head. He used his fingers to expose her clit, then sucked on it so suddenly that she bucked. He chuckled around her and went back to his task.

Eyes closed and writhing beneath him, she nearly forgot her plan. She opened her eyes and inhaled the scent of his arousal, then drew his hips down to take him into her mouth, sucking and licking and moaning until his legs shook in an effort to keep himself steady. His arousal hit her tongue, thick and salty, but she found it impossible to concentrate on his satisfaction while his mouth worked her over.

With an extra-forceful suck, she released him, and he sat up, and in the dim light she could see her wetness on his chin and the spot over his top lip. They stared at each other for a charged beat, as if remembering where they were. She pushed herself up to crash into him for another long kiss. She tasted him; she tasted herself. Then they both scrambled into opposite ends of the room.

Mallory yanked her dresser drawer open and pushed through her organized-by-color pile of bras and underpants, but he somehow was the first to find a condom, despite the chaos of his spilled suitcase. They crawled back to their spot on the rug, he covered himself, and she sat in his lap, wrapping her legs around his hips and her arms around his shoulders. She was so open and so wet that he was able to bury himself into her fast and hard, and they both gasped as she pushed her own hips against him and drove her crossed ankles into his lower back until she was completely full with him.

She had control of their movement, and she didn't waste it, pumping and pumping and gasping into his ear. Her core rubbed against him, electrifying every thrust, until she was on the edge of screaming with release. He pushed back against her, coming together with her over and over until she cried out and he groaned, and she exploded into a thousand stars and he throbbed against her sensitive insides.

They each dropped their chin on the other's shoulder and, draped all over one another, fell into a haze of warmth and sensation.

After quite a while, he lay back, bringing her with him. Her leg pretzeled between both of his, and her cheek rested on his chest, and he took her hand with his and held it.

And as they recovered together on the rug, their labored breathing mingling with the crackling and snapping of the flames in the small fireplace, all Mallory could think was that she'd lied.

There *was* something between them, but it *wasn't* merely physical, and she was desperately afraid that if she were around Carter Scott much longer, she wouldn't be able to fly away.

★ ★ ★

She didn't know how long they'd dozed there, but Mallory's grumbling stomach woke her only about fifteen seconds before her phone did.

Glancing at Carter's relaxed face and closed eyelids, she felt an icicle piercing her heart, a pain so unusual and so intense that she rolled away from him before the threatening tears filled her eyes.

There had been a small handful of one-night sexual encounters in her life and travels, and after each one, she'd been satisfied and happy to move on.

This was not that.

Her phone continued to ring in the pocket of the sweatpants she'd tossed on the bed earlier, and she scrambled to her feet and fished it out.

Trixie. A video call.

She picked it up quickly, leaving the video dark. "Hi!" she nearly shouted and realized her enthusiasm likely sounded more like mania. Many exclamation points.

"Mallory, hello! Are you and Carter both available for a chat?"

She looked down at her naked, sweaty body. "Um, yes! Yes, of course. I think he's in the … main room? I'll … get him?"

Across the room, Carter was awake and propped up on one elbow, an eyebrow raised in question. "Yeah," she said. "I'll get him."

"Oh, sure."

Mallory muted the phone and dropped it face down on the bed. "Trixie," she said, and the two of them raced around the room, throwing on clothes. Grabbing a scrunchie from the dresser, she twisted her hair into a ponytail. They both flung themselves onto the bed, wordlessly put a few non-intimate inches between them, and Mallory turned on the sound and camera, holding the phone at arm's length. "Hi! We're back."

"Hey, you two! What's on the schedule for today? You look casual."

Mallory didn't trust her own voice, but Carter smoothly took over. "Seasalter Penguin Plunge this morning."

"You both did it?"

They nodded. "We'll post soon," Mallory promised. "We needed to recover. And we saw a marriage proposal!" she added, hoping to distract Trixie from their disheveled appearances.

"That sounds amazing! I didn't want to pressure you into any particular activity, but when we were packing your box, we added swimsuits because we'd read that Seasalter has a Christmas cold plunge. I'm so glad you did it. Actually," she said, "I'm calling to let you know that Wanderlove is so happy with your content. I was so surprised to see that you decided to go with pretending a little romance after all!"

"Thank y—" Mallory started. "Wait, what?"

"We appreciate your commitment to the bit. You might not have had time to engage with the comments, but your followers are thrilled to think they're seeing you fall for each other in real time. Great job, really. It's driving a lot of traffic to our site, and you know that's exactly what we wanted. People love a love story."

"Yes," Mallory said weakly through her smile.

"Four more days," Trixie said. "Also, on Friday, there's a holiday gala at a restaurant called Muscatel's. A longtime annual fundraising event called the Fancy Dance. Although Wanderlove doesn't really sell anything appropriate for a black-tie party, we'd love for you to go as a thank-you from us. We sent the tickets to your email, and we are providing a stipend for both of you to get some really nice clothes."

Mallory was glad Carter was there to hold up their end of the conversation. "Thanks, Trixie," he said. "We're looking forward to it."

"You two keep up the terrific work, and I'll check in again soon." She winked and disconnected.

Carter turned to Mallory, and he smiled that kind of secret smile that only meant one thing. "Hi."

*Run!* But she allowed him to capture her lips with his, then to kiss his way up her jaw toward her earlobe, which he took softly between his teeth. She sighed, and he whispered in her ear, "Are you hungry?"

She giggled, despite her fear, despite her heart. "Yes."

He pulled back and examined her face, her eyes. "Was this okay?"

"What do you mean?" Though she knew very well what he meant.

"This." He gestured between them. "Us."

Us. One word. Two letters. Huge meaning.

She had sensed by the way his muscles had tensed from the smallest touch, and by the way he'd welcomed her into the vulnerable depths of his eyes, that it was more for him than sex, than an orgasm, than friends making each other feel good.

She had sensed it, because it was more for her too.

And she couldn't allow him—a man looking at houses for sale—to pin her to the ground.

But—he'd agreed to take it only as far as she allowed it. And selfishly, perilously, she wanted to do what they'd just done, again.

Why shouldn't they? Why shouldn't she? She was her own woman. She wouldn't let this take over her life. Not in four days. If she could get over a flu in four days, she could get this out of her system.

"Yes, it was okay. I mean"—she lowered her voice—"more than *okay*. It was ... fireworks. You're very, very good at what you do."

Carter managed to look embarrassed and proud at the same time.

"And I wouldn't mind doing it again."

He raised two pleased eyebrows.

"As long as we keep it, you know, casual," she clarified. "Like we said."

His expression remained, but something flickered across his face. It was gone before she could identify or interpret it. "If that's what you want."

"It is." *Right?* "Yes, it is."

He nodded slowly.

"I'm concerned, though," she said, "that Wanderlove, that *people*, think we're a couple. I'm not sure why they would." She opened her social media app and scrolled through their posts from the last two days, then squeezed her eyelids shut, opening them again only when she vowed to study them with fresh eyes.

Enlarging each pic, she stared at herself.

Oh, *God.* How could she have not seen it in her own face when she was choosing photos and videos? The blush coloring her cheeks, the sparkle in her gaze. Her smile so wide, she could count most of her teeth. All of it not aimed at the camera, at her audience as always, but at *him.*

She glanced over at Carter now, who was scrolling through his own phone, a deep groove forming above his nose.

"There are a lot of people saying some—disgusting things," he finally said. "And that's the mildest, most polite word I can use. The word I'd like to use is—"

"Don't. People on the internet are horrible. I don't engage them, and Paige blocks the worst of it."

"It's not on your account, but mine. Guys thinking we're dating, saying I should—" He cut himself off this time, with a curse combination that was admirable in its uniqueness.

"Ignore it," she said. "I don't care."

"I do. This is not what I stand for."

"Your followers are manly men."

"Manly men don't say this kind of thing. And I won't allow them to say it about—"

"This is the second time it's surprised you. You don't get trolls?"

"I do, but they're not so gross and personal. They're even worse now that they think we're a couple. Which is insane. You'd think they'd tone it down on my page if they thought you were my girlfriend."

She dragged her attention off her own phone and put a hand on his arm. "No, I wouldn't think that."

"Doesn't it bother you?"

"It's a trade-off. I get to do what I want with my life. If that's the price to pay, I'll suck it up. I hate it, I do, but I don't let faceless idiots stop me."

"If you get the TV gig, it will be worse."

"Probably. But other things will get better."

His gaze dropped back to his phone. "To be fair, there are at least ten times as many comments that are really supportive of … us."

That little big word again.

"They think we're cute together, we remind them of their own relationships, we're hashtag couple goals. They think the town is pretty and we're pretty. That's nice of them."

Mallory stood. "I'm going to get some air."

"Oh." Carter tossed his phone on the bed. "Okay, sure. Where do you want to—"

"If it's okay, I need some alone time."

If he was hurt, he didn't show it. "Sure."

"We'll meet back here in a few hours, create some content from this morning, and plan tomorrow?"

"Sounds good."

She dashed into the bathroom to change and avoid any more conversation, then walked across the room, picking up her handbag and jacket midstride. "Have a good afternoon, okay?"

*Smile. It's your best weapon. Smile like you always do.*

He smiled easily back at her. "You too."

Fighting the urge to hurl herself into his arms, she forced herself out the door.

# CHAPTER EIGHTEEN

Selene had wanted to finish crocheting a pair of fingerless gloves for Luna—so her daughter could furiously text while keeping her hands toasty—but instead of heading downstairs to join the knitters, she was sitting in the beige armchair in her third-floor apartment, listening.

Actually listening, like a creepy weirdo. Listening to Owen in his childhood room, working.

He'd moved in already—or, at least, moved in as much as he could with very short notice. He'd packed several bags, intending to return occasionally to pack up, move, and store his larger items. She'd insisted on carrying in a few things from his car, but standing in the small room with him, right where he'd be sleeping, made her shuffle uncomfortably, and she'd quickly voiced an excuse and left for her own apartment, where she was now. Listening.

So far, she'd heard the chair scrape across the floor twice, heard his footsteps creak across the hardwood floor twice, heard his muffled voice on a phone call with a client (mostly low and businesslike, but he'd let out one short burst of laughter), and heard him tap tap tapping computer keys. He had a nice keyboard, with kind of a creamy sound. She'd also heard him sneeze three times in a row, but she couldn't call, "Bless you!" because then he'd know she was there, and he'd suspect she was listening. Like a creepy weirdo.

But instead of getting up, she sank deeper into the chair, rounding her back and shoulders and laying her forearms across the chair arms, curling her fingers around the ends.

It was strange, having another presence so close, someone going through everyday motions side by side with her. She'd gotten used to the quiet over the nearly two years, and Owen's working sounds now showed how loud the quiet had been, and how peaceful and companionable someone else in her space could be.

Someone she cared about.

There had to be a chore that needed doing so she could stop sitting here, right? But the bedding had been washed, the floors swept, the kitchen and dining room cleaned. Reservations were caught up, emails were current, shopping for the week was complete. This was her short, rare down time. And she was spending it listening to the faint sounds of a man a couple of rooms away.

At least, she was able to recognize how ridiculous this was. At least, she retained some modicum of self-awareness.

Owen was a friend. A caring friend, a generous friend, a smart and funny friend. An attractive friend.

But a friend.

Even if he wanted more out of their relationship in terms of intimacy, she was certain he wouldn't overstep. He would remain what he was now: a solid, warm, reliable person in her life.

Man in her life.

Selene had never asked him about his dating situation, but she was certain he didn't have one, because on no green earth would a woman be okay with the help he gave Selene, the amount of time he spent at the Moonrise Inn with her. And if there had been another woman in the picture, he'd have gone to stay with her when he'd had to quickly vacate his own place.

If he were dating someone, this whole friendship would change, and Selene realized that when she considered that, something *pinged* under her breastbone.

Maybe he didn't want to date. Maybe he was done with relationships after his divorce, which he'd told her was amicable and mutual. Maybe he was over it.

As was she.

*Ping.*

She loved her alone time. She'd loved it even with Dan. She loved to read, to craft, to write, to binge her favorite shows, to fall into her own mind and experience her own self in the compassionate and understanding way she was unable to as a younger woman. Fifty years brought wisdom, and wisdom honed skills, and she was able to read people and herself far better than she could as a twenty-five-year-old who'd thought she had all the answers.

And if she were honest, and she could read others, she was certain that Owen—

A soft two knocks on her door startled her, but she was pleased to notice that at some point, she'd stopped listening like a creepy weirdo. She quickly picked up a book and opened it to a random page, pushing her reading glasses from her crown halfway down her nose. "Yes?"

Owen stepped in with one foot, curling his body around the door. "Hi."

"Everything okay? Do you need anything?"

"No. I'm just checking on you."

"On me? Why?"

"Why not?"

*You used to do this during my alone time, Dan. Step in from wherever you were, put eyes on me, smile, and leave with a quiet wave.*

*Yes, I did …*

She softened at Dan's approval.

"I'm doing really well," she said, and when Owen smiled, she realized she meant it.

"Hey," he said, leaning in and glancing around the room. "You don't have a Christmas tree in here."

"No, I don't. I still need to get a small one for the guests downstairs, but I've been so busy. And I don't need one up here."

"Let's go." He clapped his hands twice. "Get dressed. We're getting a couple of trees."

"Don't you have to work?"

"I did everything I needed to for today. This is now the priority. Hop to it. Jacket on."

"You don't have to—"

"I have to. I live here now. And this house knows me and will be very disappointed if I don't fill it with trees."

She tried to fix him with a stern look. "Owen."

"Selene."

She stood and moved closer to him so she could look him in the eye. "Owen, this place is not your responsibility."

He cocked his head and regarded her for a moment, and Selene worried she'd insulted this man who went out of his way for her, for the Moonrise Inn, so often. But finally he said, "No, of course it isn't. I recognize it's your responsibility. But it's my pleasure." He lowered his voice as he added, "You get that, don't you? All of this, it's always my pleasure."

*Is this okay?*

Suddenly, her fireplace clicked on with a whoosh, startling her with golden flames. She rushed over, knelt before it, and clicked it off. "That's odd. I don't think I put it on the timer."

"Odd," Owen agreed.

*Odd*, her mind echoed.

She stood and placed a hand on her belly, as if to settle something inside. Then she turned to Owen. "What are you standing there for? Let's go."

# CHAPTER NINETEEN

"What are you doing there?" Wendy leaned in, and Carter allowed her to gently take the needles from his hands, pull apart a few messed-up stitches, and give it back to him.

The knitters were meeting at Jasmine Pink's Tea Shoppe today. They'd pushed a few tables together, and the surface was covered with steaming cups, doughnuts, yarn, and various accoutrements like buttons and beads. Delilah jumped up every so often to assist a customer, but it was late in the afternoon and nearing closing time.

"This is shaping up really well," Wendy said, and he couldn't help the little bloom of pride in his chest. Her perfume was flowery, but Carter didn't know enough about flowers to identify this one. Would he ever want a flower garden? He didn't know how to tend one, but he could hire a gardener. There were so many things he could do with a yard if he had one around the house like the one Roman had shown him a couple of hours ago. He could keep bees. Or chickens. Or a horse? No, no room for a horse. A birdhouse, though. And a bat house, definitely, and in return, the bats would keep mosquitoes away.

Did he know how to do any of this? No. But that's what books and videos and classes were for. He could learn, like he was learning to knit. He shook out the yarn and regarded his project, which was almost starting to resemble an identifiable object, and it was even the object he'd intended.

Would Mallory be afraid of a beehive? He didn't think so. There wasn't much she was afraid of trying, except maybe for staying in one place.

Her skin, her dark eyes, her hair haloed around her head on the rug—her gasps of pleasure.

This situation was untenable.

He realized the chatter had died out and he glanced up to see all the women peering at him. "What?"

"You're very quiet today," Jackie observed.

"I'm always quiet. I'm the strong, silent type."

"Pssh," Brenda said. "Please. Women our age have no use for silent men. Strong, sure. But silent? Boring. Patrice here saw you with the real estate guy over at that little red house a while ago."

He shook his head. "Can someone sniffle around here without everyone knowing about it?"

"Not in a town this size," Jackie said. "You thinking about moving here?"

"I was looking."

"You wouldn't be the first to visit for a few days and decide to make it your home," Delilah pointed out. "Roman and Ana did."

"They got engaged this morning," he told them, and they all sighed. "Wait, don't tell me I told you something you didn't already know."

"It's official," Jackie said. "We've turned you into a gossiper like us."

He rolled his eyes and went back to his knitting. The repetition and the company soothed him just enough to stop him from stomping out onto the street and yelling for Mallory in an unhinged, uncontrolled manner. He hadn't seen her since she'd gone out for "air" hours ago.

Carter wasn't an idiot. Well, that was debatable at this point. But he did know what going out for air was. It was fleeing. It was running away.

And she'd told him. She told him flat out that she wasn't *commitment*, she wasn't *settle-down*, she wasn't *put-down-roots*. She was a branch stretching to the sky, pushing out leaves far above the ground.

He didn't regret anything he'd done with her. What he regretted was that he couldn't be what she needed.

Eyes on his work, he commented casually, "Anyone seen Mallory today?"

Rather than offering any useful information, Jackie said, "Interesting."

"Right?" Patrice said. "You two have been attached at the hip since you woke up screaming at each other. Is something wrong?"

"Um. No. We have work to finish, and she hasn't been back, that's all."

"What'd you do?" Beth Ann asked.

If he told these ladies what he'd done to Mallory, they'd pass out. Maybe not Jackie, possibly not Delilah ... oh, who was he kidding? These women would chuckle and probably high-five him. He settled on, "Nothing."

"Did you tell her how you feel?" Delilah asked, watching his face for a reaction he was determined not to give, but he must have, because she nodded sagely.

"It's been two days," he said. "What I feel is nothing."

"The heart knows," Delilah said, "often right away."

"My heart is five steps behind my brain on this one," he said. "And I need to use my brain."

"She's shy," Patrice said.

He looked up. "Mallory? She's the furthest thing from shy. She's out there on social media, smiling and flipping her hair and being magical."

"It's easy to be magical to a faceless crowd," Patrice said, flipping her own salt-and-pepper hair over her shoulder. "It's not easy to make a real connection. We invited her to knit with us."

He shrugged one shoulder. "Maybe she's not interested in knitting."

"She didn't say no for that reason," Patrice told him, taking a demure sip of her tea. "She was standing here in a room full of people who wanted to be friends with her, and she was terrified. She ran out of here so fast, she left a cartoon puff of smoke where she'd been standing."

"I think you're right." Brenda poked through the pile on the table, picking up a button and studying it closely. "Mallory is very lonely."

"She had no trouble with you at first, because she sensed you were prickly," Jackie said. "My guess? You weren't a threat because she thought you weren't someone who would want to get close to her."

"But then," Delilah said, "you did?"

Were these women sorceresses? How did they suss this all out so fast? Carter realized his bottom jaw was hanging open, so he clicked it shut. He wanted to ask how to get through to Mallory, but that wasn't the right question, because if she wasn't allowing him in, he couldn't force his way in.

It would be best if he left.

He'd promised Wanderlove four more days, but Mallory could handle it on her own—better than he could, judging by the way she easily dismissed her online hecklers. He could fake an emergency, and maybe Wanderlove wouldn't take him out of the running for the TV show. Maybe they'd seen enough so that they might still choose him, and he could buy that house.

Because he'd loved it.

Argh, no, he couldn't leave. He had to stay for his own future. He'd back off Mallory. No more sex. No more kissing. No more talking about anything other than work. That was it. He was a grown man who could control himself.

He remembered that he'd left Delilah's question hanging there. "I … I sort of did get close to her. But you're right. This isn't the right thing for either of us."

"I'm not sure we said that," Wendy said.

"You're absolutely right," he said, standing. "I need to get back to the inn. Work to do."

The women all glanced at one another. After a moment, Jackie held open her large tote for him to stuff his project into, then he pushed in his chair, waved goodbye to them, and exited onto Oceanview.

The cold air froze his brain cells momentarily, which he was grateful for.

★ ★ ★

The early darkness of New England in winter was depressing, but Carter was certain that once he had his home to hole up in, the short days would be permission to hibernate in the comfort of his own making. Though he didn't love it now, he anticipated loving it someday.

Rather than turning toward the lights and festivities of Broad Street, he headed in the other direction, down Oceanview to the beach. Pausing as he passed the little red house with the creaking *For Sale* sign, he noticed that at this hour, it was gray, though no less inviting. He lifted his chin to regard the moon above Seasalter, silver and full. The dark clouds crossing it offered the illusion that the moon was moving with him, and the faint sound of the lonely winter waves beckoned him.

He climbed the steps to the boardwalk, and her hair blew in the breeze like a banner. Mallory was right in the middle of the bench, clearly expecting no one, so when he sat, he couldn't help but sit close to her.

Neither of them said anything as they gazed at the water. Without the moon, they'd likely be staring into inky blackness, but the light from the sky illuminated the white crests that built up and crashed down, over and over.

Eventually, he said, "It's wild to think that this water will outlive us, outlast everything else here. Those waves have been rising and falling from the beginning of time on Earth and will continue until the end, I suppose."

She took an audible breath as if to respond, hesitated, then said, "I was about to tease you and say, thanks for talking about the end of the world at the jolliest time of year, but I realized it's not a negative thought at all. It's about what's bigger than us, and that's a nice thought, actually."

"It makes me feel less alone." He watched her from the corner of his eye, but she didn't react to the word. "It occurs to me," he said instead, "that Christmas might be difficult for you too. Though you do a far better job of hiding it than I do."

Twisting in her seat, she stared at him, so he turned his body toward her also. "How do you figure?"

"You said your mother didn't really want to be at home."

"I think what I meant was she didn't want to be home all the time. I don't think she didn't love her family."

"I understand. But it's hard, on a holiday that's about family and togetherness, to have someone so important in your life making it clear she was trapped and not wanting that type of togetherness."

Mallory didn't answer, so he forged on. "No matter how much someone loves to travel, I figure at some point, even for a short while, they need to land. Even a bird has a nest, right? Without one, you don't have a place for when you get tired. You can't rest. You can't let people take care of you."

"Christmas is a time to land, is what you're saying?"

"Yes. College students, faraway relatives. If people come home, it's often at Christmas."

Her eyes briefly narrowed in a wince, and though he could interpret it as pain or shame, he preferred to let her explain. After a minute, she said, "Well. You've got me there." Gathering her blowing hair in a ponytail in her hand, she added, "At least, that Christmas is hard. The sunshine attitude on my socials, that's not completely false, you know."

"I believe you. You are very genuine."

"I love seeing the world. Too many people don't get to experience the world, or choose not to. But yeah, this time of year, and maybe some other times, it's a bit hard not to feel … something. It's not for the reason you're saying, though."

"Are you sure?"

She pressed her lips together.

"You don't have to tell me," he said. "Though I want you to know that if you do, I won't tell anyone that Mallory Robson is lonely once in a while. Or sad. I'm not the sort to spill secrets."

"When I met you, I didn't peg you as a deep-conversation type."

"I didn't peg you as the one I'd want to have deep conversations with. But here we are."

Her thick hair still gripped in her fist, she let her head drop to the back of the bench so her face was lifted to the sky. The silvery white light bathed her face, soft and vulnerable. "We're too different, Carter."

"I know."

"I think what we did today was a mistake."

Carter hadn't expected that the pain of discovering someone really did feel something for him would be worse than the pain of thinking they felt nothing. Rather than the dull bone ache of disappointment, it was sharp, acute. "I think so too," he said, because saying anything else wouldn't have been fair to either of them.

"I'm sorry."

"Neither of us should be sorry for who we are. Maybe I'm sorry we met on Christmas, when we're both a little weaker than we'd normally be, but I'm not sorry otherwise."

Still staring at the sky, she smiled slightly. "I read somewhere that every monthly full moon has a name."

"Oh, yeah?"

"Yeah." She slipped her phone out of her jacket pocket. "I'll look it up." Sitting up straight, she tapped and slid her fingertips. "Got it. December. It's a Mohawk name: the cold moon."

"Makes sense."

"It's a symbol of endurance and resilience." She clicked her phone off.

"I like that."

"Me too."

Shivers shook her body, and she wrapped her arms around herself. "And it's cold, all right. Though starting tomorrow, there's supposed to be a bit of a warm spell for a few days."

"Seriously? It's either unseasonably warm or unseasonably cold around here."

"Complainer."

He reached out an arm, and she eyed him warily before he grimaced and gestured her closer. She inched over, and he wrapped his arm around her, rubbing her arm, trying to ease her shivers. When she spoke again, he had to bend his head closer to hers to hear her over the ocean.

"I'm sorry it's hard for me to talk to you about stuff I don't talk to anyone about. I'm not used to it."

"It's okay," he said, watching the cold moon's reflection sparkling on the ocean. "I think when we're born, we have a human instinct to trust, and there's always someone or something that breaks that trust, breaks our heart. Some people have a hard time figuring out how to trust again."

"I didn't know I wanted to."

"I guess that's the first step."

She rested her head on his shoulder, and he blew her hair out of his mouth. "How about next time you want to mope outside, you wear a hat?"

"The truth is, I don't actually own a hat."

"Unbelievable."

★ ★ ★

After posting their ocean-plunge video and photos, after pancakes at the Town Diner—where Carter and Mallory agreed that breakfast-for-dinner is ideal—and after taking some photos by the Christmas tree in the center of town, they found themselves in the Orion's Belt suite again.

"I'll take the pullout," Mallory insisted. "I'll dress in layers in case there are heat problems again. You can take it tomorrow."

How? How was he supposed to sleep with her in the next room now that he'd learned every curve of her body, heard each little sound she made in her throat when he—

"Okay," he said.

They took turns in the bathroom. Mallory lingered in the doorway. "Tomorrow is the sled race."

"If you're planning on trying to talk me into letting you win, don't bother."

Her smile lit up her face, and he was relieved. It had been hours since he'd seen her Sunshine.

"I wasn't. I was planning on asking you if we could be a team. I can't imagine anyone would beat us if we worked together."

"You're on. And listen ... leave the door open a bit so you can get some fireplace heat. Just in case."

Her smile turned a bit wistful. "Good night."

"Good night, Mallory."

Carter got into bed but lay there with his light on until her room went dark. He rolled onto his side and wondered how he was supposed to sleep.

"Carter?"

He jolted up to find her back in the doorway. "Yes?"

"My hair."

"What about it?"

"It's … it's brown. I'm not a blonde. I've been coloring it for years."

He stood, swinging his legs off the side of the bed, but he only made it to the middle of the room before she ran the rest of the way and jumped into his arms, kissing him, wrapping her legs around his waist, pressing her core against him until his hard ache made him moan into her mouth.

Never taking his lips from hers, he carried her to the bed, and they happily made a mistake. Again.

# CHAPTER TWENTY

Three days passed quickly. Mallory and Carter attended and documented the sled race—they didn't win—the Seasalter Holiday Lights Parade, an outdoor winter market, and a snowman-building contest. They tried several different restaurants for lunch and dinner. They took a sweaty class taught by Ana at Blue Ocean Fitness. They ate breakfast together every morning—earning Mallory a knowing smile from Selene. Mallory couldn't bother being embarrassed; Selene owned an inn, after all, and likely saw her share, so she couldn't be blamed for assuming.

And anyway, she assumed correctly, because Mallory and Carter spent a lot of time in their suite naked. On the bed. On the pullout. On the floor. In the shower.

They didn't discuss the future again. There didn't seem to be a need to. They both understood this wasn't a forever thing; it was a for-the-rest-of-the-week thing.

Mallory knew now that she would be heartbroken when this thing with Carter was over, but it would have to be over, and what was that saying? It was better to have loved and lost than to never have—?

But this wasn't *love*, for crying out loud. Despite a growing number of followers commenting on her posts about how nice it was to see young *love*, to see a couple falling in *love* at Christmas, that *love* was in the air. They all meant well, but they obviously didn't know what they were talking about.

Curled up together on the bed tonight, watching TV, they shared a bowl of popcorn Carter had filched from the Crafty

Ladies after spending about an hour with them. Mallory liked that despite their new need to be together so often, Carter stayed loyal to his new older friends, spending at least an hour and a half with them every day while she read a book in their room. He appreciated them and returned with funny little stories they'd told him. They'd told him tonight that he was officially a Crafty Lady now and asked him to join them on their holiday trip next year.

Mallory wondered if she could have friends like that, if it were possible for someone like her.

"Did you find a dress for the Fancy Dance tomorrow night?" Carter asked her now. They'd split up this afternoon for a while to shop.

"I did. In a thrift store."

"Wanderlove is paying, you know."

"It wasn't a money thing. It was a perfect-dress thing."

"Well, I'm looking forward to that." He kissed her forehead. "I rented a tux."

"Ooh," she said as her phone rang. She checked the screen. "Trixie."

He looked down at himself, then at her. "We're decent."

She smirked. "For a change."

His grin was sly with the secret they kept, and her cheeks heated. "Answer it," he encouraged.

She picked up and turned on the video. "Hey, Trixie!" She sat beside Carter on the couch, thankful that the popcorn bowl forced them to keep some respectable distance. She turned the phone to horizontal, so they were both in the picture.

"Good, you're both there!" Trixie said. Her expression was nearly effervescent with happiness. "I'm thrilled to say, on behalf of Wanderlove, that you've got the TV job!"

Infinite exclamation points.

Mallory and Carter exchanged a confused look. "Uh ..." Carter began but stopped.

"Who … I'm sorry, which one of us?" Mallory stammered.

"Both of you!"

Mallory blinked once, twice, then refocused on Trixie's face.

"Wanderlove is crazy about the two of you together. The public loves your chemistry. We love your talent. We want you to co-host the first season of *Wander With Love*, and we want to start shooting in January in Barcelona."

Trixie continued talking about the season and the schedule, but her words ran together into liquid syrup, and Mallory couldn't follow anymore.

A TV season? All over the world. With Carter?

Tomorrow, they were supposed to say goodbye forever. Mallory was to leave and discover her next adventure and let Seasalter and Carter crystallize into a sweet memory. If she had to spend months with him—

She wouldn't be able to sever what was between them, which was addictive and rich and satisfying. And eventually she'd be trapped in a quaint little house, a ring glittering on her finger, a boulder on her foot.

Carter was talking now, thanking Trixie, telling her that he couldn't wait, that they were looking forward to this collaboration.

*"They" means me. Carter and me.*

Then there was no more talking, just anticipatory silence. Mallory realized they were both waiting for her to say something.

"Thank you," she said, her empty voice echoing in her ears as she glued on her Sunshine smile. "Thank you. I'm really honored. This means a lot."

*I have to get out of here.*

# CHAPTER TWENTY-ONE

Carter slept fitfully and woke up out of sorts. After Trixie's call last night, things had gotten weird. Rather than discussing the opportunity they'd both wanted and worked for and were now sharing, they had both busied themselves getting ready for bed, and Mallory retreated to the TV room pullout after mumbling something like, "I'mgoingtosleepintheotherroomifthat'sokaygoodnight."

He couldn't tell if she'd wanted him to ask her to stay with him, to sleep with him, but in truth, he wasn't sure he'd wanted to. Today was the last full day of their collaboration in Seasalter, and the wordless pact had been that after that, what was going on between them would be over. It had to be.

And he'd known this whole time that it was going to be near to impossible to extricate his heart from all this, from her, but if they were to spend the next few months together traveling and filming, there was no way he'd be able to let her go when it was finally time.

It would hurt even more than it did now. And it hurt a lot now.

Her door was still closed, and he wondered if she was waiting for him to leave. An uncomfortable conversation was imminent—no, necessary—but he had no idea what his side of that would sound like, so maybe it was best to avoid one another until he could figure it out.

Carter was sure of one thing, however: He needed to back out of the Wanderlove show.

It was disappointing. For some reason, that little red house on Oceanview was calling to him, and if he were to sign the show contract, he would likely have enough money finally for a down payment, and he could build a life in the little town. He could step out of his front door and smell the salty ocean every day. He could plant mint, maybe, or parsley. He could get a cat—no, two cats. Did Mallory like cats? Probably.

He'd have to let the house go. He'd keep saving and working, and he'd find another nice house as soon as he could. It wasn't a crisis, just a delay. And Mallory would do a wonderful job on the show on her own. She'd become a star; he was certain of it. She didn't need him.

Though he needed her, and he had no idea how this need would abate.

He quickly showered and dressed, grabbed his key card, glanced at the closed door to the TV room, and left. When he got to the first floor, Owen was carrying in boxes, and he blushed cherry-red when Carter asked if he was moving into Selene's. (*Just friends*, Carter's ass. He'd seen them together. They could fool one another if they wanted to, but not him.) Apparently, Owen was staying here in between rental places, so Carter helped him move a few more boxes and bags from the car onto the third floor while Selene made breakfast for the guests.

Carter escaped the inn without any more interaction and headed up Oceanview. Instead of turning left on Broad, he crossed and continued on Oceanview, turning left instead on Evanston Street. He passed a pharmacy and a small veterinary clinic, following his nose to a small coffee shop with white twinkle lights in the window. The best advertisement was that strong scent, promising a caffeine rush that might revive him.

The bell tinkled as he let himself into Bean There, Done That, and spotted Darryl and Kyle in the corner. He lifted one hand in a lackluster wave, but they gestured him over, so when he received his oversized steaming mug, he carried it to their table.

"Out and about early," Kyle observed. "Where's that cutie you've been hanging around with?"

Carter pressed his lips together. Every morning after today, he'd wonder that. *Where's Mallory? What is she doing right now?* How many days before he woke up and didn't think about her?

"Oh, no," Darryl said. "Woman troubles in the Man Cave."

"What is a woman doing in the Man Cave in the first place?" Kyle wanted to know.

Carter folded his arms on the table and dropped his forehead down with a thud. When he lifted his head a moment later, Kyle had left the table. "Did I scare him away?"

"Nah," Darryl dismissed with a wave. "He went to get you an egg sandwich. You need sustenance for the big holiday soiree this evening."

Carter groaned. "I forgot all about that."

"I guarantee you Mallory didn't. Now, what's going on?"

"You don't need to hear all this."

Kyle, returning to the table, heard him. "No, we don't *need* to hear, and you don't *need* to share if you don't want to, but you really helped me out when I told you about my cousin getting caught up in an MLM, so I owe you one insight."

"And I'll bank one," Darryl said, "for the next time I need advice. Go on, tell the taco men your woes. We'll give you answers, even if we can't guarantee they're the right answers."

So Carter told them everything, from meeting Mallory on the highway, to their surprise collab this week, to their easy friendship and mutual decision to make it physical, to their opposite dreams for the future, to their even-bigger-surprise TV offer. He ended his monologue with his glum but determined decision to back out of the gig and let her have it.

"Well, that's the most chivalrous plan I ever heard," Kyle said.

"Well, thank you," Carter said.

"I'm not finished. It's also the stupidest."

"And the most cowardly," Darryl added.

"Hey!"

"I'm sorry," Kyle said. "I thought you wanted advice, not a pat on the head."

"You guys are vicious."

"Falling in love is vicious," Darryl pointed out.

"It's not love."

"No?" Kyle asked. "If it's not love, what is it that has you fleeing a good money opportunity, as well as Mallory's company? What is it that has you here, banging your head on the table, ready to fall on your sword? What is it … oh, thanks," he said to the waitress, who placed the sandwich in front of Carter with a wink he barely registered. "What is it that has you here, talking to us two idiots, instead of talking to Mallory about how you feel and about trying a real relationship?"

"I take umbrage at the term 'idiot,' " Darryl said.

"Fair," Kyle said, "because idiots don't know the word 'umbrage.' "

"I take umbrage at the term 'love,' " Carter said.

"Kyle's not wrong. Too bad, Carter. You need to face this situation head-on now."

"I don't think you get it. Mallory isn't just, like, a woman who simply enjoys travel. She's afraid of anyone tying her down, ever, for a day or more. She doesn't have a boyfriend, she doesn't have close friends. She avoids emotional entanglements."

"Too late," Kyle said. "She's in one. And so are you."

"But—"

"Stop talking and use your mouth to eat your sandwich. You look like shit. You need to eat."

Despite Carter's lack of appetite, the sandwich was appealing. He lifted it, impressed with its heft, and took a bite.

"It seems like your problem is that both you and Mallory think the issue is that you're not the same kind of person," Darryl said after a moment.

Carter, his mouth full of croissant, egg, cheese, and thick-cut bacon, nodded.

"I guess I'm wondering," Darryl went on, "why is that an issue? Why do you have to be alike? I would never want to date someone exactly like me. I don't need two people in my household who don't pay bills on time, who watch hours of fast-food reviews on YouTube, and who suck at bowling. That's boring. I don't want someone like me. I want someone who brings different interests and experience to the table. I want someone who wants different things than me so we can explore those differences together and have twice as many experiences as we'd each have on our own."

"Agreed," Kyle said, leaving no room for Carter to argue. "Opposites attract. That's a saying, right? Something doesn't become a saying or a cliché unless it's true. And opposites attracted this time."

"And," Darryl added, "are you even as opposite as you think? You both have parents who traveled and still do. You've both been to a lot more places than the average human. Even if she likes it and relies on it more than you do, those are actually pretty big similarities."

"The point is ..." Kyle said, then stopped, thinking. "I forgot the point, actually."

"The point is that we don't need to be the same kind of person to have a relationship that can work," Carter said.

Kyle lifted his cup and pointed it at him. "Yes. Exactly."

"Let's say you've convinced me ..."

"Nice." Kyle dropped his arm at his side, reached it toward Darryl, and they slapped palms under the table.

"How am I supposed to convince Mallory?"

"You can't convince someone to be with you," Darryl said. "You can only hope she feels the same way about you that you do about her, and that she's willing to take a risk to keep you around."

"And if she isn't?"

"Then you're correct—you're not right for each other, after all," Darryl said. "But I wouldn't give it up as a lost cause without trying."

★ ★ ★

"Opposites attract," Carter mumbled to himself as he climbed the steps to the Moonrise Inn. The rocking chairs creaked with the cold wind, as if encouraging him to sit and freeze his butt on one of the cold wooden seats. "That's why it's a cliché," he continued under his breath. "Because it's true. And if it's true, we can ..." Thinking of how he could word his entreaty, he opened the door and stepped into the sitting room. The Crafty Ladies were gathered as usual, gabbing happily, their needles flying.

"Carter!" several of them called, and despite his preoccupation, their greeting warmed him.

He said hello, darting to the stairs quickly, and they took the hint that he was on some kind of mission. He ran up the stairs to the second floor, but instead of entering the suite with his key, he knocked. When there was no answer, he listened at the door, fairly sure he heard the faint noise of the TV.

If she were napping, better not to wake her. If she were simply avoiding a conversation, he'd let her have a little more time.

They'd need to talk eventually, and the gala was tonight. He jogged down the steps.

"Hey, you," Jackie called, "you're almost done with your project. Want a little help with the finishing touches?"

"I do." There were no open seats, so he sat cross-legged on the floor, took his now-familiar yarn and needles from her, and listened to her instructions.

Several hours later, he was triumphant, and he lifted his creation like a winning goalie hefts the Stanley Cup. All the women cheered and clapped and whistled.

"You're a wonderful student," Patrice said, "and a delightful addition to our club. We're all going home tomorrow. We're going to put you on our group text, and we'll look forward to seeing you next Christmas."

Carter grinned. He'd suspected what belonging would feel like long before he'd felt it, but it still filled his soul with sparkles. "I'd be honored."

They all had pizza, and while the celebration was still going strong, he went back upstairs. Mallory hadn't come through the main room from either direction. She had to be in the room, and, with his confidence now stronger, he would suggest a real conversation about the future. Their future.

He knocked again, and when he got no answer, he let himself into the Orion's Belt suite.

The charge in the air stopped him immediately in his tracks.

Nothing appeared out of place right away. He'd straightened the bed before he left this morning, and it looked much the way he'd left it. His shoes were still on the floor, and his suitcase was—

Not next to Mallory's.

Hers was gone.

He was at the dresser in two long strides and yanked the drawers open. Empty. His throat suddenly dry, he went into the bathroom and found all her lotions and sprays and powders had vanished. Though it made no sense, he swiped the shower curtain aside, as if he'd find her crouching in the bathtub, ready to jump up with her blond hair flying and yell, "Surprise!"

The adjoining suite room was also empty. She'd left the curtains drawn so it was darker in here, and the night-light had gone on. The TV was also on, likely forgotten as she'd fled like a thief.

And how could she have fled? Wasn't her infernal reindeer Bug in the parking lot? It was. He remembered seeing it and grimacing at the red nose stuck to the front, between the headlights. Carter hurried downstairs, and outside, and circled the building, crossing the grass. Then he saw it: a back door.

Mallory had left in secret. She'd left his first knock unanswered, packed, and left while the chitchat of the knitters, or their cheering of him, or their little pizza party, drowned out the sound of her slamming her trunk and car doors, and the sound of the ignition and the gravel under her wheels.

He rounded the inn again, this time collapsing on a cold chair, squeaking it back and forth and wrapping his arms around his own body to warm himself.

No, to comfort himself.

Because she was gone.

# CHAPTER TWENTY-TWO

Mallory glanced at her GPS as she drove through Seasalter. The bridge was on the opposite end of the town from the Moonrise Inn, and though it wasn't that far, the one-lane side streets slowed her down with all the traffic lights and pedestrian walkways. There were a lot of people out for holiday shopping or to take in the sights, but it was difficult to see them, or even much of the road in front of her, because a fog was rolling in.

*I need to get out of here.*

*Before I'm trapped.*

She gripped the wheel with both mittened hands and blew a long lock of hair out of her face. The air was thick with mist that clung to the windows of her car. She turned on her wipers and let them go once, twice, before the squeak ramped up her anxiety and she snapped them off.

After crawling her long way down Broad Street, she turned right on Colony Avenue and headed toward the bridge. It was a small bridge—she remembered it from her arrival a few days ago—and the fog now completely obscured its small metal arches. Bridges always made her nervous, and when she drove over one, she usually held her breath until she was on the other side, but right now, this bridge was her path to freedom, and she desperately needed it.

She slowed to a stop behind one other car. There was a long barrier across the road, and its red lights cut through the thick chowder air. After a few minutes, she put the car in park and took her foot off the pedal, rubbing her own thighs with her mittened hands. The heat was cranked high, and she wasn't cold; she was trying to calm her nerves.

The memory of Carter dragging his lips across her inner thigh sent a quiver to her core, and she balled her hands into fists.

No. Not him. Not now. Not ever again.

She had to protect herself.

A man in a uniform-like jacket went to the window to talk to the driver in front of her, and the car in front of her made a sudden three-point turn and drove back in the direction of Seasalter.

Drawing her eyebrows together, Mallory went to shift gears and inch the car forward, but the man approached her window. She lowered it halfway and felt the humidity wind itself into her hair, threatening to drag it down. No use worrying about that now; it wasn't like she was putting herself on social media at this moment.

Speaking of social media, she'd have to repair things somehow after tearing out of the Moonrise Inn. She'd have to call Selene to explain. She'd need to apologize to Wanderlove and concede the job to Carter. He'd do really well, and he deserved a shot. She would sacrifice the job, the money, the unlimited Nirvana pass. She wouldn't be able to use it anyway, if she allowed herself to be in a relationship with Man Cave Carter. Grounded, like the good girlfriend he deserved, she would turn bitter and resentful. She would lose herself.

"Bridge is closed," the man said, apparently not one for wasting words.

"Closed? What do you mean, closed?"

"Just what it means. Closed. No one can cross until this fog lifts. Too treacherous."

"It's an emergency."

He squinted at her. "What emergency?"

Ugh, she didn't like to lie, and she wasn't good at it. "Listen," she appealed. "If I don't leave now, my life will change forever."

"Your life will change forever if your car goes off that bridge."

Mallory winced. "Is that a bit dramatic?"

"Maybe, but we don't take chances. Like I said, you'll need to wait for the fog to lift."

"When's that?"

"Do I look like a meteorologist?"

"No, but I thought you'd have a radio, or something?"

"I do have a radio, and when it's time to open the bridge again, they'll call me on the radio and tell me."

Mallory decided to try another tack. She shook her hair and turned her smile up to its high-beam setting. "Listen, I'm a really good driver."

"Look ahead of you." He pointed.

Mallory stuck her neck forward to get a closer look out her windshield. It was past dusk now, and there was nothing but inky blackness ahead of her. The lights on the arch of the bridge were the only indication that there was a bridge at all, but the lights were muted into hazy halos, and they illuminated nothing. The moon wasn't showing itself in the sky or showing anything below it.

Despite her need to leave town, her anxiety grew. She didn't want to risk a bridge she couldn't confirm with her own eyes.

"Turn around," the man said, and his voice might have gentled the slightest bit. "Wait it out a while. Better yet, come back in the morning."

Tears burned the edges of Mallory's eyes. She nodded, and he patted her car. A glance in the rearview mirror told her no one was behind her, probably because most residents of Seasalter were either occupied with holiday cheer and the ball, or knew better than to try to leave in this weather.

She was stuck.

Making her own three-point turn, she headed back toward town, but she couldn't bring herself to drive all the way up to Broad Street. She pulled over in front of a house with multi-colored Christmas lights that shone fuzzily through the fog.

*What do I do? What do I do?*

If she sat here any longer, she'd either go back to the inn and see Carter, or she'd break down and call him. Both actions would have her jumping into the emotional, sticky spider web she was trying to get away from.

Mallory pressed her forehead to the steering wheel. She pulled off one mitten and turned on the radio in time for the first line of "Silent Night."

Carter singing in German. Mallory pirouetting behind him.

She snapped the music off and checked her side mirror. There was no one at the bridge right now. She didn't know where the guard was lurking, but if she stayed quiet …

She popped her trunk and dashed out, pulling her rolling suitcase from the depths of her car. Her mind was shouting at her to think this through, to consider how she'd return for her car, to check her phone to figure out a real destination, but the logic was drowned out by the constant thrum of her heart: *Run, run, run.*

When she was about fifty feet from where the bridge probably was, she lifted her bag so the rolling wheels on concrete didn't alert the man from his car or wherever he was monitoring any vehicles that moved toward the bridge. Luckily, Mallory's dark coat and hair tucked into the inside of that coat must have blended her into the blackness enough that he didn't see her, and she walked around the outside of the barricade.

Her eyes tried in vain to pick out the horizon, or anything, but she couldn't see anything more than a few feet in front of her on the ground, so she moved slowly, concentrating on that. After a bit, the road inclined up, and she could make out the railing beside her.

Instinctively, she edged away from it, slightly closer to the center, since there were no cars and she was suddenly deathly afraid of tripping and tumbling off. She couldn't remember how far up this bridge rose, but the constantly inclining road terrified her. The fog had plastered itself to her face, creating a layer of moisture, and she wondered what the humidity was doing to her hair. Nothing good, she was certain.

She slowed her pace, telling herself it was fine, that she'd call a rideshare on the other side, once she was out of Seasalter, and go somewhere safe. Meanwhile, she needed to keep crossing.

Hearing steps, she froze, worrying the guard had followed her and would bring her back, but she realized after a moment that the footsteps were in front of her, coming toward her. Someone else, at least, had decided to cross the bridge on foot, so she couldn't be that crazy.

Who was it, though? What if it was someone she wouldn't want to meet in the dark, on a bridge, in the fog?

What was she doing?

She strained her eyes, and out of the fog he came.

Santa Claus.

His white hair and beard, as well as the white trim on his suit and hat, were easily visible. His boots' heels were hard on the ground, and he was walking with assurance she didn't feel, at a businesslike pace that she couldn't match.

When he spotted her, he stopped a moment, surprised, then kept walking until he was close enough to her to speak.

"Leaving town?" he asked.

"Yes. Are you going to town?"

"Yes. I need to attend a party. Everyone is expecting me. I can't let a foggy night and a closed bridge stop me."

"I suppose not," she said.

"And you?"

"No one is expecting me."

"But it's imperative that you leave tonight?"

"Yes." She cut her eyes to the railing.

"It's a bit of a scary hike," Santa said. "I'm used to Seasalter myself. I've crossed this bridge on foot a few times in fog and in snow."

"Yeah," Mallory said, her teeth chattering not from cold, but from not wanting to get any higher. From not wanting to walk any farther. "But, you know, I'm probably about halfway there, so—"

"You're not halfway there yet," Santa said. "It's a long walk."

"Oh." She wanted to keep going, but a growing part of her wanted to stay here with Santa Claus. She tried to recall any one thing she might have asked Santa for when she was five or six, what toy she'd been sure she couldn't survive without, but she couldn't.

"Are you okay?" he asked in a soft voice that was surprising, coming from a man who spent every December ho-ho-ho'ing with jollity. "Do you need help?"

"I …" Mallory swallowed the lump in her throat that usually appeared when she was asked anything personal. Only Carter had gotten past it so far, but this was Santa Claus. If she couldn't tell him, who could she tell? "I don't need help. I need to get out of Seasalter."

"Why?"

"Because—" She released the handle of her suitcase so it stood upright, and she tried to shove her big mittens in her coat pockets for extra warmth. They wouldn't fit. "Long story short, if I stay here, I'm pretty sure I'll fall in love, and I don't want to be trapped."

"Ah." He studied her face, and she was certain he caught the little tear that suddenly squeezed out the corner of one eye. "I thought you loved to travel. That you're a girl who needs adventure."

"I do. I am."

"So, why are you running from life's greatest adventure?"

She blinked.

"I'm a bit older than you," he continued, "and in my experience with this world, love is a challenge. It's tough, but it makes you want to be kind. It's strong, but it makes you feel helpless. It's as vast as the ocean"—he gestured behind her, toward the Atlantic—"but it lives in your own small heart. It's the greatest adventure we could go on without needing to buy a ticket or pack a bag. It's meant for everyone to have and give. And now, it's found you."

Mallory's shoulders sagged. "Yes."

"And it doesn't look the way you expected it to look."

She shook her head.

"Well, Santa drops a lot of surprises down a lot of chimneys. Would you toss it back up if you didn't like how it was wrapped? Or would you open it and see if it's really meant for you?"

"I love opening gifts," she admitted. "But I'm scared, Santa. I'm scared it will change my life."

"So am I," he said. "Because it's found me too, recently. And I'm not sure what to do. It might hurt, or it might be the most wonderful thing in the world. But as I was walking across this bridge, I made the decision to finally open the gift and find out."

"What if it's not what I want?"

"What if it is?"

She shuffled her feet, staring down at her boots, before looking back up at him. His oddly familiar green eyes pierced the fog to stare into her soul. "If it is ..." Her voice trailed off.

"I'm just a guy who gives presents to kids," Santa said. "You don't need to take my advice. But if you want to, I'd like to walk you back to Seasalter and see you on your way."

He held out his elbow, and she looped her arm around the velvety red fabric. She dragged her bag on wheels behind her with her other hand, and she realized he was carrying a large sack over his shoulder.

Santa's steps were sure, and Mallory's anxiety dissipated as they moved down the slope of the bridge. Eventually, they reached the metal gate, and he walked them around it. The guard stepped out of the fog to their left but nodded at Santa and let them pass into Seasalter without asking what Mallory had been doing on the bridge.

They walked to her car, and when she clicked her key fob to unlock it, Santa started laughing. "What?"

He pointed at her car. "Rudolph! Wasn't that the whole point of his song? On a foggy Christmas Eve, Rudolph's bright nose allowed the delivery of presents."

She laughed too. "I guess so."

"Well, get into Rudolph and see where he leads you."

"What party are you going to? Can Rudolph and I drop you off?"

"I'm headed to the Fancy Dance."

His words itched inside Mallory. She wondered if Carter had gone without her, and she wondered how angry he was with her for running, for not saying goodbye, for not acknowledging what had grown between them as more than they'd both intended.

"I had to pick up the gifts, and I got stuck on the other side," Santa said, "so I had to leave my car—er, my sleigh—there and walk. Lots of people would be disappointed if I missed this party. But no, thank you. It's only about four blocks from here, and I could use the walk to think."

"About love?"

Both corners of his white mustache lifted as he shrugged.

She tossed her suitcase in the trunk, then opened her driver's-side door and slid in. She turned the car on, and a blast of cold air hit her face from the vents. She frowned and lowered her window. "Wait. Back there, you said you know I like travel. And adventure. How did you know that?"

"Santa knows all, Mallory."

She blinked, stunned.

"I have a feeling it's going to be your best Christmas ever." He winked and gestured to the road.

Still shocked Santa knew her name, she carefully pulled out and drove toward Broad Street. She eyeballed the rearview mirror and saw Santa readjust the bag over his shoulder and start walking again.

★ ★ ★

Watching Mallory's reindeer car turn and disappear, Owen smiled through the glued-on beard.

# CHAPTER TWENTY-THREE

After writing a long social media post, Carter went to the gala. He'd rented a tux, after all. All the knitters were going, as well as Selene and Owen, Kyle and Darryl, and Delilah from the tea shop. And … it was content.

Because that's what this was about now. He'd allowed Christmas in, he'd realized—the scent of pine trees and sugar cookies and peppermint; the sounds of jingle bells, blades cutting ice, kids giggling; the tastes of hot chocolate and whipped cream and sprinkles.

And Mallory. All five senses of her.

He went to the gala anyway because it was solely his job now, and Mallory must have been absolutely repulsed by the thought of him long term if she'd wordlessly fled from the work she was devoted to and responsible for.

When he arrived at Muscatel's, he took pictures and video of the room, of the women in gowns and the men in tuxes, of the beautiful lights strung overhead and the candles on every round banquet table and the stuffed stockings on every cushioned seat. There were easily a couple of hundred people here. A band on a dais was playing jazzy holiday favorites as couples danced, and little sprigs of mistletoe hung from a few spots on the ceiling.

Carter couldn't conceptualize any unique angle for this event. If Mallory were here, they'd have plenty of ideas for video and for voice-over later, and they would laugh a lot while creating it, but right now, without her, he was artistically bankrupt. He shouldn't be, as he'd worked on travel content for a long time before meeting her, but it was as if she'd packed every ounce of his creativity and happiness in her car before she scrammed.

Her impulsive disappearance would have made it very easy for a normal man to be over her quickly, but apparently, he wasn't normal. And he'd never be again.

He leaned against a wall beside the buffet and took a bacon-wrapped scallop off an offered platter of them.

"Carter!"

Forcing a brightness onto his face that he didn't have in him, he hugged Jackie. Patrice, Brenda, Wendy, Beth Ann, and Delilah all took their turns, and when he was able to stand back, he truly admired them. He'd seen them in pajamas and in ugly Christmas sweaters and in laid-back loungewear all week. Now, in jewel-toned gowns with sparkly necklaces and earrings and upswept hair, they were beautiful, all of them.

"Wow," he said.

"Wow, yourself," Brenda said. "You clean up pretty good."

"That Mallory is a lucky girl," Wendy added. "If she wants to be. Where is she?"

As his chest deflated, they seemed to realize what was happening. But before they could say any words of comfort or advice or commiseration, Delilah looked over her shoulder and said, "There's always something to be said for a Christmas miracle."

The women parted, and Mallory was there.

The red satin dress with rhinestone shoulder straps revealed a sparkling gem at her collarbone and the dip between her breasts. A thin rhinestone belt shimmered at her waist before the dress flared to the ground. She took one more step, and a side slit revealed her bare leg from mid-thigh down to a pair of silver heels. A stack of silver bracelets graced one arm.

He didn't know when his friends had backed away, but suddenly he was alone with Mallory, and his mouth had forgotten every word he'd ever learned in his life except for the three that he couldn't say, now that she'd left him.

The three words he shouldn't want to say, but desperately did.

★ ★ ★

"I was worried you'd get stuck on the other side of the bridge," Selene said, helping Owen with his Santa bag of gifts. The Fancy Dance wasn't a children's event, but every year, the adult ticket-holders were delighted with their goody bags with crafts and jewelry and gift cards from local shops, and there would have been some very sad faces if Mr. Claus had been unable to deliver.

Selene had been lingering in the foyer, waiting for him. Though they hadn't agreed that she would, she'd ... wanted to.

"So was I. That fog is practically sentient. But I walked over, along with a lost traveler."

Selene narrowed her eyes quizzically, but he shrugged it off.

"This is my first year at the Fancy Dance," Selene confessed. "I'm glad you're here."

"How can you say that? You're friends with everyone in town."

"I am now. But ..." What could she say?

She could tell he noticed her pause, and that he was offering her a reprieve by turning his attention to the sack of gifts, rearranging and shifting and making sure nothing was crushed.

The coat check boy and girl, two Seasalter High students recruited for the task, eyeballed Selene, and now that Owen was here, she had no excuse to keep her coat on. She unbuttoned it and slid it off her shoulders, glancing down at her dress. Dan had bought the dress for her several years ago, and she was glad to have worn it once in his presence for a different event, but it had been hanging in her closet since. It was midnight blue, with a satin bodice and sleeves, and a taffeta skirt that brushed the floor.

Arcs of sparkling silver shooting stars lit up the skirt, catching the light. Her strappy sandals were impractical for winter, but the dress demanded it.

Handing the coat to the girl and smoothing her hands over the dress, she turned to find Owen's gaze fixed on her face.

His green eyes didn't waver, and he didn't clear his throat or glance at the floor or show any discomfort. He merely continued to behold her over his temporary white beard.

His stare was bold, and it was heated, and Selene accepted the challenge it proposed. She stared back.

She was somewhat triumphant when he was the one to break the silence, because she'd been tempted to and held fast. "I think," he said, "that is Cygnus."

Her lips pursed in confusion. "What?"

The coat-check kids chattered with each other, sitting down away from the window now that the rush had slowed and most of the guests had already arrived.

He chin-pointed at her. "On your dress. It looks like the Cygnus constellation."

"I don't know about that," Selene said. Dan had loved the sky myths, though. "But Cygnus, the Greek god, was turned into a swan and placed in the sky by Zeus. I forget why."

"Well, I don't know about that," Owen repeated. "But the constellation includes Deneb, which is one of the twenty brightest stars visible from Earth." He took a step toward her. "I'm no astronomer, but I'm pretty sure I've just discovered the twenty-first brightest star. In a blue dress."

He took another step toward her, but this time she matched him, so they were only a breath apart.

She searched her brain for words. Not even the right words. Any words would do. But he pulled off his white costume glove and trailed his fingers from her earlobe, down the slope of her neck, to her shoulder. With his other hand, he peeled away his white beard and mustache to reveal his jaw, his dark stubble, the outline of his lips.

Sparks fired up under her skin, and her own lips parted.

If he chose that moment to ask her a question, any question, the answer would be yes.

He didn't ask her anything.

He kissed her.

The world around them lit up, then fell into blackness in her periphery as she laid a hand on his cheek, feeling the muscles of his face move as he deepened the kiss. She tasted his tongue, which was at once different and familiar. Her nipples tightened under the bodice of her dress, pushing painfully against the satin. She gripped the red velvet jacket, wanting to tear it off and fling it into the ocean.

Owen cupped the back of her head with his bare hand, sliding the tips of his fingers into her French braid. He slid the other arm around her waist and pulled her as closer to him than she'd been to anyone since ...

Since ...

She broke away, her mouth still wet from his, her heart slamming over the neckline of the dress. The dress her husband had given her.

"Oh, no," she said. "I ... I can't ... We ..."

"It's okay," he said, and she backed away as he reached an arm out—to comfort her? To explain? To apologize?

Owen had nothing to apologize for.

And Selene was alone. She had no one to apologize *to*. Not really.

Until the door behind Owen blew open, and Luna walked in.

"Hi, Mom," her daughter said, as if only an hour had passed since they'd last spoken, as if the last six months hadn't seen them communicating mainly through painful bickering. As if she were a little girl again, eager for Christmas. "Hi, Santa."

* * *

The band played the first few bars of a new song, and the singer, resplendent in a shimmering suit jacket, crooned the first few words of "Baby, It's Cold Outside."

Neither Carter nor Mallory had said a word, but he inclined his head ever so slightly to the dance floor, and she, even more slightly, nodded assent.

He took her in his arms gingerly, as if she were a priceless crystal ornament that he wasn't allowed to touch. They moved together. Carter had trouble reading her expression and wondered if she was having the same difficulty.

"You know," she finally said, "we could discuss the sexist lyrics of this song, but right now, I keep thinking, baby, it's gross outside."

"It is. This fog is ridiculous."

They danced through another verse.

"The singer's jacket makes him look like he should be singing at a 1950s prom," she observed.

He chuckled.

"I'm usually much better at small talk than this," she said.

"You are."

"But we have bigger talk that we have to do, and I don't know how to start."

"Just start," he said. "Start wherever, and we'll manage."

He hadn't realized the song had stopped until everyone clapped that polite, black-tie clap, and the music sped up. The dancers sharing the floor opened space between them and began moving to a faster song.

Carter and Mallory dropped their arms and stopped dancing, but they stayed in the middle of the dance floor.

"I ran away," Mallory said.

"You did."

"I was scared."

"Me too."

"Of what?"

He almost said, *You first*, but he didn't want her to flee again. "I was scared of co-hosting the TV show with you. I feel ... a kind of way about you, and I was scared that working together and traveling together and being together for weeks and months would embed you so deeply into my heart that I'd have to have it removed when you finally left, so I could live without pain."

It was out there now, and he didn't regret it, especially when she said, "Oh, my God, that's *exactly* why I was scared."

"But you're not anymore?"

"I am. Aren't you?"

"No," Carter said. "I'm eager. We're both smart and resourceful and creative. Why can't we make this work if we want to?"

"You ... you want to?"

His heart, which had leaped into the sky, came crashing down to his polished black shoes. Maybe she didn't want to. Maybe this was all in vain, but this woman had dragged him out of his comfort zone so often this week that he wasn't going to back down this time. "Yes."

He waited for her to say she wanted to also, or that she didn't, but instead she said, "I went back to the Moonrise Inn to change my clothes, and I peeked at my phone. I saw the post you wrote. About me."

"I wrote it about you," he clarified, "but it wasn't for you. It was for all the horrible commenters who were saying disgusting things about you. I was over it."

Her lips twitched. "You wrote that even though you were in your Man Cave, I barged my way in and found you."

"You did."

"And that you'd never be the same."

"I won't, Mallory."

"The post went viral. You gained thousands of female followers in the last couple of hours."

"Huh."

"You didn't have to protect me."

"I did. When you … feel a certain way about someone, you have to."

She nodded as the song changed again. They still didn't move.

"Are you going to buy that house?" she asked.

"I'm putting in an offer."

They were quiet again, revelers dancing around them.

"Where were you going?" he asked. "When you left."

"I'm thinking of maybe Prague. I read that their Christmas markets run into January."

Carter didn't miss her use of the present tense. "Prague?"

"Yes."

He swallowed hard. "I have friends in Prague. When we get back to the inn, I'll give you their contact info. They're always inviting me to stay, and they'd love you." He choked a bit on the second to last word.

Mallory seemed taken aback, but whatever she was about to say next was interrupted by two women in their twenties, wearing remarkably similar sequin dresses and waving cell phones.

"Sunshine and Man Cave Guy!" one said. "We've been following you online."

"And we were at Clash of the Carols," the other said. "You two were hashtag couple goals."

"It's so adorable how you fell in love, and we all got to see it in practically real time in this cute little town, at Christmas."

"Especially because you're so hashtag opposites attract."

"So I said to my friend, we have to go to Seasalter for the holiday, and let's not wait until next year. Maybe we can find our own cute guys."

"And here we are! Hashtag girls' trip."

Carter's head spun with all the unasked-for information.

"You'd give me your friends' contact info? In Prague?" Mallory asked. "Why?"

"I started Man Cave Adventures," Carter said, "after my last girlfriend broke up with me when she realized we weren't compatible. She liked traveling. I didn't. But what occurred to me just this morning was that it wasn't that we were mismatched as travelers. We were mismatched as people. I was relieved when she left, to be honest."

"But—"

"Now, you're asking me why I'd help you travel," he continued. "It's because you're you. Because you want to go. Because I would never stop you from seeing the world. Because I would never change you. Because the Mallory I fell into ... feeling a certain way about ... loves to travel. And if you invited me, I might even join you sometimes, since I've found out that we're not incompatible. When I'm with you, I don't dislike travel quite as much, because I like being with you wherever we are. So maybe you'll go to Europe for two weeks, and I can join you in Paris for the weekend, then go home and water the garden and prepare the week's meals on Sundays and take clients from my home office. And maybe ..."

"Maybe?" she asked.

"Maybe it will be your home too. When you're tired. When you're lonely. When you're broke."

She laughed, and it sounded so much like her laughter did the night he met her that he wanted her to never, ever stop.

"We don't have to change," he added. "But we could ... adjust. Make room for each other."

The two women lingered close by, hanging on every word, but Carter didn't care, as long as Mallory was listening.

"What if I don't know how?" Mallory asked.

"You don't have to know how. You could try one time around the ice. Try singing or dancing to one song. Try one minute of playing in the coldest water in the middle of winter. See if you like it." He stepped forward and took her face in his hands. "I liked it. Because I was with you."

"I feel a certain way about you," Mallory whispered hoarsely.

Their kiss was sweet, satisfied, a sacred promise.

Carter vowed to let her go again and again, as long as they came back to this moment every time.

"Can we get a picture with you?" the two sequined women shrieked.

Mallory stepped back, her eyes shining. "Yes, of course! Hashtag Seasalter magic."

"Hashtag Christmas is not so bad after all," Carter added.

She bent her head and murmured into his ear, "Hashtag love."

# CHAPTER TWENTY-FOUR

"Hey, Mallory!"

"Hi, Paige." Mallory usually used the camera, but instead she cradled the phone between her shoulder and her ear. "I'm sorry it's so late, but you always say you never mind a late call."

"It's true, and I'm wide awake. Everything okay? I have you on the schedule to drive back tomorrow morning. How did it go?"

"Well, I got the Wanderlove show."

"What? Oh, my God! Congratulations! I'm thrilled for you!" Paige lowered her voice. "Was Carter really bummed?"

"Actually, we both got the show. We're going to be cohosts."

"Oh." Paige paused, likely to think it over. "I think this is great. It makes sense. You two do make great content together, and most people overwhelmingly love what you were doing. You should know, though, that your followers think you're a couple. Especially since Carter posted something today about you that was very—well, the kind of thing someone says when they're into someone. It's possible everyone, including him, has the wrong idea, so—"

"It's not the wrong idea. We're—we are a couple."

"You and *Carter Scott*?"

"Don't pretend like you didn't think this was a good idea."

Paige hesitated. "Okay, I admit it. You seem pretty infatuated with each other, from what we've all seen. But … wow. You and Carter are officially hard launched."

"We're going to try," Mallory said, suddenly defensive.

"That wasn't judgment," Paige clarified. "It was surprise. You don't tend to …" She stopped, probably remembering their relationship wasn't like that.

But Mallory said, "Paige, I called because I want to see if you'd like to be friends. With me."

Paige laughed. "Of course! I've been trying."

"I know you have, and—I don't let people in. Or, I didn't. But I've let Carter in. And I'm thinking it might be time to let in some friends. And I want you to be the first."

"Mallory," Paige said, "I'm so happy to be your friend. Does that mean you'll spill all the Carter Scott details?"

"I do need to keep a few things to myself." Mallory laughed. "But … some of them. Yeah."

"Yay!" Paige laughed too. "You sound—well, you always sounded like sunshine. But you shined that sun on strangers, mostly. It's nice that you're ready to shine it on people you'd like to be close to. And on yourself. You deserve happiness."

"I'm not sure what I'm doing," Mallory confessed.

"Who does? No one."

"I'm not sure exactly what my plans are today. I might go to Carter's. I might bring him to my place."

"In other words, your plans are with Carter, no matter what."

"Kind of, yeah."

"I'll talk to you later, friend."

Mallory's heart swelled. "Bye, friend."

She tossed the phone onto the sofa, went into the bedroom, stepped over the crumpled red dress and tuxedo jacket on the floor, and did a flying leap into the center of the bed. Carter's supine body bounced. He reached behind his head for a pillow, and she ducked his attack. "I almost forgot," he said. "I have a gift for you."

"You mean something other than the gift you just gave me? And the gift I'll demand in the morning?"

"Those gifts are year round," Carter said, kissing her. "No, this is a Christmas present."

"A Christmas present?"

"Yes. Close your eyes."

She did and heard him move toward his suitcase and riffle through it a moment before coming back. "Okay, open your eyes."

He stood beside the bed, both hands behind his back. "Pick a hand."

"Oh!" Mallory pretended to think, then tapped his right hand. He shuffled a bit, and she realized he was putting the present into the hand she chose. He held it out, a small blue gift bag printed with cheerful snowmen.

"I don't have anything for you," she said.

"You have everything I ever wanted. Now, open it."

She pulled it out and squealed. "Oh!"

It was a hot-pink beanie hat. The soft light from the bedside lamp caught a subtle shimmer of tinsel throughout. The hat was topped with a fluffy white pompom.

"I made it," he said. "This week. I didn't realize it would look so much like a cupcake, but it's on brand for you. I know you don't like wearing hats, but look at the inside."

She turned it inside out, revealing a pastel-pink satin lining.

"Jackie helped me sew that in, and she said it will keep your hair nice."

Mallory pulled the hat over her uncombed hair, and it felt cozy against her ears.

"Please wear it. I can't stand the idea of you being cold," Carter said.

She threw her arms around him. "I love it. I *love* it. I love that you made it. I love that you made it for me. I love—"

She squeezed harder.

"I know," Carter said. "Me too."

★ ★ ★

In the adjoining room, the night-light glowed yellow.

In Selene's living room, she pretended to read a book while she watched her daughter, sprawled in an armchair, scrolling on her phone. The lights on the Christmas tree blinked, and Selene tried to forget the recent memory of Owen threading them carefully through the boughs. She also tried to forget the regret in his eyes when he told her he was leaving today to visit his sons over the holidays and that they'd help him finish moving from his place before he came back here. After Christmas.

In the main sitting room, the Crafty Ladies chatted about the Fancy Dance, about the handsome Santa, about their newest knitting recruit and his girlfriend, and about where they might all meet next December.

Outside, the thick fog dissipated, and the crystal moon shined on Seasalter once again.

The same moon that would watch over both Mallory and Carter, even when they were apart.

# EPILOGUE

*The Moonrise Inn*

*Online Review*

*Rating: 5 stars*

*The Moonrise Inn is the hidden, sparkling gem of New England.*

*The décor here pays a graceful homage to the night sky, from the names of the rooms and the suites to the starry sitting room to the twinkle lights on the house. You might find yourself telling all your problems to Selene, the owner, but she doesn't seem to mind at all—she knows how to care for weary travelers. Her breakfasts are delicious.*

*The dining area and the sitting room are the perfect places to meet fellow guests and make lasting friends if that's your desire— and why wouldn't it be?*

*We visited at Christmas, and Seasalter, R.I., is the place to celebrate the holidays if you love skating, singing carols, and a tea shop that warms your soul. There's even an ocean-plunge challenge that we recommend trying, if you dare!*

*Also, we're still wondering if the Moonrise Inn itself is magical. Somehow it knew what we needed ...*

*At Christmastime or any time of year, the Moonrise Inn should be your getaway pick. Trust us; we're professional travelers! Check us out on Wander With Love on the Travelworld Channel, or visit us on the socials at @exploringsunnycaves.*

"Well, it does sound nice, at least," Elise said out loud. Bringing up the reservations form, she filled out *Mrs.*, deleted it and typed *Ms.*, then deleted it and went with just *Elise Kendrick*. She tried to read her credit card number through her threatening tears.

## THE END

*What happens when two people decide to keep their crumbled marriage and impending divorce a secret from the elderly family patriarch? And will Selene and Owen be able to forget what's happened between them? Find out in the next book in the Moonrise Inn Series,* Call of the Crow Moon.

# ABOUT THE AUTHOR

JENNIFER SAFREY lives in the Boston area with her novelist husband, Teddy, and their two cats, Kimura and Potus. She's a longtime freelance editor, as well as an adjunct professor at Emerson College, where she teaches a graduate course on romance novels. She grew up on Long Island. *Christmas Under a Cold Moon* is her ninth novel.

*Please visit Jennifer online:* www.jennifersafrey.com
FB: JenniferSafreyAuthor
IG: @JenniferSafrey_author
TT: @JenniferSafreyauthor

# ACKNOWLEDGMENTS

Many heartfelt thanks to all at Sibylline Press who helped bring this book into the world.

Deepest gratitude for the compassionate assistance of Suzy Vitello, Shelagh Braley Starr, and Anna Wilhelm.

Cheers to SK Duffy's mid-draft read to assure me I was on the right track when I was slightly freaking out.

Appreciation for the Art Friends, who helped me plot this Christmas book as we floated on pool toys in the hot summer.

And all the love in the world for the new Mr. Jennifer Safrey.

**Sibylline Press** is proud to publish the brilliant work of women authors over 50. We are a woman-owned publishing company and, like our authors, represent women of a certain age.